Raves for *Blind*

"*Blind Curves* is filled with a diverse cast of true-to-life lesbian characters. Shy butches, sexy femmes, closeted movie stars and dykes with disabilities, almost any lesbian can see herself or people she knows in the pages of this book...Fans of lesbian murder mystery will love this book. It's a great summer read and the first in a series. I look forward to more Blind Eye mysteries." – *Lesbian Life*

"The catfight setting for this intricate mystery is the world of lesbian magazine publishing—and because half the writing team (Diane) is the current editor of *Curve*, the plot has a patina of possibility. Some action is set in a park; that the other half of the writing team is a former park ranger adds nicely to the authenticity...With help from their dorky but able-bodied office assistant, the dogged duo clear sundry suspects before the killer—not too obvious, thanks to clever plotting—is fingered." – *Q Syndicate*

"...is the first book in a thrilling new detective series by Diane and Jacob Anderson-Minshall. The story takes place in San Francisco, the authors' home, and the descriptions are rich and lively, thus making the city itself an additional character in the novel." – *Just About Write*

"The authors put their own insider knowledge of the queer publishing world to good use, weaving a tale full of so much detail and believability that it's easy to swallow some of the more outré aspects of the book— like a detective agency which only has disabled PIs. With its expected unexpected twists, vivid characters and healthy dose of humor, *Blind Curves* is a very fun read that will keep you guessing." – *Bay Windows*

"Like the sexy derriere of its diva-femme protagonist Velvet Erickson, *Blind Curves* moves engagingly and with purpose. This clever and witty tale will appeal to mystery lovers and anyone who loves a game of cat and mouse."—Diana Cage, managing editor, *Velvetpark* magazine and author of *Girl Meets Girl: A Dating Survival Guide*

By the Authors

Blind Curves

BLIND LEAP

A BLIND EYE MYSTERY

by
Diane and Jacob Anderson-Minshall

2007

BLIND LEAP
© 2007 BY DIANE AND JACOB ANDERSON-MINSHALL.
ALL RIGHTS RESERVED.

ISBN 10: 1-933110-91-0
ISBN 13: 978-1-933110-91-2

THIS TRADE PAPERBACK ORIGINAL IS PUBLISHED BY
BOLD STROKES BOOKS, INC.,
NEW YORK, USA

FIRST EDITION: OCTOBER 2007

CREDITS
EDITORS: JENNIFER KNIGHT AND STACIA SEAMAN
PRODUCTION DESIGN: STACIA SEAMAN
COVER DESIGN BY SHERI (GRAPHICARTIST2020@HOTMAIL.COM)

Acknowledgments

We'd be nowhere without the wonderful women of Bold Strokes Books, including our patient publisher Len Barot, our copy editor Stacia Seaman, cover designer Sheri, consulting publicist Connie Ward, and our even more patient editor Jennifer Knight, without whose watchful eye we'd be writing bad TV screenplays and trying to fit them into novel format. Our family and friends get our deepest thanks for sustaining us in each of their own ways. We extend our gratitude to those pioneers who came before us—queers, lesbians, and trans folk who paved the way. And as always, we honor the real-life individuals living with disabilities—those we know personally and those we don't—who serve as role models for our fiction and our lives.

Blind Leap was influenced by the work of filmmakers Jenni Olsen and Eric Steele. Jenni, whose *The Joy of Life* is a living tribute to her good friend (and our acquaintance) Mark Finch, who committed suicide by jumping from the Golden Gate Bridge. The *Blind Leap* character Jeff Conant shares a number of similarities with Mark, including his involvement with San Francisco's Frameline Film Festival. We sincerely hope the outcome feels more like homage than creepy exploitation. We were also deeply moved by Eric Steele's controversial documentary *The Bridge*, which (inadvertently) captured Golden Gate suicides on tape and explored the impact bridge deaths have on those left behind.

Our research is indebted to the meticulously crafted seven-part *San Francisco Chronicle* series "Lethal Beauty" on the Golden Gate's dubious distinction as one of the world's top suicide destinations.

Dedication

For Stephanie Tarnoff, Denny Nelson, Gladys Stratton, and Jeremy Stevenson, and all the friends and family who have left our lives too soon. In the LGBT community and beyond, we lose far too many friends and family to both suicide and substance addiction. We don't have the answers, but we're glad that others are starting to dialog about what that means. And to all of those who've been left behind by someone who could no longer bear the pain of living: Hang in there. It's not your fault.

PROLOGUE

December 18
Golden Gate Bridge

By the time Jeff Conant's waterlogged body washed onshore nine miles south of the Golden Gate Bridge, he was nearly naked and a ghostly apparition of his former self. A streak of black amethyst bruising marred his once sun-freckled face, and what was left of his swimmer's physique was distended so much he looked like a hellish human version of Moby Dick.

At least that's how it had seemed to Velvet Erickson when the police officer shoved a photograph under her nose a week ago and asked if she knew the man in the picture. She hadn't wanted to see her childhood friend that way, and now, every time she closed her eyes, the image of his rotting, water-beaten corpse came unbidden again and again.

How could this have happened?

She pressed her body against the rust-colored railing on the northeastern edge of the Golden Gate Bridge and stared out into the Bay, where she could see Angel Island and the infamous Alcatraz. The wind whipped her long, dark brown hair across her face, pushing strands between her chapped lips and plastering damp locks to her tear-stained cheeks. The splendor of the surroundings was undeniable but Velvet saw nothing but Jeff's accusing eyes, somehow staring up at her from the empty sockets in his pale, bloated face.

Why hadn't she prevented this? How could she have been friends with him for most of her thirty-six years and not known he was desperate enough to take his own life? Had Jeff stood here, on this very spot, considering the view? In the darkness of that night on the bridge, he wouldn't have seen the beauty before her now. He would have seen the lights of San Francisco. Jumpers chose this side to make their swan dive with the ocean to their back. The ocean was cold, uninhabited, and unending. Too reminiscent of death. But the lights of the city were full of life and spoke of community and other people. Suicide might be an antisocial act, but bridge jumpers did not turn away from the city in their final hour. It was as though in death, they hoped to exchange the alienation that haunted them for the warm embrace of the city.

Velvet slumped against the railing. Her sunglasses were less to protect her eyes from the haze and more to hide her tears from passing tourists. She wanted to understand what had happened. What could *possibly* have led Jeff to leap to his death? No one saw him jump. Jeff's black Saab was discovered a month ago, on November 19, abandoned in the Vista Point, just north of the Golden Gate Bridge. There was no suicide note.

Velvet and her best friend, Yoshi Yakamota, had parked close to where Jeff's car had been found. Yoshi had elected to stay in the car while Velvet took her painful stroll along the bridge. Velvet wondered if Jeff had sat behind the wheel weighing his options for a long time that fateful night, or whether he'd gotten right out and rushed to the bridge's apex.

The California Highway Patrol officer who found the unattended vehicle in the early hours of the morning had asked San Francisco PD to do a welfare check on Jeff. He wasn't at home in his Castro apartment and his boyfriend, Tyrone Hill, hadn't seen him since the previous morning. Tyrone was anxious but not in a way that invited suspicion. Jeff's coworkers at the Frameline office had last seen him there the previous evening.

With no sign of foul play, there wasn't much the cops could do. Adults were allowed to disappear. It was a common enough occurrence: someone got tired of their life, pulled up all stakes, and took off to start up somewhere else. Plenty of people escaping from their lives didn't tell friends and family their plans, and police suspicions were not raised automatically. It made Velvet wonder what the statistics were, if so many people disappeared on their own accord. Where did they all go? Did they return to their old lives eventually, or were they like those fugitives from the seventies who disappeared and became entirely new people, never once contacting the loved ones they left behind? Or people in witness protection. How did anyone just do that—vanish and never look back?

The honk of a passing car drew her from her thoughts. In just a few hours' time, the Golden Gate Bridge would be packed with cars squashed against each other like sardines in a tin can. Commuters would inch slowly toward the city only to crawl back to the northern feeder towns in Marin and Sonoma counties eight hours later. At night, the traffic thinned out and vehicles would cross the span at irregular intervals. If a jumper didn't want to be seen, he usually made his date with the bridge after dark.

Velvet knew more than she wanted about what it meant to jump off the Golden Gate Bridge. Just eighteen months ago, the *San Francisco Chronicle* had published the last of her four-part series on suicide and the bridge. During the months of research that went into the article, she'd interviewed emergency personnel, medical examiners, family members of suicide victims, and even one of the few survivors of the fall and its aftermath. The Golden Gate had the dubious distinction of being one of the world's most popular and reliably lethal suicide destinations. Velvet suspected the natural beauty of the surroundings, the architectural wonder of the bridge itself, and the special cachet that came with making a newsworthy leap probably drew people who'd never made a splash in their lives.

Jeff's body was spotted by fishermen nine miles south of the bridge, three weeks after he went missing. He was short one hand and his limbs were badly damaged, but despite the weeks submerged, he was still vaguely recognizable. The cops had told her it was a fluke they'd found his body at all. Bodies float, but only while they're buoyed by gases formed in the process of decay. Once the fish start munching through the remains, they break into the body cavity and let out the gas. With nothing to keep it afloat, the body sinks to the ocean floor, joining every other skeleton to be broken down.

The working theory was that somehow Jeff had gotten hung up on something, perhaps caught in the fishing lines of an old trawl and tethered, floating just under the surface for a week or two until whatever he was caught on broke loose when his hand came off. This horrible thought was enough to make Velvet sob uncontrollably every time she thought of his lonely death.

With Jeff missing, she'd spent Thanksgiving Day as she'd spent nearly every free moment since he disappeared—searching. She'd posted his picture on telephone poles and in businesses from San Francisco to Russian River to the north, and as far south as San Jose. She'd walked the beaches of Marin, San Francisco, and San Mateo. She'd hired a boat to speed her around the edges of the Bay. When the searching had taken her to places only a jumper's body would end up and she'd found nothing, she'd briefly convinced herself that Jeff was vacationing in some exotic locale and would call her one day and laugh about the trouble he'd caused. She was angry with him for the journey he'd chosen instead.

Her psychologist, Artemis McDermid, ever the spiritualist, had a theory she thought would comfort Velvet: that dying amidst spectacular geography reminded people of their Creator and would help them merge with their God. *Bullshit*. The bridge had been convenient. No need to buy a gun or access prescription medication—the bridge was its own murder weapon. All you had to do was close your eyes and step into the void.

Suicide by bridge was horrific. Anyone who thought going off the Golden Gate was a coward's way out hadn't read the *Chronicle* series. You pull a trigger, and you expect life to end in an instant. You take a flying leap off the bridge, on the other hand, and you know you've got moments of sheer terror as you fall. And it's not the fall that will kill you, it's the impact. At eighty miles an hour, the speed of the fall, water is like concrete. When she'd written her piece Velvet had actually gone around saying how jumping was incredibly ballsy. Now she found the act reprehensible in its selfishness. Suicide was so unfair to those left behind; Velvet was mad as hell that Jeff could have done this to her.

She'd always thought of him as bright *and* courageous, and somehow she couldn't see Jeff settling for his fifteen minutes of fame post-mortem. His life had seemed too full of promise. Was he trying to make some kind of point? Hadn't he read her articles? He'd always told her he read her work, but maybe he'd just been shining her on, being polite. *Asshole*. Once he'd gotten something in his head he'd always been so damn resolute. He couldn't have become a successful clothing designer, then changed careers to become executive director of the world's largest lesbian and gay film festival without that determination. Was his death another final act of stubbornness?

Why hadn't he told her what he was considering? She'd just reconnected with him, for godssakes. Who reconnects with one of their oldest and closest friends and then takes a flying leap off a bridge? Did he intend to say good-bye? Velvet desperately wanted to talk to him one last time. She wanted to tell him all the things she'd never said about how much she loved him and needed him in her life. She shouldn't have let Tyrone drive her away. She wanted to know why Jeff jumped—*and why he didn't leave a note?*

He'd phoned her the day before he vanished, leaving a message on her voice mail. She'd thought he was just confirming their next lunch date or wanting to pick up their last conversation where it had left off: Chase Devlin, the producer he was working with. Jeff's message was vague, almost uncharacteristically so. What if he'd wanted to tell her something that was weighing on his mind? If she'd gotten back to him right away, would he still be alive?

When the flowing of her tears slowed to a gentle stream, Velvet turned from the Bay and the cold wind. Pulling her jacket tighter around her, she strode back along the pedestrian walkway to the Vista Point.

CHAPTER ONE

Five Weeks Earlier

Yoshi Yakamota felt hot. Hot, cramped, and uncomfortable. AJ Johnson had talked about this concert for weeks, so Yoshi did not want to express her discomfort. She and AJ had been dabbling in courtship, a will-they-won't-they two-step that had established solid ground for a friendship...or more. Tonight Yoshi hoped to clarify, once and for all, which one was meant to be.

As a private investigator, she noticed subtle clues; it was her job. So she'd recognized that the LGBT hip-hop concert held great significance for AJ. Her excitement about the event was more than a subtle clue. With nearly a year of policing the San Francisco Bay Area's East Palo Alto neighborhood under her belt, AJ was longing for a return to her hometown of New Orleans. Her post-Katrina dislocation and subsequent move west had left her somewhat brokenhearted. Yoshi hoped the concert would lift her spirits.

Perhaps the rare outing would do the same for her. She spent far too many nights at home, alone with the ghost of her father. It had been his home and he still seemed to inhabit the residence and her dreams. He was hungry and yearning. He wanted justice. One day she hoped to give it to him.

Soft fingers grazed lightly across her forearm and Yoshi felt someone's breath on her neck. *Velvet Erickson.* She could always recognize the journalist's unique scent, even in this crowded room. Velvet said something, but Yoshi could barely hear her over the cacophony. She dipped her head, sending her hair sweeping across her shoulders.

"Are you okay?" Velvet asked.

"Yes." Yoshi was not entirely certain she was being honest. The truth was, this situation was all a little overwhelming and she was feeling more than just prickled by the heaving crowds.

Her eyesight, which had been slowly degenerating for a decade, had all but ceased to exist. Just a month ago, she had still been able to distinguish large objects: this tall, dark blob a person; that low and long one a couch. But now the encroaching darkness had all but eclipsed the world around her, and here she was packed into the El Rio with numerous other queer folk, yet she felt entirely alone. It was disconcerting. She was glad Velvet and Tucker had joined her and AJ for a double date.

Velvet, an investigative reporter for the *San Francisco Chronicle*, had been Yoshi's best friend for years. They had also been lovers, once upon a time. Yoshi adored her, even if she frowned on Velvet's love-them-and-leave-them dating style. She was particularly concerned about her friend's interest in the much younger Tucker Shade, the receptionist at Yoshi's private investigation firm, Blind Eye Detective Agency. It had never turned out well when Velvet dated one of Yoshi's employees. But Velvet and Tucker had seemed so smitten, there was no point in trying to separate them.

The crowd tightened around Yoshi, jostling her as they did. She could almost feel them sucking the oxygen from the room. She was just becoming claustrophobic when the first performers came on, announced as the Deep Dickollective, a men's troupe. Yoshi could tell that Velvet and Tucker were already in their own little bubble, and AJ was transfixed.

Yoshi could understand why the New Orleans native was thrilled to be in a familiar environment, and even more so after discovering LGBT artists performing the musical style she loved. There was no equivalent for Yoshi, even in San Francisco, no lesbian performers specializing in Japanese *kayo-kyoku*. Kayo-kyoku was a type of Japanese pop music blending Western and Japanese scales. The melodies of these pentatonic scales mixed the trills and grace notes common to traditional folk songs and *shamisen* of earlier times with the sophisticated rhythm and strong beats of Western pop.

The crowd screamed with delight, leading Yoshi to conclude that this audience was primarily composed of members from a younger generation. They intoned a deep, baritone whoop that was probably one of those "holler backs" AJ had told her to expect. The emcee introduced a performer named "Katastrophe," and Yoshi was subjected to another swell of the crowd, then near-deafening noise. The floor vibrated. Was the audience stomping their boots? Yoshi couldn't tell. The pulsating staccato steps of low, sustained booming sounded like a Japanese Taiko drumming troupe.

She smiled and let her mind drift to San Francisco's Taiko Dojo. Her body responded as she recalled the feeling of every molecule vibrating to the unparalleled sound of the prized O Daiko drum, a round rope-tension drum carved from a single piece of wood. The tree trunk that spawned the O Daiko must have been enormous. The one-ton, twelve-foot-high drum, the largest in the Western hemisphere. dwarfed its drummers. Some accountant, who had not understood the remarkable spiritual and cultural value of the O Daiko drum, had assigned it a monetary worth of half a million dollars.

Another rush of the crowd slammed Yoshi backward, knocking her toward the floor, and snapping her consciousness rudely back to the El Rio. AJ's arm was around her waist immediately, keeping her on her feet.

"He's tight, huh?"

Yoshi supposed the comment was in reference to the rapper who had just performed. Not a hip-hop fan, she remembered "Katastrophe" as a transgender man called Rocco Kayiatos. She'd met him once at a book signing for his novelist girlfriend, Michele Tea. They were local celebrities in San Francisco.

The next act, Kritik, initiated a litany of purple prose. Yoshi only understood every third lyric, but what she did get made her alternately smile and cringe depending on the singer's sexual frankness.

Velvet, who had drawn close to Yoshi again, whispered in her ear, explaining that Kritik's entourage was a cute, chubby drag king troupe known as the Bois of Boise—which Yoshi assumed was a tongue-in-cheek reference to the infamous fifties roundup of gay men that had disgraced that city. If she recalled correctly, the event had been dubbed the "Boys of Boise." The reference appeared to be wasted on this audience.

She nearly shouted her reply but still her voice was all but drowned out. "Thought-provoking, if this generation was aware of anything that occurred before a Bush was in the White House."

"I know. And the song they're lip-synching is an old Conway Twitty ditty."

Yoshi ran a flattened palm above her hair. It was a motion she had used since college, a pantomime that indicated something went over the subject's head.

"Where'd AJ disappear to?" Velvet asked.

Yoshi shook her head. She did not voice her thoughts: *Perhaps to regale one of the performers with testimonials as to how righteous or tight she found them.* She berated herself immediately. She had difficulty understanding modern urban slang, but knew full well that when AJ spoke the street dialect, she was not doing so out of ignorance. What Yoshi always found funny was hearing white youths from suburbia adopt urban slang without any awareness of its racial heritage.

"Feel old yet?" Velvet asked.

It took Yoshi a minute to realize Velvet was referencing both the music and the audience. "*Please.* I felt old before these kids were learning to drive. Tonight I feel positively Paleolithic."

"Guess who Tucker and I ran into?" Velvet said. "Jeff and the boyfriend."

"Jeff Conant? How is he? I haven't spoken to him in ages."

"I know. It's been too long for me, too. Seeing him made me realize how much I've missed him. We haven't seen each other as much since he started dating Tyrone. I don't know why Jeff even fell for him, he's such a dirtbag."

Before Yoshi could comment, Velvet rushed on. "I know it's not *just* Tyrone. We've both been so crazy busy the last few months—Jeff with the film festival, me with the whole Rosemary Finney fiasco. But Tyrone just seems to monopolize all of Jeff's time and energy. It makes me so mad."

"Gosh, I have no idea what *that* would be like," Yoshi remarked.

Velvet apparently heard the sarcasm in her voice. "Tucker and I aren't that bad."

"Of course not," Yoshi responded with mock sincerity, still raising her voice to be heard over the crowd.

"Tyrone's just going to have to get used to me. Jeff and I have been friends forever," Velvet said, as though Yoshi could have forgotten their history. Velvet loved to reminisce. "We're family, damn it. He was my first boyfriend—when we were both fourteen—and we've been friends since we were in grade school together."

Yoshi often wondered what it would be like to have family. She supposed all only children tried to imagine a life with siblings and their offspring. Her mother had passed away when Yoshi was five. After that, her father had been her best friend, and then he, too, was taken from her, killed several years ago. Aside from Velvet, she did not have family, not even in the queer sense of the word. She wondered when she would *really* adjust to being so alone.

"Anyway," Velvet rattled on, "we made a lunch date. I'm thinking Blowfish. Their sushi is to die for."

AJ tumbled into them, so breathless with excitement she could barely string together a complete sentence. "Yoshilicious!"

Yoshi was surprisingly fond of AJ's recent moniker for her.

"There'll be another concert next week!"

Wonderful. If this was modern music, Yoshi was having serious doubts about her interest in attending future concerts. Her idea of an ideal musical experience was classical string and percussion orchestras at the conservatory, operatic theater performances, and the Twelve Girls Band on National Public Radio. The instrumental sounds of a dozen Asian women playing traditional instruments were so haunting Yoshi was nearly breathless every time she heard a performance. *That* was music.

She had also attended a few memorable concerts with Mai Lee, an elder in San Francisco's close-knit Japanese community. Yoshi's father might have failed to recognize his tendency to treat her like a son, but he had acknowledged his failures to properly enculturate her and had all but handed her over to community grandmothers like Mai, who schooled her in Japanese culture and tried to shame her into behaving like a proper Asian lady.

Very little of this education stuck. Yoshi's heart hadn't been in it. She had found something intriguing in the feminine accoutrements of fashion, skin-care products, and enticing aromas, but she rejected the traditional Asian notions of femininity. Now, after spending time with AJ, who had come up in the entirely African American neighborhood of New Orleans's Ninth Ward, she was beginning to wonder if she had missed something.

The next performer was an emcee from Minneapolis whose name

Yoshi did not catch. As this person took the stage, the crowd let out a collective bark. What were they saying? Dog meat? Do me? Doughy? Dougie? She could not decipher the noisy acclamations for the life of her. When she was knocked into *again* she tugged on the pocket of the nearest trousers, thinking they belonged to AJ. They did not.

After sincerely apologizing to a bemused owner and her irate girlfriend, Yoshi bumped into a man's broad chest. He smelled of a spicy mix of clove, menthol, and camphor.

"Yoshi? Yoshi Yakamota?" The voice hinted at a Latino heritage.

Thank God. Someone who knew her. At this point she did not even care if she knew him.

"It's Detective Chico Hernandez with the SFPD. My dad was Bud Williams's partner."

Yoshi assumed Hernandez had provided his professional information not because he was on duty but because she had encountered him in the context of his work. Chico's father, Jose Hernandez, was the chief of police in San Jose. He owed Bud Williams a debt of gratitude that sometimes proved to be useful. When they were both detectives, Bud had taken a bullet meant for Jose. He had been paralyzed below the waist and was a reluctant retiree of the San Francisco Police Department.

Yoshi had inherited Bud when her father passed away and left her in charge of his PI firm. Some people adjusted well to a change in their abilities. Bud had not. Yoshi surmised he had always been sexist, surly, and heterosexual, but his personal tragedy had made him bitter and hard to motivate. He was the Blind Eye Detective Agency's own grumpy old man. Bud's tactics could be a bit unorthodox. But when he got it in his mind to solve a case, he could not be deterred, and this made him an invaluable resource. Unfortunately, the cases he became obsessed with were not always those Yoshi was paying him to investigate.

Chico Hernandez was Bud's main source inside the SFPD. Evidently the young detective was vulnerable to guilt trips and reminders of the personal debt his family could never repay. Yoshi shook his hand. Although she had met him before, she tended to coordinate with a more senior detective in the SFPD, Ari Fleishman. She had never encountered Chico Hernandez at a social event.

He introduced her to the man with him. "This is my partner, Rick Pallin."

A warm, beefy hand closed around Yoshi's. "Charmed to meet you," Rick said. "FYI, that's *romantic* partner. What?" The latter comment seemed directed at Hernandez rather than Yoshi. "I don't want her to think I'm another cop. Don't try to put me in some kind of cop closet, Chico. I won't put up with that."

Rick dipped his head close to Yoshi's so she could hear without him shouting. "I'm teasing him. When you've been together as long as we have, you don't care who knows what."

Yoshi hinted she was feeling a little claustrophobic in the tight quarters of the club and Rick gallantly escorted her outside, keeping one arm around her waist as they exited. She was certain he could have whisked her into the air without the slightest exertion, and yet he was far from brutish. Once outside, he entertained her with witty banter that helped her relax. The humidity hinted that storm clouds were passing above them, waiting for the warmth of the next day's sun before they could let loose their rain. She shivered in the cool night air and Rick removed his jacket and hung it around her shoulders. If she were straight and he had been her date, she would have swooned into his arms.

Why wasn't AJ this attentive? Were they not on a date? Yoshi sighed at the thought. Perhaps lesbian dating was not as exciting as Velvet liked to think. Or perhaps Yoshi was not built for dating. She did not favor Velvet's one-night-stand approach, yet she found dating rituals cumbersome and awkward. Generally, she avoided romantic entanglements. She had not been in a *serious* relationship for nearly a decade, not since she and Velvet called it quits and agreed to go back to being friends. She had taken a chance with AJ. They had a certain chemistry between them, a spark she had not felt in a very long time. Perhaps she should have allowed that feeling to pass. They always did. Eventually.

Hernandez's partner entertained her, regaling her with elaborate stories detailing the adventures they had encountered in their five years together. His intriguing tales and droll observations distracted her from the chill and facilitated the passing of time.

"There you are." AJ's statement suggested she had spent some time searching for Yoshi inside the club, an assertion Yoshi did not quite believe. AJ smelled of sweat and she was breathing heavily, presumably from singing, dancing, and ignoring Yoshi. She made no effort to apologize for interrupting Rick's latest tale.

Yoshi introduced the two of them, thanked Rick for his kindness, and returned his jacket. Much to AJ's consternation, Rick insisted on escorting them to the safety of AJ's recently acquired Escalade before he returned to the club.

"Your dawg there, he think I can't take care of my breezy?" AJ asked, turning the key in the obscenely adorned vehicle she cherished.

Yoshi responded with a noncommittal monosyllabic reply and settled into the comfort of the Escalade's bucket seat. The vehicle was a recent acquisition, financed through a police auction. While it was clear that AJ enjoyed Yoshi's company, it was equally obvious that her feelings for Yoshi paled in comparison to those for her Escalade. The vehicle was a greater status symbol than an attractive woman, and AJ did not need Yoshi. As a new butch in town, she was in high demand.

The lesbian community in San Francisco fell victim to the same demographic pitfalls as a remote island population. There were only a limited number of available partners, and within the population relationships became quite incestuous, with exes dating exes. When new arrivals drifted in on the metaphorical tide, they offered all the thrills that those overly familiar exes did not. AJ could have a dozen new suitors before she arrived back at her Hayward studio apartment.

They were not headed to that apartment now, but to Yoshi's single-level home in the Richmond district. After they exchanged a few niceties, AJ flipped on the CD player. Heavy chords and rapid-fire rhyming echoed off the oversized vehicle's windows. Yoshi did not try to make conversation; AJ had announced her listening priorities.

After a while they came to a halt and AJ said, "We're here."

Against her better judgment, Yoshi invited AJ inside. She did not want to face her father's ghost alone. Not tonight. Unlocking the door and stepping over the threshold, she was back on familiar ground and no longer at the mercy of strangers. Here she knew exactly where everything was, where the gold-quilted settee was to toss her coat on, how to throw her house keys and land them on the bird's-eye maple hall table without even a pause. Here she was no longer disabled.

In the home she had grown up in, and in the Blind Eye office, it was as if Yoshi were no longer blind. She was strong, capable, and independent. She was a private investigator who, despite her failing sight, had continued to manage her business with a modicum of assistance. Over the past few years she had found methods to work around her gradually increasing blindness, but tonight, at the El Rio, she had been incapable of extracting herself from a situation she found difficult to cope with. Worse yet, although Rick Pallin had not let on, it was clear that he had seen her fear and neediness. Hers was no longer just a private shame, tonight it was a public humiliation. A humiliation made all more sharp because others could plainly see that not only could she not care for herself, but she had to be rescued by a *man*. Yoshi felt like she had single-handedly set the feminist movement back twenty years.

Slumping on the divan, she fought off tears. She wished she had told AJ to go home. Then she could cry all she wanted, without anyone witnessing her at her weakest and most vulnerable.

AJ slid next to her and stroked her hair. "*Ma chérie*, don't cry. What say you?"

"No." Yoshi rolled her head from side to side to reiterate her unwillingness to converse, even when AJ filtered her questions with Cajun dialect. She had been bottling up her fear and isolation for years now. She worried that once she popped the cork on those emotions, she would no longer be able to control them.

AJ's sweet breath warmed Yoshi's face, and her calloused fingers traced invisible patterns on her cheeks. She allowed herself to soften under AJ's touch. Her body ached to be held and soothed. And below the surface of that need, another swam impatiently; it was a darker desire that whispered promises about becoming lost in physical passion, subverting her emotional pain and rigid posturing by surrendering herself to another.

Hungrily pulling AJ atop of her, Yoshi caressed her face, her fingertips relaying data to her brain that translated into a more complete image forming in her mind's eye. The bump on AJ's strong nose was a relic of a rough-and-tumble past, as was a scattering of small scars on her forehead, cheeks, and chin. Yoshi traced AJ's parted lips and was surprised when AJ gently captured her wandering fingertip with her teeth. AJ's tongue darted out and tickled the sensitive webbing where Yoshi's fingers joined her palms.

Yoshi prickled with excitement. She drew her noncaptured fingers over the back of AJ's hand where the prominent veins crisscrossed like the sinewy hoses fire fighters lugged over their shoulders to douse hungry fires. AJ had the opposite effect on Yoshi, stoking a fire that was racing down her body like a wick dipped in gasoline.

Yoshi pressed her lips against AJ's. Their tongues entwined. One of them moaned. AJ removed Yoshi's cardigan and Yoshi felt a button on her oxford shirt pop off as AJ hurriedly pulled it open and pressed her face between Yoshi's small breasts. Her nipples were pert under her bra. AJ freed her arms from her own oversized sweatshirt, and let Yoshi pull the Beefy-T over her head. Below that AJ wore a men's tank undershirt. Yoshi imagined how the stark white of the shirt must look against AJ's dark skin. She smiled and ran cupped hands down AJ's muscular arms.

When she lifted the bottom of AJ's undershirt, AJ pulled her hands away. Yoshi nodded, understanding that to mean AJ wanted to leave it on. It was cute, how the butchie girl wanted to cover herself even though Yoshi could not see. Yoshi unhooked the belt around AJ's loose-fitting jeans, which immediately fell to her ankles. AJ's rough hands pushed aside Yoshi's bra and cupped her breasts as she nibbled the nipples. There was no protest this time. No third-date plan. No safe words.

Yoshi wrapped her fingers in AJ's short hair and pressed her down. It had been a long time between lovers for both women and within seconds, like greedy vines climbing an Ivy League dorm, their limbs were woven so tightly it was hard to remember where one ended and the other began. When Yoshi did orgasm, she was nearly unaware of her surroundings, unhinged by need, lost in pleasure. Their bodies were soon drenched in sex and they hydroplaned, sliding across each other. By the time her back arched in final upheaval, Yoshi's mouth was dry and her breathing ragged. Exhausted, she slipped into sleep almost immediately.

In the morning when she awoke, she and AJ were still heaped on each other on the living-room floor, clothes half on, half off. She untangled herself and quickly pulled on clothes before AJ stirred. What they had had belonged to the night and it should stay there. When they'd fallen asleep together, Yoshi had understood, as clear as if AJ had whispered it in her ear, that this would be the extent of their romantic relationship. It was not that they were sexually incompatible. It was not that at all. There was just this sense that they had given each other something they both needed and they might never need each other that way again.

Yoshi was a little relieved.

CHAPTER TWO

Velvet circled the block around the postmodern brick building that housed Blowfish, the Mission District's chic, urban sushi restaurant. Passing one more filled parking spot, she muttered curses under her breath. With more vehicles on the streets than parking places, San Francisco's parking situation had gone from merely bad to simply God-awful. She should just get rid of her beloved Celica, but she couldn't bring herself to part with it.

A true Los Angeleno, Velvet saw her car as far more than a conveyance. It symbolized her freedom to up and leave whenever she wanted. It reflected her self-determination and independence. She didn't have to be at the mercy of cab drivers or the schedules and limited routes of public transportation. She could come and go on her own terms. Even after a decade away from her home city, Velvet wasn't willing to let all that go. She might not have the patience to circle the block endlessly searching for an open space, but she most assuredly did *not* have the patience to depend on her ability to flag down a cab.

She was just about ready concede defeat when she hooked a parking space on her fourth time around the block. Walking west on Mission Street, she spotted Jeff Conant sauntering her way. He cut a dashing figure with his trim, muscular body and fashionable business suit. He was so grown-up.

When they met up at the corner, Velvet could see that Jeff was practically glowing, a wide smile on his handsome face. The other night at El Rio, the lights had been so low she'd barely gotten a look at him. Now she could see him in all his glory. Although his once flowing locks had succumbed to male-pattern baldness, Jeff kept what was left trimmed close to the scalp, and the style accented his features. His white teeth were offset by a deep golden tan. The pudginess that had plagued him in his twenties had given away to a gym-toned body. He exuded confidence.

They hugged, holding each other almost too long, perhaps giving passersby the mistaken idea that they were a hetero couple.

"It's *so* good to see you," Velvet drawled in a perfect Valley Girl twang. The speech pattern she'd been cursed with since growing up in Southern California resurfaced in the company of Jeff, her parents, kids from her old neighborhood, and people she'd known in high school.

"I know!" Jeff swooped her curvaceous body into his arms, easily lifting her feet from the cement. He swung her around like she was a little kid or they were replaying that ubiquitous image of the Times Square, post–World War, civilian-kissing, returning solider.

Velvet was a little light-headed when he set her back down and she clung to his broad shoulders for balance. Jeff slung an arm around her waist and they ambled together, up the street and through the doors of Blowfish.

The restaurant was the type of place San Franciscans took their New York friends to prove the West Coast had culture. Low-slung wooden beams and hanging miniature lamps vied for attention with two video displays showing Japanese anime, and prints from Asian sci-fi animation movies that graced the walls.

Their cheeks had barely graced the bench seat cushions when Velvet, no longer capable of holding in all of her questions, burst out with, "So, how's life? Is it treating you well? How's work? Life? Love?"

"Ah, love. Despite your many complaints, I am *still* in love with—" Jeff paused to let the waitress fill their glasses with water from a stainless steel pitcher. He took a drink, furtively watching Velvet's face as though monitoring potential expressions of emotion or unspoken opinion.

She tried to keep her smile pleasant and her eyes projecting an objective interest she did not feel.

Jeff repeated, "I am still in *love* with…my job at Frameline." He smiled deviously. "Seriously, I had no idea I could be treated this well by a job. Frameline's really the most *amazing* organization, and all the staff—they're just awesome."

"I'm so glad, Jeff. You deserve it." This time Velvet's smile was genuine. "I love what you guys are doing this year with the free community-center screenings. It's such a great opportunity for people to see the films. Every time I've gone to a screening it's been packed to the gills."

"That's great to hear. My assistant, Davina, has really taken off with that project. She's managing it so I don't have to. You know, we started holding the free screenings to increase interest in our home DVDs."

"You just launched those, didn't you?"

Jeff nodded and they both glanced up as their waiter approached. Young and hip, she sported a hummingbird tattoo on her right wrist and eyebrows pierced with mismatching rings. She wore a white T-shirt with Blowfish's smiley punk puffer-fish logo plastered in the center and exuded a disdain bred from the comforting knowledge that an endless supply of restaurant patrons were clamoring for the chance to fill her tip jar.

Lowering her eyes from the girl to the laminated menu, Velvet wondered when she'd become a stodgy old broad. Although this was a lunch break and she would have to avoid slipping into an afternoon coma, she ordered her old standby, a triple-dirty vodka martini. Jeff chose a sake Bloody Mary. *Bloody hell.* In her head, Velvet heard the adorable Brit actor Hugh Grant say the words, and pictured a scene in *About a Boy,* but the phrase could just have easily come from any of several hundred British films.

"Quit stalling and *spill*," Jeff demanded. "Tell me about the girl from the other night—Tucker? Have you turned cougar on me? She looked a little young."

"Yes, *Mother*, she's ten years my junior."

"Oh, my God. You've got a girl toy!"

Velvet smiled. Nobody got her quite like Jeff did. "Girls my age just can't keep up with me."

"You mean lesbians your age are all settling down and having kids, and that *terrifies* you."

Velvet didn't respond. She didn't have to. He knew her better than she knew herself. She had met Jeff when they were both eleven years old. Velvet's mother had made a play date with Annie Carroll, a sweet towheaded girl from around the block with a slight overbite, a smattering of freckles around her nose, and a scoliosis brace that all made her, ironically, Velvet's first female crush. Annie had a crush, too. Hers was on Jeff. He had feathered blond bangs, piercing blue eyes, and even more freckles. He wore a retainer that seemed to get lost every time they ate lunch, but even then, Jeff was trendier than Velvet ever could be, left to her own accord.

Fortunately, Jeff had taught Velvet everything he knew about style and grace. The rest she gleaned from movies, glamour magazines, and *Sex in The City*. For a few months in high school, they'd played at being lovers, a word much too sophisticated to describe their futile attempt to be teen sweethearts. Velvet was almost a member of the Conant family by that time. She adored his parents, Charlie and Charlene, and knew the family secrets.

As time went by, she and Jeff had danced in and out of each other's lives with jobs, lovers, and moves that sometimes stretched their contact from daily to monthly. Still, they were close enough to rarely see each other and yet feel deeply and permanently connected. Every time they reunited, it was as though they'd never been apart; they slipped right back into reading each other's thoughts and completing each other's sentences. Though she hated to sound flaky and what she called "new-agey," Velvet liked to think of them as soul mates. Very queer soul mates.

"So," Jeff continued, "you get them when they're young and too naïve to recognize one-night stands for what they are, an opiate to keep them oblivious of the world around them until it's too late."

"Whoa. When did you become such a nihilist philosopher?" Velvet swirled the skewered olives around her vodka and olive juice concoction.

"It's *not* nihilism, dear. And you're avoiding the subject. Again."

"I'm afraid the shock might kill you. She's Yoshi's assistant—"

"That's *hardly* shocking, although I thought you weren't going to do that anymore." It was a statement, not a question.

She punched him lightly. "That isn't the shocking part, you jerk. We've gotten kind of serious."

"Really?" He narrowed his eyes at her, dubious. "Define serious."

"I've been seeing her for a couple of months and I'm still not tired of her." Velvet raised her hand and bent her fingers over one by one, ticking off her main points. "She has not only spent the night, but she does so *regularly*."

Jeff, well aware that Velvet generally sent her conquests packing as soon as they finished their sexual transaction, looked fairly impressed.

"And..." Here came the real shocker. "Since our first week together I haven't slept with anyone else."

"You're having a monogamous patch?" His mouth was attracting flies. "God, Velvet, that *is* serious." He shook his head as if he still didn't believe what he had heard. "Velvet Erickson has a *girlfriend*? Go figure."

"I know. It's the weirdest thing. It's not like I ever *said* I'd be exclusive, but it's just worked out that way so far. I haven't *wanted* to be with anyone else."

"Are you feeling well?" he joked.

Velvet bit one of the olives off its toothpick, took a drink, and swilled it around in her mouth like a wine taster, allowing the bouquet to settle on her taste buds. "I'm not sick. I feel as horny as ever. I just always seem to want to express it with her."

"You haven't gotten bored?" She knew he asked not because *he* equated monogamy with boredom, but because he knew she did.

"We haven't run out of positions." Velvet grinned.

Jeff plugged his ears with well-aimed forefingers. "Blah blah..." Then he got serious. "Well, tell me about her. If she's going to be my sister-in-law, I might as well hear all the dirt."

"Are you ready yet?" Their waitress was back.

Velvet still hadn't even glanced at the menu. She didn't need to. She knew it by heart. She ordered for both of them. A handful of signature rolls including her all-time favorite, the Ménage à Trois, which combined salmon, salmon skin, *ikura*, and *tobiko*. When the girl left with their order, Velvet attempted to adequately describe Tucker Shade.

"She's from Idaho, of all places. She's kind of a weird farm girl and she's got some emotional baggage—"

"Don't they all?"

"But I'm, like, totally smitten. She's whip smart, a little naïve..."

"I know how you like that." Jeff smirked.

She acknowledged him with a smile. Ticking off the high and low points, she regaled him with colorful stories of her last couple of months: meeting Tucker, Yoshi's failing eyesight, being accused of murdering her nemesis Rosemary Finney, the headway she was making with her shrink, and the investigation she was doing for the *San*

Francisco Chronicle into an ex-gay camp from which two kids had run away. Her contention so far was that the kids were still in the Bay Area, probably living on the streets in the Haight-Ashbury neighborhood.

Their rolls arrived. Velvet finished off her martini and dug in. Between bites, she continued bringing Jeff up to date. There was the latest celebrity gossip, news from back home, even those cute kitty shoes she got at Torrid last week. When they were done with the rolls Jeff insisted they split an Angkor Wat for dessert.

One bite of the banana, rum, and ice cream confection and Velvet pleaded her case: "I'm way too full to eat any more. So, what's new in your life?"

In between bites, Jeff answered, "I have to say, I'm really looking forward to next year's film festival. It's going to be great."

"Really? You can tell already?"

"Yes. I've screened some of the early submissions, and I have to say, if they continue in this vein, our program director is going to have a hell of a time picking this season's lineup."

"Do tell." Velvet, a film buff herself, was intrigued.

"Oh no, you don't." Jeff wagged a finger at her. "I'm not going to be your source inside Frameline so you can break the news. You'll have to wait for the program like everyone else."

Velvet pouted.

It did not melt his resolve. He changed topics. "Tyrone and I are still together. It's going well, even though we do have our ups and downs." He paused, looking sideways at nothing in particular. Velvet wondered if he was deciding exactly what not to tell her and how much to disclose.

Jeff had two obsessions, his new job and Tyrone Hill. The model turned actor had enchanted Jeff, the *auteur*, so much he seemed oblivious to the drama Tyrone brought to every situation. A clothing designer by trade, Jeff had fallen into the world of filmmaking—as he seemed to fall into a lot of things in his life while Velvet worked her ass off for hers—after he designed all the costumes for an independent gay film. Being on the set, fitting costumes and designing on the fly, Jeff fell in love, both with film *and* the star, Tyrone Hill.

Tyrone's roots in San Francisco's indie film world were deep, and by hanging out with him and his friends, Jeff had absorbed the ins and outs of new queer cinema. Within a year he'd sold off his haute couture line and used the proceeds to fund his move into gay filmmaking. First Jeff picked up a bulky and antiquated old-school camera from the Bay Area Video Coalition, a guerrilla nonprofit organization that trained San Francisco's indie filmmakers in production methods. Later, as his skills grew, he purchased new equipment and began exploring the medium through collaborations with other filmmakers and the producer Chase Devlin.

After his first film, *Loving Randall*, went to festivals across the country and sold out to audiences at Frameline, Jeff found his name started to open doors. When the executive director position came up at Frameline, the country's largest film festival for LGBT films, he applied immediately and was delighted when they picked him for the job.

"But all couples do—at least those that stay together more than a few days. Once you get past the honeymoon period with Tucker, you'll see what it's like."

Velvet hadn't thought of her relationship as being in a short-lived phase that would soon be superseded by routine and compromise. The idea disturbed her.

"What's Tyrone doing now?" she asked.

"Well, he hasn't really worked for a while. He thought he had a gig in New York, so he flew out there for a couple of weeks, but he had to come back because it fell through. He's mostly just meeting with people, going on auditions and stuff."

"You don't sound happy about that. Is something wrong?"

"No, no. It's just really tough being an actor, you know. He's having a difficult time with all the rejection."

Velvet thought the answer was bullshit, but she played it cool. She didn't want to drive Jeff away after having just reconnected. Not being the kind of woman to hold her tongue, she had made no secret of her dislike for Tyrone and her opinion that Jeff deserved something better. The first inkling she'd had about Tyrone's *problems* was at a cocktail party in honor of *Loving Randall*.

Jeff's closest friends and new film buddies converged on the Foreign Cinema restaurant in the Mission District, gathering to toast Pinot Noir and imagine the future of queer cinema. The Foreign Cinema offered French cuisine in a theater setting. *Loving Randall* played in a continuous loop on the restaurant's large movie screen. When glasses began to run dry, Tyrone had volunteered to go out for more wine.

Hours later when he still had not returned, the party fizzled out. By the time Velvet left for home, Jeff was still making excuses his guests didn't believe.

A few months later, Velvet had happened upon Jeff and Tyrone at The Café. While she and Jeff caught up, Tyrone made his boredom clear by fidgeting and rolling his eyes. Clearly he thought that a conversation that was not about him wasn't worth listening to. He excused himself to go to the restroom, and when he hadn't returned thirty minutes later, Jeff went looking for him. Velvet thought the boy toy was probably in the men's room getting high. But, as it turned out, instead of blowing smoke, Tyrone was blowing something else, or more precisely, *someone* else.

Since then Velvet had turned down a number of offers to get together with Jeff and Tyrone for social events. She always cited her workload but the truth was, she didn't relish the idea of spending time with Tyrone, or worse, listening to Jeff ramble on about what a great guy his partner was. But she loved Jeff dearly, and when he insisted that he and Tyrone were in love and begged her not to judge him harshly or interfere in their relationship, she had decided to follow the old adage: If you can't say something nice, don't say anything at all. All the same, she'd been relieved when Jeff mentioned Tyrone would not be joining them for their lunch date at Blowfish.

Steering toward a less personal topic, she asked, "What are your plans for Thanksgiving? Are you going down to L.A.?"

"Maybe next year. This year we're going to a friend's. How about you?"

"Tucker claims to know how to cook. I'm putting her to the test." She glanced at her watch. "Damn. I hate to say this but I have to get back to work."

"I know, me too. But it's been so great to see you again."

They paid the check, embraced, and promised to get together soon. Outside, they found that gray storm clouds had drifted in from the ocean and were snacking on the midday sun.

As Jeff walked Velvet back to her car, he asked, "Vel, have you ever met Chase Devlin?"

"Your production partner?" Velvet recalled that Devlin and Jeff were currently working on a new, as yet unannounced, film. "No, why?"

"Just curious. I thought you might have run into him some time."
There was a slight quaver in his voice.

Velvet searched his face. His features suddenly seemed darker
than they had earlier. The glow she'd seen earlier was gone, or was it
just the change in the outdoor lighting?

Trying to lighten the mood, she teased, "You're not trying to set
me up with a boy again, are you?"

Jeff humored her with a smile. It brought some light back to his
face. "God, no. It's nothing. We'll talk more later."

"Okay, text me to set up lunch sometime between now and
Thanksgiving. Cool?" Velvet was suddenly melancholy about their
parting, not entirely trusting that they would catch up again as soon as
she hoped.

They hugged one last time and whispered into each other's ears
like they had since they were thirteen.

"Love you."

"Back at you."

Getting in her car, Velvet teared up. It had been way too long
since they had last talked. She promised herself that she wouldn't let
as much time go by without seeing Jeff. Despite her firm intentions, as
she pulled away from the curb and watched him grow smaller in her
rearview mirror, she felt disheartened.

She had no idea that her unease was a premonition of terrible
things to come.

CHAPTER THREE

December 18
Golden Gate Bridge

Yoshi was no stranger to heartache. Jeff Conant was just the latest in a trail of loss that stretched back to her childhood. As she waited for Velvet to return from her sorrowful walk on the bridge, she thought, *At least Velvet knows the person lost to her.*

Yoshi could barely remember her mother. The face she imagined when she thought of her was not her mother's actual face; it was an invention, Yoshi's guess at what her mother might have looked like. She did not know for sure. She recalled her mother's smell, the touch of her hand, the sweet, soothing sound of her singing Japanese lullabies. But even though she had her sight as a child, she could not conjure up a memory of her mother's face.

Her father had not been the kind of man to capture his wife's beauty with a camera. He had expected her to be there in their home when he wanted to see her face. Nanako was only twenty-four. Too young for cancer, she had never had a mammogram. By the time they made their diagnosis it was too late. The cancer had already metastasized and spread throughout her body. She was gone six months later. In his grief, Yoshi's father could not even bear to hear her name, and he cut off contact with their extended family back in Japan.

It was three years now since a stranger had stolen Hiroki Yakamota's life, and Yoshi still hadn't recovered, not really. A consummate professional, she had been careful to keep her emotional wounds well hidden. It did no one any good to know the depth of the fear that had stalked her ever since Hiroki lost his battle with a six-inch blade; her friends and coworkers would not understand her anxiety. They would assume that her job put her in proximity to the kind of perpetrator who had stolen her father's life, and therefore brought up the horror of her loss. But that was not it. Not at all.

Yoshi feared that without someone like Hiroki in her life, she would not longer function when the last light in her eyes faded and she was plunged into an eternal darkness. Her father had been her rock, her best friend. He had also been her caregiver when she needed one, and her cheering section when she had doubts. He had been her reason for working hard, the reason she was even in this field of private investigating. That fate would take him from her as well, even though it was twenty-five years after the death of her mother, seemed anything but fair. And now that she had lost both Hiroki and her eyesight, she wondered if it was time to admit defeat and hang up her PI credentials.

The sound of footsteps interrupted her thoughts and the driver's side door cracked open, letting in the cold and humid winds of San Francisco's December. Without a word, Velvet slid into the Celica. Yoshi detected the scent of salt water. It was probably a combination of tears and the coastal breeze pregnant with seawater molecules. She covered Velvet's hand with her own and did not interrupt the silence by verbalizing her sympathy. Velvet's skin was chilled from the elements.

"Why?" Velvet demanded, as though Death hovered nearby, willing to give up his secrets when properly queried.

"I'm sorry," Yoshi said, knowing it was not enough.

She squeezed Velvet's hand before releasing it like one of the rehabilitated birds of prey that wildlife specialists regularly set free from the hills above the Golden Gate Bridge. She imagined hawks soaring over the bridge and the ocean. Circling on once-broken wings, they offered hope that Velvet would recover, too. Her emotional wounds would heal and she would fly again. But it would take time.

As Velvet accelerated rapidly away from the parking area, the G-force pressed Yoshi hard against the back of her seat and gave her stomach the sensation of roller-coaster rides. She imagined Velvet's foot slammed on the gas pedal, pressing the lever until it kissed the floorboards.

Yoshi gripped the door handle. She understood Velvet's need for acceleration, and she knew that when first exiting the scenic turnout a driver had the advantage of an extra lane. But this wouldn't last long;

in only four hundred feet it turned into an exit ramp for Sausalito. She muffled her concern; it seemed unwise to utter a panicky sound when Velvet would need all her concentration to keep them on the road.

Given the steep incline leading to the Waldo Tunnel, which linked them to the rest of Marin County, revving the Celica up to speed in the short distance was a tremendous feat. Leaning forward in her seat as though her weight would propel the vehicle forward, Velvet coaxed the car to 45 m.p.h. and, just as she was running out of pavement, swerved sharply into the freeway slow lane. A horn blared behind them as an irate driver was forced to reduce his speed.

"Fuck you, too," Velvet yelled, releasing her pent-up emotions by pounding on her own horn. It echoed off the walls of the tunnel and elicited responses from other drivers.

She glanced sideways and saw Yoshi tighten her grip on the door handle. For a split second, Velvet worried that inertia would propel her friend over the emergency brake and she would slam into Velvet, making her swerve into the path of a big rig, and they would both die. But Yoshi was clinging to the door frame like she had the same idea in her head, too.

"He's gone," Velvet said. "Relax. We're fine."

Yoshi let her relief out in an exaggerated sigh and released the handle.

"Why couldn't *he* have been the one to jump?" Velvet asked, not expecting an answer.

Yoshi did not try to give her one.

❖

International maritime law dictated that wherever a floater first touched land, that would be the jurisdiction responsible for the case. In most Golden Gate suicides, the Coast Guard pulled the body from the water and hauled the victim to Fort Baker. This meant that the Marin County coroner's office was assigned the unenviable task of identifying jumpers, notifying family members, and performing the autopsies. Marin County doesn't have a morgue. They contract out with a funeral home to hold the deceased and subcontract a pathologist to perform autopsies on site, next to the embalming room.

Velvet pulled into the shining white gravel lot of the Russell and Gooch Funeral Chapel in the town of Mill Valley. She parked by the side of the building. It was not nearly as creepy as she remembered it from a late-night visit during her research for the bridge suicide piece. On that occasion, she'd been summoned to the Fort Baker beach, where she'd joined Guardsmen holding silent vigil over the Golden Gate Bridge's latest victim. The body was transported to the funeral home in a Mercedes station wagon instead of a hearse, a fact that for some reason had dismayed Velvet. She'd watched the gurney being loaded into the back, acutely conscious of the lack of ceremony. Somehow the routine nature of the removal seemed an ignominious end for someone who'd chosen to make a dramatic departure from life.

The funeral home had given Velvet the creeps that night. In the ethereal light of dusk, hulking oak trees hovered threateningly overhead. Their branches had reached out like hands to grab her under the pale light of a half-moon. They quavered in the breeze and sent shadows scurrying across the gravel. She had wanted to follow them, running away from the eerie building.

Now, in the light of day and with Yoshi by her side, the place didn't seem nearly as dark and foreboding as it was in her memories or during the nightmares that plagued her for months after writing the bridge series. Back then, she had gotten access to an actual bridge autopsy. Her presence had only been tolerated because she had not known the victim and Marin County supervisors had wanted her there. They did not appreciate that their county was the final destination for Golden Gate jumpers and wanted her to share the gruesome details with *Chronicle* readers so the good citizens of the San Francisco Bay Area would understand that the bridge did not promise an easy death. In fact, quite the opposite. It was like one of those "scared straight" programs where kids visit morgues to see the bodies of people killed by drunk drivers.

Velvet had arranged today's meeting with the Marin County medical examiner so that she could verify the cause of Jeff's death. She still couldn't quite believe he had killed himself. She needed an expert to tell her there was no doubt.

"Are you sure you want to come?" she asked Yoshi.

"I think I should hear the facts, also."

Velvet tucked her tiny digital voice recorder in her bag, stepped out of the Celica, and slung the brightly hued satchel over her shoulder. She waited for Yoshi to get out on the other side of the car and they walked together around to the front of the building. It took both of them to force the heavy ornately carved wooden door open. Inside, the funeral home was as quiet as a church.

Velvet pressed a button on the wall next to a leather love seat whose duplicate graced the opposite wall like a mirror image. Although the call button elicited no discernable noise, she assured herself that it would summon the funeral director and she sat down next to Yoshi to wait. A satin burgundy curtain covered the doorway into the funeral home proper and helped muffle sounds from the other rooms.

It had taken investigators from the Marin County coroner's office several days to conclusively identify Jeff's body. It came into the morgue without identification and they hadn't had much to go on. Velvet knew the standard protocol was for an investigator to meet with California Highway Patrol officers and compare notes. The length of time Jeff had been in the water might have complicated things. Although the CHP had found his vehicle in the Vista lot, that had been several weeks prior and might not have come to mind instantly. Eventually the investigator had compared notes with the SFPD and made the connection.

The remains of jumpers were often in a condition that made visual identification difficult. Jeff's driver's license descriptors would have been compared those with the unidentified body, but medical examiners also liked to have identifications confirmed in person by a family member. None of Jeff's lived nearby, and they would not ask his parents to come up from L.A. until they were all but certain the body was his. He didn't have any tattoos or piercings that could have enabled a positive identification.

Instead the photograph of Jeff's swollen body had been shown to various people who knew him well. Velvet, Tyrone Hill, and Jeff's Frameline coworkers had all confirmed his identity. The investigator then obtained a DNA sample for comparison. Tyrone had already provided San Francisco detectives with Jeff's toothbrush and strands of hair from his comb. Velvet had the impression from the cop who'd shown her the photograph that they were just working their way through the formalities, as they did with every suicide. She'd pressed him for more information and he said there was nothing to suggest foul play. The state of Jeff's apartment aroused no suspicions, and the lack of a suicide note was no big deal. Some people never left one.

Velvet had trouble believing Jeff would have signed out without telling anyone why. The man made movies. Surely an unscripted exit would have been too untidy for his liking.

Her reverie was interrupted when a tall, brooding man pushed aside the burgundy curtain and stepped toward her with his hand outstretched. "May I help you?"

Velvet stood and shook the proffered palm. "We're here to see Pamela Carter. She's expecting us."

The man nodded solemnly. "Right this way."

He held the drape open while Velvet and Yoshi ducked under, then he stepped around them and led them down the hallway. At first, Velvet thought he was leading them to the morgue room, where rows of white crosses and Stars of David hung from the wall like decorations. Instead, he directed them to a small vestibule.

"Dr. Carter will be right with you," he intoned before disappearing behind another curtain.

Velvet couldn't help but think about the last time she'd been here. The memory started like a photograph, a still image of a naked man stretched across the metal table. The smell was unforgettable, an aroma of rotting meat mixed with soggy, mildewed clothing and the antiseptic scent of hospitals.

The medical examiner had made the Y incision with her whirling saw and Velvet had thought she was going to faint. Or throw up. There was blood everywhere. Dr. Carter explained that a broken rib had punctured the heart and caused massive internal bleeding. When she noticed Velvet gulping like a fish, she politely provided a trash can for her to throw up into. Velvet closed her eyes, trying to neutralize the memory. The man on the slab suddenly had Jeff's face. He stared up at her with big eyes and mouthed something that looked like, "Help me." The ME yanked her hand from his chest and triumphantly hoisted his still-beating heart.

Velvet swayed on her feet, unable to switch off her imagination.

Yoshi caught her before she fainted.

Yoshi was so strong. And not just physically. But Velvet wasn't, not today.

"I can't do this," she said. "I thought I could, but—"

"It's all right," Yoshi assured her. "This is why I came with you. I am capable of managing the interview alone. Would you like to meet me back at the car?"

"Yes," Velvet said before fleeing from the room.

❖

"Hello?" The woman spoke in a hushed tone appropriate for the funeral home environment. "Oh, I'm sorry, I was expecting Velvet Erickson." She strode briskly into the room and lifted Yoshi's hand. "Pamela Carter, Marin County Medical Examiner."

Yoshi could feel the rough wrinkles and elevated veins on the back of the woman's hand. They bore evidence of the stress of a long career steeped in death and tragedy. With her palm against Carter's, she also felt a smooth dustiness that was probably talcum powder from inside latex gloves. Tools of the trade.

"Velvet needed some air," she explained. "She requested that we meet without her. I am her friend, Yoshi Yakamota. Also, I am a private investigator."

"Have you been hired by Mr. Conant's family?"

"No. This is a personal matter. Jeff was a friend of mine, also."

"My condolences to both of you," Dr. Carter said. "I know this is difficult."

"Yes. Thank you." Yoshi appreciated the ME's concern. The woman sounded sincere.

"How can I help you?"

"Velvet is having difficulty accepting suicide," Yoshi confided. "She was wondering if there was anything out of the ordinary about his autopsy."

"Does she have reason to suspect foul play?" Carter asked.

"Not anything significant. There was no suicide note, and Jeff did not seem the type to have ended his own life." Yoshi paused. "I recognize that disbelief is quite usual for friends and family. You must hear these sentiments expressed often."

"Yes." Carter acknowledged. "Suicide is hard for surviving family and friends to accept. Most can't believe that their loved one was so desperate yet didn't reach out."

"Velvet has always had sharp instincts," Yoshi said. "If she is concerned, I've learned to listen. So I would appreciate anything you can tell me, Dr. Carter."

"Are you sure you want to know?"

"In my profession, I am quite accustomed to the frankness of autopsy reports."

"All right. It's not pretty. Death by bridge never is."

"I understand." Yoshi braced herself.

"The good news is that it looks like he died on impact."

Velvet would be relieved. Yoshi verified, "COD was multiple blunt-force trauma?"

"That's right. The lung weight and blood strontium comparison appears to rule out drowning. The absence of mucus bubbles around the mouth and nose further suggest the subject did not survive impact."

Yoshi nodded. It was something of a relief to know he had not suffered further after the fall. "Anything else?"

"Do you want me to walk you through it?" Carter waved something that sent a small breeze toward Yoshi.

A file folder, Yoshi surmised. The autopsy results. "Please."

Carter opened the file.

"There was extensive bruising, signs of massive trauma, and several compound fractures. A purple discoloration covered the abdomen and midsection. The third and fourth left ribs were fractured by the impact and propelled through vital organs. Aside from the usual lacerations associated with this kind of death, his organs were healthy. The subject's sternum, skull, clavicle, and pelvic bones splintered and lumbar disks three, four, and five ruptured."

The list sounded typical for the effects of a human body impacting the San Francisco Bay at eighty miles an hour.

"Those injuries are consistent with a fall from two hundred fifty feet," Carter shared her conclusions. "What is atypical is the jagged traumatic amputation of the right hand just below the wrist, and the shattered bones of the proximal and distal rows that all appear to be postmortem injuries. From the decomposition and the rate of formation of adipocere, I feel confident in stating that something prevented the body from completing the typical cycle of sinking to lower, cooler depths. This DB remained in more shallow waters."

Yoshi frowned. "So what does that mean?"

"I believe your friend's body was hung up on something that kept him floating near the surface for seven to fourteen days. It seems likely that when his hand was severed, it freed his body from whatever he'd been entangled in."

"I see."

"Additional postmortem scrapes and scratches most likely occurred when emergency personnel recovered the body. Subject was HIV negative. The tox screen came back clean."

Yoshi took a moment to process the information. "Was there anything *at all* that could suggest this wasn't a suicide?"

"Being in the water so long means most trace evidence washes away. I did look for unusual wounds or evidence that might indicate whether this was an accidental fall or homicide. The injuries sustained, although they could have originated from some other force, were consistent with a bridge suicide. So, at this point suicide is my official conclusion. If there were other indications of foul play I might reconsider. But so far the evidence indicates your friend jumped off the bridge. In my opinion, no one does that unless they intend to kill themselves."

Yoshi found the ME's logic convincing, but would Velvet? "I recall reading a statistic, something akin to eighty-five percent of Golden Gate Bridge suicides have had previous attempts. I understand that there was no evidence that Jeff…"

Pamela Carter shuffled through the report again. "No, you're right, neither my physical examination nor the background investigation found any indication of previous attempts. Still, we get a fair number of newbies."

Yoshi suspected that despite the compelling evidence of suicide, Velvet would still be dissatisfied. Jeff was her oldest friend, after all, and Yoshi sensed Velvet needed to *understand* what led to his untimely death. She wanted to believe he had been a victim of something more than a secret suicidal impulse.

"Oh, there was one odd discovery," Carter said.

"What's that?"

"We found some unidentified debris in his lungs, with traces of sodium tripolyphosphate."

"That hardly seems unusual." Yoshi wrinkled her brow. Jeff had probably inhaled water before he died. "Where would the chemicals have come from if he died on contact?"

"It sounds more peculiar than it is. With bridge suicides we have actually found much stranger things. Sodium tripolyphosphate is used in dishwashing detergents. It gets into the storm drains somewhere around the bay and works its way into the bay itself. There was likely a pocket of the chemicals that your friend may have floated through or bobbed along with."

"Interesting." Yoshi was not sure what else to say.

"But not helpful," Carter concluded. "Because it does nothing to prove it was not suicide."

Yoshi nodded. She thanked Carter for her time and slowly made her way out of the mortuary. She understood the ME's quandary. Without evidence of foul play, or pressure from the police to rule Jeff's death suspicious, or some injury inconsistent with a fall from the bridge, there was no reason to assume anything but another tragic suicide.

But Yoshi also knew that when Carter said "consistent with a bridge suicide," that did not rule out all other possibilities. Of course, it was not likely that Jeff had been dead before he went over the bridge. If blood had not been pumping through his veins at the time of the fall, you would expect the injuries to be different. All in all, Yoshi thought as she left the building, Jeff's death was probably no more complicated and painful than it appeared to be: the unexpected suicide of their friend.

CHAPTER FOUR

Sighing, Yoshi pressed the buzzer again. She should have made the cab wait until she was inside the door. A vehicle was in the driveway but no one was answering her announcement. Maybe Velvet had walked to the nearby market. It didn't sound likely, but Yoshi decided she would sit on the steps and wait for a while just in case. She turned her back to the door and had just slid into a seated position when she heard footsteps darting along the hardwood-floored hallway. She had never known Velvet to be so light on her feet.

The door pulled open and the sweet aroma of sex and perfume wafted through the screen door.

Someone inhaled sharply. "Oh, Yoshi, I...I..." Tucker Shade stammered. "I didn't expect you."

Yoshi could detect the embarrassment in Tucker's voice. Even though Yoshi was well aware of her employee's sexual entanglement with Velvet, sometimes Tucker acted like she was still in the dark. Her young protégé's shyness was kind of cute, but Yoshi could not help wonder why Tucker reacted nervously whenever she was nearby.

The rustling of fabric suggested Tucker was hurriedly tucking in her shirt and smoothing out the wrinkles of clothes that had probably been recently crumpled on the floor. No wonder Velvet had not rushed to the door. She was probably still getting dressed.

Yoshi swallowed a chuckle. "Good evening, Tucker, is Velvet there?"

"Uh, yeah."

"Are you going to invite me in? Or do I have to wait out here on the steps all night?"

"Oh, God, I'm sorry. Of course." Tucker helped Yoshi to her feet, held the door for her, and then followed behind her.

Yoshi trailed her hand lightly along the wall, locating the arched entrance to the living room.

Tucker paused at the closed bedroom door across the hall, cracked it open, and called softly, "Velvet? It's Yoshi."

Yoshi heard her friend Velvet's unmistakable voice purr in response, "I'll be right there."

Yoshi was almost to the couch when Tucker darted past her and returned pillows that had been discarded during the lovers' recent tryst. Yoshi caught herself wondering where else the two had consummated their relationship. Was Tucker Shade a kitchen table kind of girl?

The bedroom door open and Velvet waltzed into the room in a rustle of flowing garments. When she planted a kiss on Yoshi's cheek, she smelled of mint, cocoa butter, and sandalwood.

"What brings you by?" She sat down on the couch so close to Yoshi that their thighs touched.

"There's a board meeting of the Golden Gate Bridge, Highway and Transportation District this evening."

"And?"

"It's a special public meeting for members of the public to make comments about the possibility of a suicide barrier. Or maybe it's just about the possibility of starting a study to analyze the feasibility of thinking about a suicide barrier," Yoshi joked. "You know bureaucracies. I thought you might want to go with me."

Velvet was quiet for a moment, as though considering the idea. Then Yoshi heard the faint jingling of dangling earrings as Velvet shook her head. "No, I don't think so. Thanks anyway."

"I'm sorry, did that sound like a request? I meant to say that I am here to accompany you to the meeting and I am quite willing to drag you kicking and screaming if that is what is required. You simply must address what happened, Velvet. I think this meeting is the perfect environment to allow you to feel like you are making an effort to change the situation."

"Why? It's not like that'll bring Jeff back."

"No, but it might prevent other people from meeting his fate."

"I don't care about other people," Velvet offered as a weak defense.

Yoshi slid her arm across the back of the couch and wrapped it around Velvet's neck, gently coaxing Velvet toward her. Velvet laid her head on Yoshi's shoulder and wept. Yoshi stroked her hair.

Tucker came into the room and set drink glasses on the coffee table. She didn't say anything. Yoshi imagined the younger woman glaring at her and wondered what gave her that impression.

"What did you say?" Tucker demanded. "She was doing fine until you showed up. Here I am working hard to keep her mind off…things, and you're here for two minutes and she's crying?"

Yoshi was surprised by Tucker's accusation and the tone of her voice. As her boss, Yoshi had never heard Tucker speak that way before.

Velvet wiped her eyes and sniffled. "It's okay," she assured Tucker with a forced lightheartedness Yoshi was familiar with.

Yoshi shook her head. "Tucker, you do realize that it is acceptable—even necessary—for people to grieve? Velvet has every right to cry."

Tucker flopped down on the La-Z-Boy recliner. "I know," she said contritely. "It just tears me apart seeing my honey suffering like this."

"That is one reason why it might actually be wise for just Velvet and I to go to the meeting."

"She's probably right, honey," Velvet said to Tucker. "It might be nice for you to have a break from taking care of me. And I don't know that I'll be able to speak, but I would kind of like to see what they say at this meeting."

"Fine." Tucker's voice implied a pout. "Just go."

If Velvet hadn't made a feeble attempt at a chuckle, Yoshi would not have realized Tucker was teasing by acting offended.

"If Velvet comes home miserable," Tucker announced, "I'm going to blame you." She directed the comment at Yoshi and laughed at the end as though the threat was just a joke.

Yoshi wondered how it was that being around Velvet gave Tucker the self-confidence to speak her mind so directly, when at work she acted shy, nervous, and unsure of herself. Maybe she was showing off in front of Velvet, like a little boy acting tough for Mommy's friends.

❖

Every bridge suicide seemed to inspire renewed demands for the construction of a barrier along Golden Gate's pedestrian walkway that would prevent future suicides. The debate had been simmering since

1937. Over the years, there had been seven attempts to design a structure that would quell the Golden Gate Bridge Highway and Transportation District board's concerns. Board members had argued for decades that a suicide barrier would be too expensive, unsightly, or ineffective. Their detractors accused the board of valuing aesthetics over human life and insisting on a standard no design could guarantee: one hundred percent effectiveness. Before the board would even consider a barrier, they required a two-year feasibility study likely to cost millions of dollars. The board had repeatedly said that they would not divert bridge funds for such a study, effectively stymieing any progress.

In response to renewed public pressure to reconsider their decision against the barrier, the GGBHTD board had reluctantly scheduled several public meetings to hear comments. The first of these was taking place in the Golden Gate Bridge Administration Building. The building sat at the periphery of San Francisco, right at the very brink, on a cliff top overlooking the Golden Gate where the ocean met the Bay, mere yards from the Golden Gate Bridge Toll Plaza.

Yoshi and Velvet found a couple of seats near the front of the boardroom and listened to various speakers discuss actual case histories and research statistics.

After someone spoke about the Kevin Hines case, that of a nineteen-year-old jump survivor who realized he didn't truly want to die, Yoshi heard the noise of a chair pushed back.

"I'm Jenni Olsen," a woman said. "You might be familiar with my film *The Joy of Life*?"

From Velvet, Yoshi knew that Jenni Olsen was an "institution" in San Francisco LGBT film circles. A former Frameline employee, the soft butch white woman had made a film that helped renew the debate about the Golden Gate Bridge suicide prevention barrier.

Olsen offered to set up a private screening of her film or provide DVD screeners for the Bridge Authority board members to view. They declined the offer.

Not to be daunted, she continued, "I made this film in part as a tribute to my friend Mark Finch, who committed suicide on the bridge twelve years ago. Mark was a lot like the most recent victim, Jeff Conant. In fact, they both held leadership positions at the LGBT film festival organization, Frameline. They both died on rainy nights and no one saw either of them jump. Mark left his leather briefcase leaning against the pedestrian railing, but his body was not found for six weeks.

His family and friends had to wait six agonizing weeks, six weeks of hoping he had run away or been abducted, or…" Her voice cracked and trailed off. "Mark was my friend, but he was so much more than that. He was a pioneer, the first person to organize a gay and lesbian film festival. He developed the format every LGBT film festival uses today."

Yoshi had not known Mark Finch, but she was stunned by how similar his story was to Jeff Conant's. She knew Velvet shared her sense of déjà vu; she could feel her fidgeting nervously and could sense the tension radiating from her body. Yoshi thought it would help Velvet to stand and bear witness to her story, her loss, but she also knew it would be a difficult thing for her to do. Just when Velvet seemed about to stand and speak, a deep baritone voice beat her to it.

Velvet let her plentiful ass sink back onto the uncomfortable chair as a barrel-chested, bearded man cleared his throat theatrically and addressed the board. He wore dark blue jeans and a navy suit jacket over a light blue dress shirt with no tie.

"My name is James Harden. I'm also a documentary filmmaker." He glanced toward the back of the room.

Velvet followed his gaze and was surprised to catch sight of a black woman with long braids hoisting a large film camera to her shoulder.

"Over the last year, I've been filming the Golden Gate Bridge. And I've…" Harden shuffled nervously. "I've captured more than a dozen suicides on tape."

A moment of silence passed as his statement was processed, and then chaos erupted. It seemed as every person in the room was speaking at the same time and they were all asking, "What?" and "How?" and "Why didn't you step in to stop this?"

The board's director, Eric Wideman, slammed something hard against the long table, banging it like a gavel and shouting "Order" as though he were a judge. When the noise finally lowered to a murmur, Wideman—who, Velvet noted, wasn't as broad as his name might suggest—said, "Excuse me, sir, but that sounds like an issue better addressed with us in a private venue rather than this public hearing."

"No!" The whole audience seemed to respond with one loud voice.

"With all due respect," Harden replied, "my project is completely aboveboard. I was issued a permit from the Golden Gate National Recreation Area to install four remote digital movie cameras and download images for a documentary film. Having unexpectedly borne witness to these tragic events, I feel I must speak out on behalf of the victims and add my own voice to those here tonight," Harden swept his arm around to indicate those gathered in the room, "in asking you to install a barrier and end this tragic loss of life."

The board members shifted nervously in their seats. Director Wideman's face turned a darker shade of red. The man to his right turned sideways in his chair with a cell phone raised to his ear. Velvet wondered whom he was calling. When the call was over, he set the phone on the table and leaned over to whisper in Wideman's ear. The director nodded and stood.

"As managers of the Golden Gate Bridge, we share the public's concern about the people who kill themselves on our structure. Our deepest sympathies go out to the families and friend of those so determined to end their lives. Unfortunately, there will always be depressed individuals. If the bridge were unavailable, they would simply find another location or method of killing themselves.

"It seems," he continued, "that every decade or so, interest will pique and we'll review designs for a suicide barrier. We have had to reject all of the architectural designs because they threaten to ruin the beauty of the landmark while failing to provide a foolproof deterrent to bridge suicides. Best estimates for cost of a barrier are in the neighborhood of *twenty* million dollars. Now, I'm sure you're all aware that Bay Area motorists are unwilling to pay a ten-dollar toll simply to cross the Golden Gate—even *if* it was guaranteed to reduce deaths—and we have no way of knowing whether it would."

Velvet couldn't sit still any longer. She stood. Her voice cracking with emotion, she insisted, "According to the San Francisco Suicide Prevention, nearly 1,250 people have committed suicide on the bridge since 1937. Are you saying that their lives weren't worth a hundred and fifty thousand dollars each? When you personally make—what is it— sixty thousand a year or more just to sit on this board? My friend, Jeff Conant, was the bridge's most recent victim. He was thirty-six years old. He had his whole life ahead of him. In less than three years he'd make what you're saying his entire life wasn't worth!"

Several people applauded. Velvet was just getting warmed up, but before she could say anything more, she heard the door open behind her and saw Wideman glance up and smile.

"Thank you all for your compelling testimony," he said in a voice that expressed more relief than appreciation. "I'm afraid the public portion of our meeting has now come to an end."

The disappointment in the room was audible.

"We're adjourning the public hearing early in order for the board to deal with an unexpected, urgent matter that has just came up."

Grumbling, the attendees slowly stood and shuffled toward the exit. One protested, "Don't think this is over!"

The door opened wide to expose two uniformed police officers standing in the foyer. *So that's who the board member called.*

Velvet bent down to Yoshi and whispered in her ear. "I'll be right back. Wait for me."

She pushed her way through the flow of the crowd to get to James Harden. The filmmaker was shrouded from view by a throng of people, probably the family and friends of people who had died on the bridge this past year. They were swarming him, all asking the same thing. Like Velvet, they wanted to know if a loved one's final moments had been caught on camera. Had someone witnessed their swan dives after all?

The two police officers stepped into the meeting room and began asking members of the public to leave. Velvet sighed. She returned to Yoshi and helped her to the aisle. There Yoshi extended her white cane—probably more for the police's benefit than her own, Velvet thought. They pushed their way out of the room and through the crowded foyer to the crisp evening air. They walked the short distance to Velvet's car, which was parked in sight of the main door.

"Do you mind if we wait here for a while?" Velvet asked.

"I insist on it," Yoshi said. "We have to talk with that filmmaker."

Velvet smiled and squeezed her friend's hand. Yoshi always understood.

"I don't know if you recognized any of the board members," she said, watching the door like a hawk, looking for the filmmaker or camera woman amidst the dispersing crowd. "But I did. I had no idea Tom Ammiano sat on the board."

Yoshi nodded. "Ammiano supports a suicide barrier—earlier this year he accused other members of 'nickel-and-diming human life.'"

"Really? How do you know that? He didn't say anything tonight."

"It was in the paper," Yoshi replied snarkily. "You should try reading it—what with you working there and all."

Velvet was offended. "I *do* read the *Chronicle*." She lowered her voice and spoke her admission from the side of her mouth. "I just don't read it cover to cover."

Yoshi tsked.

"I'm amazed that Ammiano got on the bridge board," Velvet remarked.

She recalled that the nineteen-member board was drawn from the six counties that originally put up bond money to build the bridge. Of San Francisco's nine seats, three went to city supervisors like Ammiano. Various counties like Napa, Mendocino, and Del Norte had one seat each. Velvet was surprised they got to have a say on bridge management, being so far away. Surely no one commuted to San Francisco from Del Norte. That was one of the primary criticisms of the board—that too many members represented counties that didn't use the bridge.

"Are the board members elected or appointed?" Yoshi asked while they were waiting for Harden to exit.

"They're appointed by each county's board of supervisors, or by a conference of the county's mayors."

"So they are insulated from public criticism?" Yoshi noted.

"Yes. No threat they won't get reelected." Velvet sighed. "I hate that kind of thing. It seems so undemocratic."

They spoke occasionally over the next half hour as they waited for their quarry to emerge. The camerawoman exited first, went to a nearby van, and loaded her equipment. She returned to the entrance, leaned against the outside wall, and lit a cigarette. Shortly afterward, James Harden joined her and two immediately began an animated discussion.

"Let's go see what kept him so long," Velvet said.

They caught up with him on the sidewalk. Yoshi waited while Velvet introduced them, then stuck her hand out. Harden shook it.

"So what did *they* want?" Velvet asked.

He snorted. Yoshi imagined him rolling his eyes.

"They filed an injunction preventing me from airing the film, continuing the project, or even talking about it—can you believe that?"

"When did that happen?" Yoshi asked.

"Apparently the guy who interrupted the meeting was actually the Bridge Authority's lawyer."

From the slight change in the direction of his voice, Yoshi ascertained that he'd turned to address her. As her eyesight had deteriorated, she'd learned how to tell a lot from the sound of a person's voice. The Doppler effect aided her efforts. Sounds changed depending on their direction and how close or far away they were. She was learning to think like a bat.

"Didn't you get a permit?" she asked.

"Yes. But they're saying that I misled the permit department about the purpose of the film."

"Did you?" Velvet asked bluntly.

"Not intentionally. The truth is, I originally imagined this project as one in a series exploring the interaction between a national monument and nature—the fog, ocean, sun, moon—but now, with the footage of suicides, I feel I have to honor that in film. I've started interviewing family and friends of people who died, and I want to give voice to their loss."

Yoshi put her hand on Velvet's shoulder. "Our friend—"

"Yes, I heard. I'm so sorry." He sounded authentically empathetic.

"Have you…" Velvet's voice was husky with emotion. "Did you see him? It happened in November. His car was found at the bridge on the nineteenth."

"Myself? No."

"Are you sure?" Velvet sounded crestfallen.

He responded quickly. "I may have captured his…the event. I'm working with four cameras and ten months of film. I'm nowhere near caught up to date."

Yoshi withdrew a business card and handed it to Harden. "Will you contact us if you find anything we should be aware of?"

"Sure. I mean, assuming I resolve this issue with the board." He took the card. "Blind Eye Detective Agency. Was the death suspicious or something?"

"We have some concerns," Yoshi said.

"I wouldn't have imagined one could be a blind detective. That's amazing. You must have an interesting story."

Yoshi shrugged. She didn't think her story was all that compelling. "It's what I know how to do."

He chuckled. "I know what you mean. Filmmaking is in my blood,

I don't think I could stop even if I wanted to. Which reminds me." He turned to Velvet. "Would you be interested in speaking with me? For the film? I mean, when all this legal shit blows over?"

"Of course." Velvet's answer surprised Yoshi.

"Let me get your number."

After the two exchanged numbers and Harden departed with the camerawoman, Velvet explained, "Maybe he'll be more eager find out about Jeff if I'm willing to appear in his film."

Yoshi nodded. It was hard to believe that Jeff's last moments might have been captured on film. Velvet would probably do anything to see that tape—but was that the wise thing to do? Surely it would be even more traumatic to actually witness his jump.

As Yoshi climbed into the Celica, she told herself that it was premature to worry. For all they knew it could be months before the legal issues were resolved and the injunction lifted. Perhaps the Bridge Authority would win and prevent the film's release. She could certainly think of arguments for doing so.

❖

"What can you tell me about why people commit suicide?" Yoshi asked Dr. Artemis Jones.

They were in the psychologist's second floor office, sitting in the private room where Artemis conducted her counseling sessions. Yoshi couldn't come here without recalling how she had angered Artemis the first time she'd been in this office. At the time, Yoshi would never have thought that Artemis would become a friendly collaborator. But after providing information that helped the Blind Eye detectives solve the Rosemary Finney murder, she had become a resource. Yoshi found her insights useful in shedding light on motives and behavior. Facts could speak for themselves, but sometimes, when data was not easy to interpret, a good PI used her own instincts or those of someone who knew a great deal about the type of crime under investigation.

Artemis had firsthand experience working with suicidal individuals, particularly those who had been dissuaded from preceding Jeff off the Golden Gate. Yoshi wanted to obtain her specialized insight.

"No one really knows *why* people commit suicide," Artemis said, immediately reducing the likelihood that Yoshi could check what she knew of Jeff against list of symptoms and determine if he was the "type."

"Sometimes, the person least aware of *why*," Artemis continued, "is the victim him or herself, at the moment of the decision. Suicide is the eighth-leading cause of death in this country—and the third for fifteen- to twenty-year-olds. Around three percent of American adults will attempt suicide in their lifetime."

"Are all these people depressed?" Yoshi asked. Velvet was adamant that Jeff had never been treated for depression and had never spoken of such feelings to her.

"That's debatable," Artemis said. "Physiologists will argue that low serotonin levels prejudice a person to commit suicide, while sociologists point to forces outside the individual."

"I had not realized that *sociologists* studied suicide."

"Oh, yes, absolutely. In fact the very *field* of sociology was founded in part on the discovery that suicide rates had a sociological base."

Yoshi had expected to learn something today, but had not expected to be surprised by the information. Artemis went on to explain that a French sociologist had discovered that single people were more likely than married individuals to take their own lives. She reeled off various facts unfamiliar to Yoshi. Protestants were more likely than Catholics or Jews, urban residents more likely than rural folks. Men were three times more likely to complete a "successful" suicide, while women were three times more likely to make "unsuccessful" attempts. People with children were at the lowest risk, and the predominant age group was 20–35.

Jeff had been thirty-six. He did not have children. Yoshi wondered if he had wanted them. She had never had that kind of conversation with him. Velvet had always said that *if* she ever planned to conceive a child she would do it with Jeff's contribution. Yoshi wondered if Jeff had made the same assumption.

"Those who are socially isolated are more likely to kill themselves," Artemis said.

Again, this factor did not jive with what Yoshi knew about Jeff. His family, while far away geographically, was close emotionally. He had a partner, friends, and a social life.

"Unrelieved sleep disturbances and insomnia may lead to suicidal action." Artemis ticked off other factors. "And we believe that drugs and alcohol also play a role and may even unleash latent depression and suicidal urges that were otherwise controlled."

Jeff consumed alcohol regularly and had casually used recreational drugs. Could his use of these substances have led him to kill himself? Yoshi thought there would have been previous signs of mood change if these substances affected Jeff profoundly. She continued to compare the factors Artemis listed against what she knew about Jeff. He had not made any earlier attempts and there was no history of suicide in his family, as far as she knew, but she would have to ask a family member to be sure.

"Stress?" Yoshi queried.

"Recent childbirth, or a recent loss of a loved one, job, money, or anything that affects prestige and self-esteem can be factors," Artemis said.

Yoshi intended to speak with Jeff's other friends, family, and his partner Tyrone to develop a full understanding of his mental state in the weeks leading up to his disappearance. She hoped to have a chance to do so at Jeff's memorial service.

"Is there a formula?" she asked. "Say those with eight out of ten of these factors will kill themselves. Only five and they won't?"

"I wish it were that simple, but no, I'm sorry." Artemis sounded slightly amused. "People in my profession look for certain clues. Something like eighty percent of all suicides exhibit warning signs about their intent."

Yoshi wondered if Velvet had noticed any of the clues Artemis identified: expressing suicidal thoughts, being overtly anxious or overwhelmed with guilt or shame, rigid thinking, impulsive behavior

"They don't seem capable of creative problem-solving," Artemis mused aloud. "Sometimes their behavior is very impulsive, as though they have no sense of possible consequences."

Yoshi paused to reflect. A moment later, as a new direction presented itself, she asked, "Can you tell me what kind of perpetrator might try to cover up a murder as a suicide?"

Artemis took her own moment before answering, "You mean instead of making it look like an accidental death?"

Yoshi found the question interesting. Artemis had just identified a key point. If a murderer was going to cover up a crime by fooling the authorities, he or she was faced with a conscious choice: make it look like an accident or like a suicide. Why choose suicide?

"I suppose suicide is more personal," Yoshi murmured.

"Yes. Loved ones will be hurt," Artemis said. "The person who commits suicide can be discredited, and the method or location could hold special meaning for the perpetrator."

"The bridge would be a particularly dangerous location to kill someone, or dispose of a body," Yoshi said.

"It would be easier at night, without all the traffic, of course."

"But there are security guards, especially post nine-eleven." Yoshi was deep in thought. Someone would have to pay close attention to the security if they wanted to pull off a fake bridge suicide. Yoshi contemplated asking Velvet but decided to keep her thoughts to herself. Velvet was having enough trouble accepting what had happened without Yoshi validating her doubts.

Besides, why would anyone want to kill Jeff Conant? If Yoshi wanted to explore alternative theories around his death, the first factor she would need to examine was motive.

CHAPTER FIVE

Sitting at her desk at the Blind Eye office, Yoshi was happy to hear Velvet in the reception area. She had worried that Velvet would be too depressed to come and she would have to attend Jeff's memorial by herself.

"You ready?" Velvet asked from the doorway.

"Yes, of course." Yoshi turned off her computer, cleared her desktop, and hustled from her office, closing the door behind her.

She had assigned Tucker to stay behind and complete some research. Bud should arrive soon to monitor Tucker's work and do some of his own.

Velvet led the way into the hallway. A moment later, as the doors of the historic Flood Building's ornate elevator closed behind them, Yoshi shared the news she had saved to distract Velvet from her deepening depression.

"I have offered AJ a position as a private investigator with Blind Eye."

"Really?" Velvet's voice was flat.

"Are you surprised?" Yoshi had expected more of a response and had planned her argument accordingly. "I have previously expressed my need to bring on another investigator, and we have both witnessed AJ performing proficiently in that arena."

"Won't it be a problem?" Velvet attempted interest. "I mean, because you two are hitting it together?"

"We did go on several dates and—" Yoshi did not share the details.

The elevator doors opened on the ground floor and they crossed the wide foyer.

When Velvet did not make a shrewd but lascivious comment, Yoshi knew her best friend was even more depressed than she had originally thought.

"That night of the concert it became obvious we are not a good fit." Yoshi listened to the echo of their voices off the high ceilings.

"So what was it?" Velvet asked, sounding a little more like herself. "Was it that trans woman asking AJ if she was FTM?"

"I beg your pardon?" Yoshi scoffed. "Of course not. Why would I care about *that*?"

"Uh, because you're a big old dyke and you don't want anyone thinking you're dating a dude—even one who used to be a girl."

"That is utterly ridiculous." Yoshi shook her head. "*I* know AJ is a woman. I believe I am fairly progressive when it comes to issues of gender. I think my own performance of gender, in fact, has to do with…"

"I know, I know," Velvet interjected. "Your conscious rejection of your masculine upbringing, your missing mom, yada yada."

"Thanks, Velvet." Yoshi sighed halfheartedly. "I always appreciate your thoughtfulness."

"Okay then, what's wrong with AJ?" Velvet prodded.

"There is nothing *wrong* with her."

"Is it the age thing? Because I know with Tucker and I—"

"It could be our ages," Yoshi acquiesced, knowing she definitely did *not* want to hear the details of Velvet's physical relationship with the Blind Eye receptionist. "Or the chemistry between us, or perhaps the quandary that we're from different cultural backgrounds and it can be challenging to surmount those dissimilarities."

"Hmm."

They crossed the street to the parking garage and entered another elevator.

"Here is an example: the outfit she wore that night?"

"Her thug chic?"

"I am entirely serious about this, Velvet. Does that make me a terrible person?"

"Unfashionable, at least. You do know that look's totally hot right now, don't you?"

"For lesbians?" Yoshi found that hard to believe. "I thought it was exclusively the apparel of teenage boys. It strikes me as unprofessional. What adult lesbian wears her pants down around her knees?"

After the short elevator ride, they exited and walked around the corner where Velvet fed the fee machine. "I'm sure the look wouldn't pass a lot of office-attire regulations, but it's the casual style these days, and a lot of women like it."

"Well, I am not a fan," Yoshi said as they entered the third elevator. "I prefer women with more of a classic style of fashion. Suit coat, tailored shirts."

"Maybe I should set you up with Marion Serif—if she weren't still love-crazy about that pilot of hers. Marion's a classy dresser. So does AJ always dress that way off-duty?"

"She does not always wear the droopy drawers, but she does dress more urban ghetto than I would prefer. She is so attractive in her uniform, it is a shame she has to take it off."

"And yet you're thinking about taking her cop job. Have you talked to her about it?"

"God, no."

On the third floor of the parking garage, they stepped off the elevator and walked through the cavernous parking structure, their voices echoing against the distant walls.

"You do realize that most butches don't know the first thing about dressing themselves, right?" Velvet said. "You have to help them develop style. Take Tucker. Surely you've noticed she's better dressed these days."

"Could we possibly go longer than fifteen minutes without your bringing up the topic of my employee?"

"I'm just saying that her fashion sense didn't just happen. Are you really going to break up with AJ because of the way she dresses?"

"We have not been serious enough to break up. It's not that I am not fond of her. I am. She is intelligent and sexy and it has been considerably stimulating to be with her. She has certainly introduced me to a distinctive world. I simply may not fit within it."

"What about expanding your horizons?"

Velvet unlocked the passenger door of her Celica and stood there as Yoshi settled into the seat.

"I may have assumed the two of us would share commonalities, as we are both lesbians of color. I realize now that was an incredibly naïve presumption. Do you know that all these years I have never had a genuinely close African American friend? I believe I now understand why."

Velvet shut the door without responding. She took a long time to round the vehicle and open her own door.

"I did not mean that in the way it sounded." Yoshi rushed to correct the seemingly un-PC sentiment. "I merely meant that my path did not cross with those of African American lesbians. Certainly Bay Area demographics played their part—I am certain you've noticed that the neighborhood where I reside is primarily Asian American. But despite AJ and I both being minority women, where we do have differences, they are quite extreme. We are from such different worlds."

"Yeah. Africa and Asia."

"You think you are being funny," Yoshi retorted. Unlike Velvet, she found this topic very serious. "Our communities *are* marked not only by our ethnic heritages but by how our ancestors came to be in this country and how they have been treated since their arrival. While it can be tiresome to be a model minority, I have always been securely middle class and I cannot truly comprehend what life is like for a working class black lesbian—especially one who, like AJ, is routinely mistaken for a black man. Racial profiling carries deeply disparate consequences for each of us."

"Yeah, it sucks for me, too, you know." Velvet sounded serious this time. "First off, I've got this lily-white name and I was adopted by the Waltons. I had to figure out on my own what my heritage is. And then, when you say you're a Native American, everyone thinks you belong in a museum or something. It's like one day I'll find my birth parents and they'll be on display at the Natural History Museum." Velvet paused. "This conversation is getting *way* too heavy. AJ would be a great addition to Blind Eye. And she'd probably jump at the chance to get out of East Palo Alto PD."

They drove through downtown San Francisco in silence. Rush-hour traffic stalled their progress, and Yoshi could feel Velvet's stress levels rising with every annoying honk. The traffic-light changes resulted in no forward motion. Yoshi's sense of time told her they were probably running late.

"I'm still having a hard time believing Jeff killed himself," Velvet said when they were several blocks from the Castro Theatre where Jeff's memorial was to begin shortly.

Yoshi was not surprised to hear Velvet express her reservations once more. She had been through enough grief cycles to understand that denial was just part of the process, and she wanted to be patient with Velvet. Still, despite her willingness to consider other possibilities, she had found no reason to believe Jeff's death was anything but self-inflicted.

"It is entirely understandable that you are struggling with this, Velvet," she said. "It *is* hard to imagine that someone we cared about could choose to end his or her life. In retrospect, none of the person's struggles seem worth dying for. But depression is a powerful motivator. You know yourself that it's easy to live with depression without anyone around you recognizing the mental-health issues you're dealing with. Perhaps that was what was happening for Jeff."

"But why wouldn't he tell me? Why would he lie and tell me things were great? We made plans to get together again."

"I don't know. Perhaps he did not want anyone to prevent him from carrying it through."

"Maybe." Velvet sounded doubtful.

Yoshi remained silent as Velvet parked the car. The grieving process could not be rushed. Each phase would take as much time as it needed to.

❖

In the darkness of the Castro Theatre, music signaled the close of Jeff Conant's film *Loving Randall* and accompanied the film credits that were undoubtedly scrolling up the screen. That the instrumental refrains quavered with aching sadness served as fitting closure to both Jeff's life and the memorial itself.

From the scuffing of feet on the cement floor and the sound of seats snapping closed, Yoshi deduced that the house lights had just illuminated the grievers, who responded by exchanging their tears for meaningless chatter, as though embarrassed by their grief and wanting to deny it. This might be a memorial, but the Castro Theatre was no house of worship or stilted funeral home. Although it had seen its share of tears, shed at gut-wrenching dramas or escaping through eyes squeezed tight from giddy laughter at campy classics like *Vegas in Space*, when the house lights came on, they signaled time to dry your eyes and return to the stickiness of real life.

Beside Yoshi, Velvet scrunched down in her seat as though she hoped it would swallow her whole. Her low sobs were audible. She took Yoshi's hand and squeezed it wordlessly, indicating she was ready to relinquish the safety of her seat. For Yoshi, the noise that echoed throughout the room slowly resolved into clumps as mourners drifted together into small social groups. She sensed someone shuffling up to them as they stood.

"Velvet." The voice was as silky as the soft fur on the bunny rabbit her grade school had kept in a wire cage. Yoshi thought she heard a subtle resemblance to Jeff.

"I'm so glad you made it." Charlene Conant pulled Velvet into a hug.

"Charlie." Velvet used the nickname that made Jeff's mother and father sound like a doppelganger gay or lesbian couple who shared the same name. "I'd like you to meet my friend Yoshi. She's the private investigator I told you about."

Yoshi remembered seeing pictures of Charlene. She was a fiery redhead who had retained her looks well into retirement. A former model, she must have bent down to shake Yoshi's hand, and Yoshi wondered if the diminutive intelligence of some models was the consequence of thin air from their higher elevations. In Yoshi's grip, Charlene's hand was small and frail, the skin cool and papery. The kind of hands that suggested she had spent a lifetime avoiding physical labor.

"Your eyesight doesn't hamper your investigations?" Charlene was straight to the point.

"I manage," Yoshi replied.

"She does more than manage," Velvet said in Yoshi's defense. "She cleared *me* of murder and saved my ass from jail."

"If Velvet trusts you, that's good enough for me. I'd like to hire you to investigate my son's death."

Charlene's straightforward manner was a welcome characteristic in a potential client. Particularly if she would be equally frank about her son.

"You don't think it was a suicide?" Yoshi asked.

"No." Charlene was vehement. "He wouldn't do that to me."

"You were close?"

"Yes."

Whether Yoshi accepted Charlene's case depended on how the older woman answered the next question. "How well did you know your son?"

"As well as any mother can know a gay son who wanted to spare her the details of his casual drug use and the particulars of his sexual proclivities."

Yoshi nodded. Charlene had been honest—even with herself. It was safe to take her case. "I would be willing to look into it *un*officially," she offered.

"I want it to be *official*," Charlene insisted.

"You might not fancy what I discover. It could be worse than not knowing."

"Are you saying you won't do it?" Velvet sounded hurt.

"No, I would be honored to investigate the case. I just want to be sure you are prepared—"

"I am," Charlene insisted.

"All right," Yoshi said. "We can set up a meeting in a few days, when you are up to it."

"I want you to start now," Charlene said. "I know who did this."

Yoshi raised an eyebrow.

"It was that shiftless boyfriend of his, Tyrone Hill. Tyrone was ruining him. He had already bled Jeff dry. Charlie and I offered to help out—financially, but Jeff wouldn't agree to our terms. He always was such a stubborn boy."

"What terms?"

"They wanted him to break it off with Tyrone." The voice of Jeff's brother, David, closed in on them as he approached.

"It was for his own good," Charlene said.

Before David could blame his parents' meddling for Jeff's death, Yoshi changed the direction of the conversation. "Allow me to play Devil's advocate here. Was there anything that might have caused Jeff to be depressed?"

"Just the opposite," Charlene assured her. "He was so excited. He had just found out he was going to be a daddy."

"A daddy?" Velvet asked, her tone conveying *You've got to be kidding*.

"Oh yes," Charlene said. "I'm so sorry they had to leave early, I'd like you to meet Theresa and Isabelle."

"Who are Theresa and Isabelle?" Velvet sounded impatient.

"They're Jeff's baby mommies," David joked. There was no humor in his voice. Yoshi imaged that his eyes were without shine, the matte orbs of dark grief she had seen so many times staring from her father's face.

"Maybe you saw them sitting behind us?" Charlene said. "They're a lovely mixed-race couple. Isabelle—the mother—is from the Caribbean. Very beautiful. They worried about the impact of all this stress on the baby and decided to leave early."

Yoshi felt Velvet stiffen next to her.

"It's the one good thing in all of this," Charlene murmured. "At least a part of Jeff will live on."

Velvet gripped Yoshi's arm tightly as though to keep from falling over. *That was my sperm!* The exclamation sounded in Yoshi's head as clearly as if Velvet had spoken it aloud. She had not.

Yoshi squeezed Velvet's hand to show she understood. As long as Yoshi had known her, Velvet had been dedicated to her career success above all else, but there was also a part of her that longed for children. She kept postponing, waiting for a more appropriate time when she was in a long-term partnership and they could provide their child with financial stability and a stay-at-home parent. Despite being a modern career woman and feminist, Velvet believed it was best for a child to have a primary care provider during the first three years, which had been found so critical to healthy development. The truth was, Velvet had imagined *she* would be the stay-at-home mother, perhaps moving into freelance writing so she would not have to sacrifice her career. Yoshi knew Velvet had always assumed that Jeff was the built-in father for the baby she would have one day. Now he was gone and another lesbian couple was carrying the child that rightfully should have been hers.

"I need to sit down." Velvet clung to Yoshi's arm like a frightened child but still managed to direct them to a quiet corner of the theater. She collapsed into a fold-down seat and began to sob.

Yoshi stood behind her with a hand on Velvet's shoulder. She did not attempt to soothe her friend. She remembered how utterly annoying mourners had been at her father's wake, so driven to keep her from shedding tears. It was as though her grief caused them such pain that it had to be prohibited at all cost. Yoshi would not do the same to her friend. She allowed Velvet to cry without intrusion.

Now that Blind Eye had been *officially* hired to investigate Jeff's death, her approach could become far bolder. Although Yoshi had little reason to believe Jeff's death was *not* a suicide, out of loyalty to Velvet she had already set her minions to work, digging into the circumstances around his passing. In any suspicious death, the first person of interest was the person closest to the victim. In this case, that was Tyrone Hill. Earlier in the day, Yoshi had conned East Palo Alto PD officer AJ Johnson into tailing Tyrone Hill tonight. She had heard enough from Velvet to recognize that Tyróne's relationship with Jeff had been less than smooth sailing.

Yoshi slipped her Braille cell phone from her purse and quickly typed in several text messages. The first was directed to AJ. "The shadow is now official, please get *close*."

She addressed the next to Tucker instructing her to wake Bud, roll up their sleeves, and prepare to get dirty. They would need to dig much deeper.

❖

Velvet's sobs shuddered to a stop and she sniffled one last time, like a vehicle exhausting the last of its fuel. "Let's see what else Jeff didn't tell me about his life." She lowered her voice. "Do you think I knew him at all?"

"Everyone has their secrets, Vel."

Yoshi's remark did not seem to soothe Velvet's concerns.

They wove through the throng of mourners who milled about in the theater's screening room and lobby. Every few minutes someone would recognize Velvet and come speak with her. By her friend's mannerisms, Yoshi quickly deduced which of these old acquaintances Velvet believed had information relevant to the case. Mostly she spoke with clipped, no-nonsense language, sharing quick condolences and choking back tears. With other memorial attendees, however, Velvet played prison interrogator.

Yoshi shook hands with someone Velvet introduced as "Robbie." He had smooth, slight hands, a solid handshake, and a gossipy nature.

"I can't believe *he* has the nerve to be here," he whispered loudly as though he had a secret he wanted the world to know.

Yoshi felt the movement of air as Velvet whipped around to see where Robbie was pointing.

"Isn't that Chase Devlin?" Velvet asked.

"Yeah, that's right."

"Why shouldn't he be here? Jeff knew him."

"Not as well as Tyrone." Robbie drew a dramatic breath. "Tyrone knew Chase in the biblical sense."

Yoshi could hear the smirk in his voice.

"While Tyrone was with Jeff? That *bastard*!" Velvet exclaimed.

"Totally."

"How is it you came by this knowledge?" Yoshi asked, hoping to determine the validity of his claim.

"I saw them going at it." Robbie gave the smug sniff of a man who had enough dirt to guarantee himself an audience. "I was at Martin Cohen's Tarts and Vicars party. I was a tart, of course, they have the best costumes. I was in this whole sort of Dr. Frankenfurter two-piece and…"

Yoshi interrupted by clearing her throat, hoping to nudge Robbie back on track.

"Anyway, I walked in on them doing it in the coatroom, along with a half dozen other people. No one stopped. Devlin was on top, of course, and Tyrone was stoned out of his mind."

"That's the kind of thing what happens when you're always *partying*." Another man expressed his moral judgment. Yoshi recognized his voice immediately. It was her friend, Detective Ari Fleishman of the San Francisco PD.

"That's true." Robbie sounded less like he agreed with Fleishman and more like he recognized Fleishman's law enforcement background and did not want to look like a meth user himself. "Tyrone's become a total tweaker."

"Are you familiar with Tyrone? Professionally?" Yoshi asked Fleishman as Robbie drifted away.

"He was busted six months ago on possession. Judge gave him a slap on the wrist, first-time offender and all. Since then he's managed to keep his nose clean—I mean, we haven't busted him—but it's probably only a matter of time."

"You think he's still using?" Yoshi asked.

Velvet remained unusually silent.

"Yeah. Jeff was worried Tyrone had become more than a casual user."

"He spoke with you about Tyrone's drug use? When was that?" Velvet queried.

"Just a few weeks ago. He said Tyrone's behavior had become increasingly erratic and he was using more and more. And it wasn't just confined to PNP."

"PNP?" It was not an acronym Yoshi was familiar with.

"Party and play," Velvet said before Fleishman could answer. "Gay guys use meth and then have sexual marathons. Jeff and I talked about it sometimes. He said he couldn't imagine going to a club without it. Tyrone must have really gone overboard for Jeff to get worried."

"So there is a good deal of crystal meth use in the gay men's community?" Yoshi asked.

"Absolutely." This time Fleishman responded. "It's a huge problem. Especially as meth use is becoming linked to increasing HIV rates."

Velvet walked away as Detective Fleishman rambled to Yoshi about the hazards of meth. She thought of the movie *Salton Sea*. Val Kilmer played a guy who was willing to become a meth user and go undercover in the tweaker underworld to find the guys who killed his wife. Would she do the same to avenge Jeff's death? Maybe with Blind Eye on the case, they could finally learn what had really happened.

Velvet glanced around the room and spotted Tyrone Hill standing by the exit with a small group of friends. He was hard to miss, a mahogany god, as the girls at her hair salon would say. He was tall with almond-shaped eyes, a scruff of black facial hair, and a beautifully shaved head. The first time she'd met him, Velvet nearly mistook him for the supermodel Tyson Beckford. But now the difference was striking. His skin, once so perfectly flawless it looked like it had been airbrushed, was spattered with tiny blemishes. Still, if he was a meth addict, it certainly hadn't ruined his looks. Not yet. He had none of the scabs from picking at his skin, the sunken cheeks, or rotten and missing teeth that characterized advanced methamphetamine use.

Not taking her eyes off him, she darted through the mingling crowd until she stood in front of him. "You bastard, how could you?"

She smacked his chest with both palms, knocking him backward. Surprise crossed his face. He regained his footing quickly and held his hands out in front of him angled like a praying mantis. He crouched on bent knees and Velvet remembered Jeff mentioning Tyrone had a black belt in karate. Where was her friend Marion Serif when she needed her? Marion had been a pugilist in her younger years, before she started publishing her lesbian magazine, *Bent*.

Not one to back down from a fight, even one where she was so obviously outmatched, Velvet stood her ground. She'd learned how to fight dirty defending herself from Latina gang girls after inadvertently wearing the wrong colors in the disputed hallways of L.A.'s high schools. Tough situations had always been easier when it was the two of them, Jeff and her, against all others. But the man in front of her had ruined all that. He had taken Jeff away from her.

"You killed him!" She could hear the wail in her own voice, which came out louder than she'd expected. Around them, people turned and stared. She barely noticed them. She was intent on Tyrone.

Confusion crossed his features. He dropped his hands and stood to his full height. "Hey, girl," he said with a voice as soft as Fox News.

"*You* killed Jeff," she said again and jabbed her forefinger at his chest. "How could you do that to him?"

He shook his head. "What're you, mental? Jeff killed *himself.*"

"Is that right?"

He nodded.

"Then you're the reason he jumped, you bastard."

One of Tyrone's friends stepped forward. "Come on, that's *harsh.*"

"Oh, that's harsh? Your *friend* here is a cheating man-whore and a drug addict. Maybe he's a batterer, too."

Velvet turned back to Tyrone in time to see pain flicker across his face. She didn't care. She wanted him to hurt. She wanted him to feel like his heart had been ripped from his chest and shown to him. That's how she felt.

"You use him as a punching bag?" she demanded, pushing into his personal space. She kept her eyes on his face and saw something ripple in the muscles of his jaw. Was that barely contained anger? "Did you throw him off the bridge to cover the bruises?"

A low rumbling growl escaped from his throat. He grabbed her by the shoulders and lifted her plus-sized voluptuous body as though she were an undernourished model. She smiled through her fear. Wasn't this proof that Tyrone was violent? She kicked at his shins with her new Emilio Pucci cork-heel sandals.

Before she could find out how far she'd pushed him, Ari Fleishman was there, peeling Tyrone's fingers from Velvet's shoulders. When Velvet landed on her feet, Yoshi hustled her away.

Velvet's anger surprised Yoshi, but she reminded herself that Velvet had a right to be angry. A right to be irrational. Still, she thought it better not to mention that. She directed Velvet toward the source of city air and street noises. They had almost reached the door when a large body with a feminine scent blocked their exit.

"Velvet. Remember me? Davina Singleton? I worked with Jeff."

"Of course," Velvet replied.

Yoshi heard the clap of the woman's hands around Velvet's outstretched palm. There was a moment of silence as though Davina was attempting to covey emotions without words. She opted for a meaningless remark. "It's good to see you, Velvet. You look good—I mean, I'm sorry."

"It's okay. You do too, Davina."

"I don't know what to say."

"I know." With a strained throatiness, Velvet said, "I mean, why? Why would he have done that?"

"It's a nightmare. I can't believe it."

Yoshi detected a note in each woman's voice that explained the slight change in atmosphere. The air seemed heavier. They had stepped closer together, their scents mingling, their clothing clinging with static in a couple of places. Yoshi was disappointed that Velvet did not immediately put the kibosh on any ideas Davina might have by mentioning Tucker. She hoped this did not mean the couple was having troubles or that Velvet's nomadic eye was wandering again. Before the encounter could turn into a flirtation, she interrupted.

"Davina, was there anything going on at work—anything out of the ordinary?"

"Just the same old," Davina replied after a few seconds. "Raising money and screening films."

"Did Jeff seem depressed or anything?"

Davina hesitated. "No. I don't think so."

"But?"

"It can be stressful, always working overtime on a shoestring budget and dealing with producers and directors. Some of them don't take rejection well."

"Really? Did you ever hear of anyone threatening Jeff?"

"Not physically. But some of them get very worked up, leave a hundred voice mails, send angry e-mails saying they're going to ruin him. That he's an idiot who wouldn't know original creative thinking if he stepped in it, that kind of thing. We had this one nut job who camped out in front of our office yelling about how the whole system was rigged and you couldn't get your film screened unless you bribed or blew the right guy."

"Is there any validity to that?" Yoshi asked.

"There's no casting couch at Frameline." Davina's response was rote, as though she had been over the same ground many times. "We screen films blind. We often don't know who sent what. Of course, sometimes it's still obvious, but Jeff would never, ever have asked Jennifer Morris to schedule a film he didn't believe in, not even if the producer offered an enormous donation."

"Do you think I could get a list of people who might've held a grudge?" Velvet asked, transparently eager to put names to anyone who might have harmed their friend.

"You think someone drove Jeff to kill himself?" Davina asked. "Or are you saying…no…You don't think he was *murdered*?" She spoke the last word in a whisper.

"I don't know," Velvet said. "I'm just looking for some answers. Struggling to understand."

"We all are. It's crazy."

"Davina, who will be taking over Jeff's position?" Yoshi asked

"Jennifer Morris. She's our program director. She'll be taking over temporarily until we can find a suitable replacement. We hope to have his successor in place by the festival season."

"Do you think it would be possible to speak with Jennifer in person?"

"She already left, and I'm afraid I'm about to do the same. But I'm sure she'd be happy to help, if she can." Turning to Velvet, Davina added, "Feel free to give me a call if you ever need to talk." She withdrew something from her pocket and handed it to Velvet.

Was it a business card with her number? Yoshi wondered.

Yoshi and Velvet said their farewells, and a few minutes later, as they walked toward Velvet's car, Yoshi mentally assembled a persons of interest list:

Tyrone Hill, as the boyfriend, had to be at the top of the list, with his drug use and philandering. Methamphetamine use could cause paranoia. Did it also lead to violence? Could any of Tyrone's drug connections have something to gain from Jeff's death? How bad was Tyrone's addiction? Was his behavior a financial burden as well as an emotional one? Could this have pushed Jeff over the edge? She needed to pin down Tyrone's alibi for the time of Jeff's death, and she needed to locate his dealer.

Charlene Conant was desperate to disprove suicide. Was there a life insurance policy that would not pay out for suicide? Who was the beneficiary? Had Jeff left a will?

Theresa and Isabelle, the lesbian couple expecting Jeff's baby. What had been their custody agreement with Jeff? Was it amicable? Had they taken out an insurance policy on his life, as some couples did when the donor was not an anonymous party but might have some involvement? Would they or their child benefit from Jeff's death?

Chase Devlin. What role, if any, did this producer and business partner play in Jeff's personal life? Was their business relationship a good one? Did Jeff know about the sexual encounter with Tyrone Hill? Was there more to their liaison than a single encounter?

Thwarted film producers or directors. Davina Singleton had revealed that some of these individuals were angry at Jeff or hoped to influence his decision. Blind Eye could obtain a list of names from Davina and consider if any of those with that motive would have had the opportunity and means to permanently retire Jeff. Could replacing Jeff alter the festival lineup? Who stood to gain from that?

Frameline's interim director, Jennifer Morris. Could she have enough of a stake in Jeff's death to be a suspect? How was she chosen for the position? Did she know before Jeff died that she would take over his job?

CHAPTER SIX

"D o you party?" a bald white guy with a salt-and-pepper goatee asked AJ. He held out a small mirror with two thin lines of off-white powder.

They were standing in a darkened corner of the video dance bar inside SF Badlands, a cruisy gay club filled with mostly clean-cut twentysomething white guys. AJ had tracked Tyrone here twenty minutes ago and got in without a hitch. If the blond bouncer posted at the door noticed that AJ was a chick, he didn't mention it. She'd gotten used to being mistaken for a guy but figured it wouldn't happen in San Francisco, where everyone was so used to seeing butch women.

She'd been lost in thought at the time, musing on Yoshi's offer to work at Blind Eye Detective Agency. Guess the girl could separate her personal feelings from professional ones. Could AJ? That night together had been hot and Yoshi was an amazing lady, but in the end AJ knew they weren't right together. With Chantal they'd been two flames meeting and burning brighter, but with Yoshi their fires burnt at odds, putting each other out. Sure, the sex had been *hot*. But what would it be like to work for the hottie you'd hit it with?

And then there was the work itself. AJ had problems as a cop, being as how she'd been the only female officer for almost a year in her squad. But then AJ had worked a task force that took down some heavy-hitting politicos and she'd racked up street cred, and now SFPD had hit her up to put in for a lateral transfer. They talked like she'd be short-listed for one of them bitchin' spots on narco. Could be couple of years away, but could she pass it up for PI work?

Yoshi had called her earlier, offered her the chance to get a feel of rollin' Blind Eye style, and she was tailing a brother. The DB's SO was their top POI. Though AJ thought in acronyms, using stand-ins for "dead body," "significant other," and "person of interest," Yoshi had not said it quite like that. She wasn't sure what tracking Tyrone Hill would uncover, but AJ had agreed to play along. Give her a chance to try the job on and see how it fit. And Yoshi had agreed to pay her under the table just this once, so the department couldn't get riled about her off-duty activities.

AJ had followed Hill inside Badlands not long after the Conant memorial service, surprised the bouncer man took nothing more than a cursory at her ID. He did notice her Louisiana driver's license. Her CO would have a shit fit if he heard that she still hadn't gotten herself a California license. They'd gone and given her a twelve-month deadline, so she still had three months to decide if she was gonna stay so far from her N'awlins home.

"You forced out by Katrina?" Blond bouncer asked her the question everyone did when they found out where she grew up.

"Yeah," she said. It wasn't the whole capital-T-truth. She'd made it through *Katrina*. It ain't been Katrina that'd put New Orleans in the ground. Bush and his cracker cronies were responsible for the breached levees, for her dead peeps. Even them broken levies didn't send her packing, it'd been broken *trust*. Trust in her fellow police officers. Trust they hadn't deserved. Trust they'd quickly betrayed for selfish gain.

The bouncer had passed back her ID and AJ had bounded into the darkness of the bar. Her eyes had since adjusted, but she still couldn't see Hill anywhere.

Tucker had told AJ a secondhand story about Hill blowin' guys in the john, so she ventured a peek through the men's room door. She didn't see him there. Spying some guy with his trousers around his ankles, she backed out. She passed a pool table and circled around to the bar. There was Hill, accepting a mixed drink on the rocks in a short glass. He was with two other guys.

AJ asked for an Abita beer, then settled for some local ale the bartender recommended. She took a long swig. *It'll do.* She worked her way through the room, heading down the long corridor that seemed primed for groping. When some guy's hand bumped against her crotch, she wasn't sure if it'd been an accident or if she'd gotten cruised. Whichever, she was glad she was trying out a packy; it'd pass manual inspections.

"Pardon," she said, sidestepping the errant hand and the guy's gaze and continuing to the front lounge where the tank-topped throngs had multiplied. *Shit,* she thought, *this is a lot of dudes.* She moved back to the video bar, and seeing Tyrone, planted herself between his group of friends and a trio of white dudes with seemingly matching goatees.

"Do you party?" The guy who asked earlier had found her again. Turned out his name was Kirk and he was interested in chatting her up and apparently getting her high.

"I don't do coke, man." AJ came up in the eighties, back when crack was king and bangers ruled the hoods at home. Too many fly girls turned into crack hos, too many of her peeps gunned down, and lots of fucking black men serving time in the big house. She knew there would always be a market for drugs. But she didn't want to buy into it and so far she hadn't and maybe she was stronger or maybe Jesus helped her stay tough. Whatever it was, she hated what cocaine did to her community.

"It ain't cocaine, it's crystal. Sure you don't want a hit?"

She shook her head. These guys had a world between them and the streets she'd come up in. Why'd they risk it all for a drug rots your teeth out? Middle class gone and gotten so fucking bad they'd snort meth to escape? What the fuck?

"What's the attraction?" she asked.

Kirk snorted. "Hey, guys, we got ourselves a virgin! This kid's never gotten amped. He wants to know what's the big deal."

The guys snickered. AJ didn't respond.

"You're young enough for an all-night round of clubbing and fucking, but some of us old guys need a little pick-me-up," Kirk said, winking at her.

"You're missing out if you haven't fucked while partying with Tina," one of Kirk's clones insisted, as though using slang for the dope would make it more attractive.

"Don't listen to 'em, kid." The words came from the left. "That shit'll fuck you up. Ruined my life."

AJ was surprised to find Tyrone Hill sticking out his hand. She shook it firmly.

"Tyrone," he said. He pulled out a wallet and passed her a photo of Velvet's dead friend, Jeff. "Me and my boyfriend."

"He's hot," she said, as though qualified to judge.

"He was." Tyrone stroked the picture with his forefinger. He kept his head bent, but she saw the tears in his dark eyes.

"He killed in Iraq?" AJ asked. Back home in the hood that'd be a reasonable guess, if a death wasn't gang related.

Tyrone looked at her like she crazy. "He was *gay*," he said, like it ruled out military.

AJ pretended like she got it. He slipped the photo away. She wondered if she'd lost his attention. She remembered learning in police academy: Sit back, listen, ask open-ended questions.

"Ya blame your tweaking?"

He nodded and pulled out a pack of filtered Camels. He offered her one. She hesitated. Back in the hood, everyone smoked. Once she'd got to California she'd learned smokers were second-class citizens. She'd been trying to give it up. But she liked pairing smoking and drinking. The vices went together.

She accepted a Camel, jabbed it between her dry lips, and bent over his lighter. Her lips had been chapped since she moved here. No humidity. She sucked the smoke deep into her lungs like an asthma patient inhaling from an oxygen mask.

Tyrone started talking like it was a relief to have someone listening. "Started out where we'd just be speedin' to keep up with our homies at the club."

"We?" AJ looked pointedly at the homies playing pool.

He shook his head. "We'd gone from using at clubs to sharing a hit before sex."

"Why? What'd it do for y'all?"

"Makes it so you can go all night long."

Sounds exhausting.

"Then I started wanting it more and more. Jeff wouldn't do it with me, and it got so I'd do just about anything for a fix." Tyrone lowered his voice. He seemed embarrassed. "I'd pick up tricks online who could offer me refreshments."

AJ wanted to capitalize on his chattiness. She leaned forward and kept her own voice low. "Ya cheatin' on your boy? Keeping it on the down low?"

"*Cheating?*" It caught on his tongue like a foreign language. "What are you, a *lesbian*?"

She stared at him. *What gave it away?*

"You just come out or something?" Tyrone demanded.

Sure. She nodded.

"You'll find," he spoke slowly as though he'd just discovered she was a second grader, "a lot of gay guys just aren't built for monogamy. It's just not in our natures. Jeff and I had an *arrangement*. We could fuck other guys."

"Bareback?" AJ asked about wearing protection. It seemed reasonable.

Tyrone blushed. It could be hard to see the blood rising to dark-skinned cheeks, but AJ'd had practice. She used to make Chantal blush all the time. Back before the levees broke, before Hurricane Katrina, before Chantal broke her heart.

"Like I said, crank ruined my life. When I'm high it's like gay sex *isn't* unsafe. It's such a relief. We got our family saying gay sex is a filthy, dirty sin. Then AIDS comes along and now gay sex can kill you? That's what it means to be gay? It's soul crushing. That's just so depressing." Tyrone stared at AJ intently as he was passing on something critical. "I've always found bottoming difficult, you know? Childhood issues, I guess. But when I'm on crystal, I'm an insatiable bottom. When I'm high, suddenly getting fucked is no longer unmanly. It's awesome."

He offered to buy AJ a refill. She watched him closely until he returned with their drinks. He wasn't talking like a guy.

"You make meth sound spiritual."

"It is. It is spiritual. I wanted it more and more and I started booty bumping."

Booty bumping? It sounded like another name for kicking it. Or some kind of ass-bumping dance step.

"You dissolve crystal in water, then you shoot the solution up your ass," Tyrone explained.

That's nasty. AJ hoped her face didn't reveal her feelings.

Tyrone smiled as though happy to make her uncomfortable. "The high hits you almost as fast as smoking, but it don't fuck up your lungs."

AJ did not get men sometimes.

"Problem is, if you booty bump and then bottom, it can increase abrasion, 'specially if you're banging raw. I...well, I've done a lot of things I'm not proud of. When you're high you forget about everything else." He seemed to want to say something else but couldn't bring himself to do so.

She thought about what he was telling her and what she knew about homies on the down low. "You positive?"

He nodded.

"Ya give it to your boy? That how he died?"

"No." He was adamant. "Jeff was still HIV negative." He hung his head. "But he killed himself because of me."

"'Cause of the drugs?"

"Yeah."

"He leave a note or something?"

"No."

"Then how d'ya…?"

"Day before he did it, he tells me he can't live with me like this anymore. Thought he was going to leave and I begged him to stay…But then…"

"Damn, dawg, that's tough," AJ said with full genuineness.

They sat in silence. AJ finished her beer. When Tyrone's friends returned from playing pool he turned his back to her. She jumped at the chance to leave. She'd heard all she could take.

She'd tail Tyrone Hill when he left.

AJ crossed the street and hopped in her pimped-out Escalade. She was still pumped about snagging such a tight ride. Probably seized from some drug dealer before being sold at police auction.

From the comfort of the classy ride, AJ weighed Tyrone's statements. Did his meth use drive Jeff to suicide? What was it Tyrone wasn't proud of? Had he turned violent? AJ knew firsthand about drugs changing personality. Weren't tweakers paranoid? Under the influence, he could have seen Conant as a threat. Tyrone seemed so distraught, though. Plus, AJ wondered aloud to herself, could she even trust his memory? Meth does a lot of damage to user's brains as well; maybe Tyrone was filling in the blanks in his head with what he thought was likely.

Okay, so Tyrone said he'd had a open relationship with Jeff Conant. Was that true? Had he been honest with Conant? Did the deceased know about him riding bareback? Tonight she had a lot to think about. It was far from over, especially if Tyrone was using and really could stay up for days at a time.

❖

Tucker was a little peeved at being left behind while Yoshi accompanied Velvet to Jeff's memorial. *She* was the girlfriend, after all.

She should've insisted on being there. A sexy, voluptuous femme like Velvet really shouldn't go anywhere without a handsome butch on her arm. Without Tucker's presence, how would other butches know Velvet was taken? A whole string of girls would want to take Tucker's place. She might've captured Velvet's heart, but she wasn't foolish enough to forget about Velvet's wandering eye.

Although Velvet was the one who had insisted she stay behind, Tucker had no doubt Yoshi put her up to it. She'd hinted that Tucker would be "collaborating" with Bud on Blind Eye's hush-hush investigation into Conant's death. It sounded like an excuse. Yoshi probably didn't want Tucker at the memorial in case Velvet noticed the distracting chemistry between them. Yoshi was too classy to let anything happen, of course. Velvet was her best friend, and Tucker was in the lowly role of receptionist.

But that wouldn't always be the case. She'd begun taking night classes at the Sam Brown School, a San Francisco institution that trained private investigators, and when she was done there she could be a PI herself. Then she'd be Yoshi's colleague not her subordinate. Eventually. For now Tucker was only 30 hours into the 212-hour program. *And* she still needed to rack up another 5,000 hours working with a licensed investigator. Thank God her day job counted as time served. That would greatly reduce the three-year sentence she'd originally calculated and make it so she'd get her own license sooner. Then she'd finally be Yoshi's colleague and their attraction could blossom.

Bud's cough intruded rudely on Tucker's fantasy and she immediately felt embarrassed about the way she'd gone from thinking of Velvet to dreaming about Yoshi. Rationally, she knew her attraction to her boss was absurd and would never come to anything. So why couldn't she get over it? Velvet was every girl's dream. She was sexy and smart, successful and fun, soft and curvaceous on the outside while tough-as-nails assertive below the surface. *And* Tucker had really fallen for the voluptuous journalist. So why couldn't she banish thoughts of Yoshi?

Bud coughed louder. "Yo, princess, you awake over there?"

"Yeah."

"Your thingie's going off."

"My thingie?"

"Your cell phone."

"Oh right. I forgot I had it." Tucker hadn't gotten used to the device yet. She'd never had a cell phone until Yoshi assigned her a Blind Eye one so they could talk business even when she was out in the field.

Tucker was kind of a country bumpkin, not used to having fancy high-tech gadgets. She was from a small farm in an area of Idaho that seemed immune to the advancements of technology. In junior high she'd been sent home from school for wearing a T-shirt with the slogan, "Welcome to Idaho, set your clocks back twenty years." The principal had never appreciated her sense of humor. Or her style of dress. He didn't think her suit, jacket, and tie combo was appropriate for a girl.

By high school plenty of kids had their own cell phones. Even more of them had their own vehicles. But not Tucker. She'd had to ride the bus all the way up to graduation. At least she'd finally gotten seniority over bus seats. That final year, when the orange bus pulled over at the dirt road that led to her home, she could pick any bench seat she wanted and, without a word, the littler kids would quickly vacate it for her.

Tucker fumbled with the buttons on the phone. The ringing stopped. Thinking she'd found the answer button, she said, "Hello?"

No one was there. Damn. She stared at the screen.

"Hey, I got a text message!" She wondered how long the message had been waiting. Hours, probably.

Bud grunted noncommittally.

Just because the old sourpuss didn't appreciate her excitement, it wasn't going to get her down. This was, after all, her first text message.

"It's from Yoshi," she announced, sort of disappointed it had not been Velvet sending her a little "miss you" note or something, but Velvet was probably still too upset about her friend killing himself. "Hey, the investigation's gone official."

Bud didn't seem interested. "Yeah?"

"Jeff's mom hired us. I guess she wants us to look into Jeff's death."

"Really?" The sarcasm dripped from Bud's voice. "And I thought she'd hired us to find Jimmy Hoffa."

Tucker made a face at him. "Now that it's official, we should probably get to work."

Bud didn't answer. He returned to reading the *Playboy* he'd smuggled into the office under the cushion of his wheelchair. Just because Yoshi insisted he work late didn't mean he was going to break a sweat. Hell, he was probably only there to babysit the kid while Yoshi and that steamy reporter, Velvet, were working the memorial.

This whole Conant case was a bunch of nonsense. Everyone knew the fag offed himself. Even Yoshi didn't think his death was suspicious. She was just throwing Velvet a bone. *Bone.* He chuckled in his head. He'd like to throw that brick shithouse a bone of his own. If he only had one to throw. Ever since the hot lead of a bullet seared through his spinal cord, he hadn't been able to get a bone to save his life. Or his marriage.

He shook the thought from his head.

Yoshi had probably just given them the assignment so the kid would have something to practice on, playing investigator on a case that wouldn't matter if she fucked it up. Well, if the boss wanted to throw good money his way to watch the kid play dress-up, who was he to say different? But that didn't mean he wanted to play along.

"Where should I start?" Tucker asked.

Bud sighed. *Damn.* Before the text message, the kid had been content to quietly play make-believe all by herself. Now Yoshi'd gone and suckered some grieving mother into funding an all-out investigation, and for what? The guy had taken a swan dive off the bridge. God knows, Bud understood what could send someone over the railing. If he could get over the railings without legs, maybe he'd have done the same. He wasn't interested in pretending this was a real case, but now that Yoshi had a bee in her bonnet, Tucker had gotten all serious about doing the work. Wouldn't you know it? Now she needed her hand held or something. God forbid she do anything on her own.

Okay, granted, that wasn't *always* the case. On the Finney murder, she'd actually put her country-fried knowledge to good use, figuring out how a horse played a role in the murder. But that was just a stroke of luck. He wouldn't want to turn her loose on real evidence in a real case, not that this was a real case. That was the point, Bud concluded, returning to his first thought. Yoshi was trying to train Tucker and because of her own limitations, Bud could already see how that was going to play out.

He grudgingly responded to Tucker's query. "We start by finding out everything we can about the victim. Then we move on to looking at the people close to him. The boyfriend, coworkers, whatever. Doing that, we establish more elements of the case. We keep spiraling out from there, clearing POIs as we go and narrowing in on *suspects*."

"Fine." Tucker obviously hadn't noticed he was only explaining all this because he had no choice. She looked thrilled. "Actually, I already got some stuff on Jeff Conant."

Tucker's computer screen was open to Detective Magic's Web site, where they could access everything from a subject's child support payments to their police record. "Got a TRW report and checked out his financials. Looks like he's maxed out on some of his credit cards and cleared out his savings a few months back."

Bud stuck the *Playboy* under his seat cushion and rolled closer to Tucker's desk. "Okay, there are four main reasons why men need money. Drugs, booze, women, gambling. So let's look for evidence of gambling or drug use."

"I checked his online activity, there's no Internet gambling."

"How about drugs?"

"Jeff told Velvet he dabbled in recreational drugs, but it sounds like his boyfriend Tyrone might be a regular."

"Did you look into Tyrone's background? The partner is always a good POI to start with."

Tucker entered Tyrone Hill's information into the Detective Magic database. Luckily he lived with Jeff, so they didn't have to sort through a dozen Tyrone Hills living in the San Francisco Bay Area.

"He doesn't have a driver's license. Isn't that weird?" Tucker asked naïvely.

"Not in San Francisco, it's not. Plenty of people don't drive, like Yoshi."

"Oh, right. What do they use for ID?"

"They get state ID cards."

"That makes sense. Hey, he's got a record."

"For what?" Bud maneuvered his chair so he could see the computer screen over Tucker's shoulder. He was disappointed with what he saw. "Is that all?"

"It says he was arrested for possession of controlled substances."

"Yeah, but see he barely had enough for one hit, so he obviously wasn't dealing and they let him off with probation."

"But if he's using again, wouldn't that get his probation revoked and send him to prison?"

"Not likely." Boy, the kid was green. It was like she'd lived her life in a box. "Prison overcrowding being what it is, they wouldn't waste their time with a small fry like that. Plus first-timers have to go through a rehab program these days, instead of doing hard time. Cops'd probably just try and flip him."

"Flip him?"

"Turn him into a snitch, a CI? A confidential informant."

"Couldn't that get him killed?"

"He's so low on the food chain that doesn't seem a plausible. Move on. Is he broke, too?"

The kid took a moment to pull up Hill's credit report. "It doesn't even look like he has a bank account. Closed six months ago. Couple of past-due balances and his credit card accounts frozen. You think all this is from his drug use?"

Bud nodded. It was a likely deduction.

"What's his 'Net use like?"

Tucker maneuvered through a few windows. "Mostly porn sites."

"Really?" Bud perked up his ears. Finally something of interest. He glanced at the screen. "Eew." Two guys were doing things they most definitely should not do, unless maybe they grew up behind prison bars.

"*Gay* porn sites," Tucker said.

Bud wrinkled his nose and waved his hand in front of his face as though she'd just cut one. The brat hid a smirk behind her hand. She thought she was so funny.

"I'll check for chat rooms." Tucker typed at the keys and pushed around the mouse.

Bud rolled away while she searched through Hill's history. He didn't want to accidentally see the wrong popup and turn queer. "What'd this guy do for a living?"

"I don't think he has a job."

"What about Conant?"

"He was the executive director of the Frameline film festival."

"We'll want to talk to some of his coworkers."

"It looks like some of the chat rooms are places where gay guys hook up."

"Can you track what he wrote?"

"No, I can't, not through this program."

"Too bad. If he was picking up guys online, one of them could be involved. I mean, if there was actually a crime."

"You don't think there was?"

The kid was so wet behind the ears she probably didn't think anyone would kill themselves.

"When it looks like shit and smells like shit, I don't think it's a chocolate bar."

"Gross." Tucker was silent for moment. "I don't think it should be illegal."

"What?"

"To kill yourself," she said, surprising him. "It doesn't seem anybody's business but your own."

"Yeah." He tried to think of something else to talk about. "Let's put together a list of people to talk to. Write down Hill and the film festival people. Write down their hours and phone numbers, too, in case we need it while we're driving around."

"Is that what you've got planned for tomorrow?"

"I don't know if it'll be us, but yeah, someone will have to chat with our POIs."

Tucker opened a Word document and started typing, her hands flying across the keys. They trained girls to do that kind of thing. Nobody had taught him, and it showed. He was a hunt-and-peck man. His aversion to computers might have something to do with the fact that he'd never bothered to hone his keyboard skills. He didn't trust those machines. He didn't trust anything he couldn't stare in the eyes of to get a sense of its character.

"What else we got?" Bud asked when Tucker stopped typing. "You say Conant's family is all from out of town?"

"Yeah, but apparently they're really tight."

"So, no animosity there?"

"Not as far as I know."

Either that meant the Conant family had no dirty laundry or they just didn't air it in public. Maybe the boyfriend could tell them which. Bud thought for a little while before mentioning some other ideas. The kid happily typed everything he said into the computer. It beat having to scribble his thoughts down himself.

"We ought to get someone to go through Conant's apartment since Hill lived there, too."

"Won't the police do that with a search warrant?"

Slowly, with exaggerated patience, Bud said, "They would if they thought this was a murder, but seeing as it's a suicide, they've got better things to do with their time."

"Then how are we going to get in there? Do you think Tyrone will let us search the place?"

"We'll just have to ask, won't we?" Bud replied in an irritated singsong. "I'm guessing the bereaved boyfriend will want to help in any way he can. Otherwise how would that look?"

"Guilty."

"Catching on," Bud muttered. "Going through their place will give us a picture of both our victim and main POI. Kill two birds with one stone." He thought some more. "Didn't Yoshi say she was going to have that cop tail Hill?"

"AJ? Yeah, she's on it now. He's in a nightclub."

"Perfect. That makes it a good time to check out his domicile, while we got a tail on him. You got her number?"

Tucker's forehead wrinkled like one of those butt-ugly shit-poo dogs. "But isn't that breaking and entering?"

"No, that's Private Investigation 101."

"Still—" She avoided his eyes.

"Where's your sense of adventure? You worried about my legs or something?" He smacked a thigh with an open hand. It was like hitting someone else. He felt nothing.

She was cautious about answering. "Well, yeah."

"Don't worry." He waved aside her concerns. When they got to Conant's house he would tell her the punch line—she was going to have to do the breaking and entering all by herself. He had to smother a chuckle when he thought about it.

CHAPTER SEVEN

As Velvet pulled away from the curb, Yoshi broke the silence that had followed them from the Castro Theatre.

"What was that with Davina?" she asked.

"What do you mean?"

That was the type of question suspects asked, stalling for time and hoping the interrogator would tip her hand. Perps would hold back on providing information until they believed the interrogator already had it and maybe could even prove their malfeasance. Yoshi was disappointed to hear the stalling question from her friend. But she did not back down.

"You two were flirting."

"I don't know what you're talking about." Velvet was defensive. "Even if that's true, what's it to you?"

"I don't want to see Tucker hurt."

"It's none of your business, Yoshi."

"Actually, it is. I remember explicitly requesting that you *not* become involved with yet another of my employees. You did anyway. Now that you and Tucker are an item, I have a vested interest in your staying together. I would be disappointed if your grief-muddled decision making resulted in my having to recruit another employee."

"And why would it?"

Yoshi sighed. "Because that is exactly what happened with my previous receptionist. When you broke off with her, she spent work hours pining until I had to let her go. And my administrative assistant, Catherine Hildenbrand. She just left town…"

Apparently, Velvet had no intention of dignifying Yoshi's snide comments with a response. She was silent for a moment before switching subjects. "If you were thinking Jennifer Morris might have had something to do with Jeff's death, you're way off. I've known Jennifer for years. She had nothing to gain from his death."

"She's Frameline's interim director now," Yoshi said. "Perhaps the job will become permanent."

"No. She doesn't want it. Before Jeff joined Frameline, Jennifer shared director responsibilities with Michael Lumpkin, and when he left, they offered the full position to her. She turned them down, so they created the director of programming position specifically for her."

Yoshi accepted her friend's assessment, knowing Velvet covered the annual LGBT film festival for the *San Francisco Chronicle* and was well versed in the inner workings of the Frameline organization. Still, she could not depend on Velvet's assurances alone. Someone would have to speak to Jennifer Morris in person before her name could be crossed off the POI list. Blind Eye would need to confirm her alibi and assess her truthfulness. In addition, Yoshi hoped to press Morris for more insight into Jeff's professional life and any problems he was having at work.

"Davina mentioned irate filmmakers and producers," Yoshi said. "Do you put any stock in the idea that someone associated with the festival could have killed him? Perhaps a producer who believed that his film would have a better chance of being added to the roster under Jennifer Morris's tenure?"

"No, I don't buy it. As director of programming, Jennifer was already in a position to actually choose the films to be shown at the festival. Offing Jeff wouldn't have changed the lineup or improved anyone's chances of having their film chosen."

"Okay." Yoshi accepted Velvet's insight. She carefully chose her next words. "Davina indicated that Jeff might have been under some stress recently—"

"I keep telling you, he didn't kill himself. Why can't you just accept that?" Velvet drew a sharp breath and released it with the shaky deliberation of a woman struggling to control her emotions. "I can't believe you could be so damn hypocritical as to take Charlene's money when you've already made your mind up."

Yoshi did not try to defend herself against her friend's outburst. She did not make a statement about the importance of critical thinking in the field of private investigation. She did not say that most deaths that appeared to be suicides were just that, not carefully concealed murders.

She touched Velvet's arm, trying to convey her sympathy, to connect over this divide separating them.

Velvet shrugged her off. "It seems so obvious what happened."

Yoshi had never known Velvet, the investigative reporter, to insist on the "obvious" without completing thorough research to back up her contentions. It was so strange, the way that grief impacted a person's very reasoning skills. From an evolutionary point of view, Velvet's response seemed entirely ineffective. After a lion killed a hunter-gatherer tribal member, it would seem like survivors needed greater, not lesser deductive reasoning so they would not suffer a similar fate. Instead, Velvet seemed intent on clinging to faulty reasoning.

"That bastard Tyrone," Velvet said. "He probably killed Jeff in a meth-fueled rage and then dumped him off the bridge to cover it up. The fall and impact would have obscured the injuries before death."

"Do you have any reason to actually believe Tyrone had been violent with Jeff?" Yoshi asked. The first she had heard of the accusation was when Velvet confronted Tyrone at the memorial.

"You mean, how could I have missed the signs? What kind of person wouldn't notice their friend was being abused, is that it? Or are you saying you think I'm making this up? That I'm what? Delusional?"

"Of course not, I just—"

"If I'm so delusional, maybe you'd rather walk home than stay here and ride with me. God knows *what* I'm likely to do next—in my delusionary state, I might confuse red for green or a sidewalk for a freeway entrance—"

"Velvet, don't be ridiculous."

"Oh, now I'm *ridiculous*?"

"I did not mean—"

Velvet yanked the wheel sharply to the right, hit the brake, and ground to a stop. "Get out!"

"Velvet, please." Fear clutched at Yoshi's insides.

"No. I can't deal with you right now." Velvet began to sob.

"It's all right."

"No, it's not! Why can't you just support me? Is that too much to ask?"

"You are asking me to just make a blind leap and accept your hypothesis that Jeff Conant was murdered by Tyrone Hill, all without the smallest shred of evidence that a murder was even committed.

You know that I don't work that way. I will examine all possibilities, including the possibility that no crime has occurred." Yoshi touched Velvet's shoulder.

Velvet jerked away. "Oh, right. What was I thinking?" The sarcasm dripped from her voice to the steering wheel. "I'm *just* an investigative reporter and Jeff's best friend. What would I know? You're the brilliant detective. Clearly I'm in your way. So just go."

"If that's what you really want."

Yoshi pulled the car's door handle. With the click of the releasing latch, the door swung open, letting in a blast of cold air. Surely Velvet would reconsider. She would not, when it came down to it, leave Yoshi stranded, alone at night and unable to see.

Velvet did not try to stop her.

Yoshi vacated the vehicle.

Velvet did not speak.

Yoshi shut the door and Velvet pulled away from the curb. Yoshi stood there listening to the Celica drive away. Velvet was just making a point, teaching her a lesson. At the intersection she heard the Celica turn a corner. She would just circle the block and then return, apologizing profusely. Yoshi would admit she truly believed Velvet had abandoned her. They would chuckle about the practical joke, and Yoshi would make an effort to compliment Velvet on her ribbing: *Good one, Velvet. You really got me.*

The minutes ticked by. Yoshi strained to hear the sound of the Celica returning. With each approaching vehicle, she perked up and waited for the vehicle to pull to the curb near her. One by one, the cars continued past, their drivers oblivious to her growing panic.

Velvet was not coming back. She had truly abandoned her to the darkness.

Yoshi extracted her cell phone, felt for the appropriate keys, and entered one-one-one, the code for Velvet's stored number. She ticked off the moments in her head while the signal bounced to a satellite dish and back down to Velvet's mobile. The call went straight to voice mail.

At the beep, Yoshi apologized profusely for her regrettable word choice. She hung up and dialed Velvet's home number. She got another message and apologized again.

She called the Blind Eye offices, where she had left Tucker a few hours ago. There was no answer. After four rings, the message center picked up. Yoshi hung up, and from memory, typed in the code for Bud Williams. Once again she reached voice mail. Likewise for Tucker Shade. What was the point in supplying Blind Eye's employees with cell phones if they were simply going to turn them off or ignore them?

Not bothering to leave a message, Yoshi ended the call. She started to enter the speed-dial code for her favorite taxi service, then stopped. *Oh, damn.* She did not know where she was, and she could not provide directions to a cab driver. Yoshi tried to recreate the drive from the Castro Theatre. She had not paid attention. She had been too busy angering Velvet. God. All she knew was that she was somewhere between the Castro and the Blind Eye office in the Flood Building downtown. What was she going to do?

Yoshi tried to fight off the terror sneaking up on her. She hated this. She hated being so damn vulnerable. Hot tears stung her eyes. She swiped angrily at them. *Get it together*.

She was a smart, strong, independent Asian woman. She could do this. A woman blind from birth had run the grueling thousand-mile Iditarod through the Alaskan tundra. By God, the least Yoshi could do was navigate her way to some place familiar. Then again, a half dozen seeing-eye Huskies had accompanied Rachael Scdoris on *her* adventure, and the only dangerous predators Scdoris had to contend with were polar bears. They might be voracious hunters, but they were nothing compared to the predators loose on San Francisco streets. Everyone knew to stay away from polar bears; even Yoshi wouldn't ask a wild animal for directions. But human predators were much more difficult to detect. And defend against.

She should not travel downhill. Doing so might point her directly at San Francisco's shadier neighborhoods, the Tenderloin or Bayview. Depending on where she was to begin with, strolling uphill should steer her back toward the Castro neighborhood or to Nob Hill. Either would be preferable to the other options.

Yoshi returned the cell phone to her purse and pulled out the white telescoping cane. At least she had that with her. Remembering that Velvet had pulled over to the right to let her out, she started walking back the direction they'd come. She tapped her way to the end of the block where her cane dipped off the curb.

Most of San Francisco's intersections were not equipped with the chirping jangle that indicated to the blind when to walk and when to stop. This was just one reason Yoshi preferred a friendly cab service that could take her directly where she wanted to go. These days, she limited walking to situations where she had the advantage of familiarity, having mapped them in her memory from years past.

Now Yoshi waited nervously at the corner of a street she did not recognize, listening to the sound of cars driving through the intersection. The traffic parallel to her seemed to flow through the intersection without stopping. This meant there was no stop sign. Yoshi waited a little longer. She still had not heard cars slow or idle and she determined, therefore, that there was no signal light either. Thus, the traffic on the street perpendicular must have a stop sign and would need to come to a stop before continuing through the intersection.

Yoshi cautiously stepped off the curb. When no drivers responded by honking or shouting warnings, she hurried across the street. It seemed a very long time before her cane bumped against the far curb and she stepped back on safer ground. When she did, she felt as triumphant as if she had crossed the distance on a tightrope strung high in the air.

It was merely one lone street, and yet it served to restore her confidence. *I can do this.* Now the statement was made with conviction, instead of as a positive-thinking mantra meant to reassure herself. She could successfully traverse the streets of San Francisco, using her senses to deduce when it was safe to cross. But, she thought as another wave of trepidation washed over her, could she truly navigate? Just because she could walk down sidewalks and cross streets did not mean she knew where she was heading. And what if she was attacked? Could she defend herself?

If her father were with her now, he would not tolerate her self-doubt. Hiroki Yakamota had insisted she learn defensive moves in preparation for just such a situation. He had enrolled her in karate, kickboxing, judo, and jujitsu, hoping to find one at which she was particularly skilled. An image came to her of her adult self shrunken to age seven or eight, wearing her white karate *gi*, standing with other children her age on a padded floor. Her father stood against the wall of the gym, the look on his face clearly conveying an odd mixture of disappointment, bemusement, pride, and love.

Yoshi could almost hear him speaking to another parent, his Japanese accent still thick after a decade in the United States: See the girl with the long dark hair? The one who lost every match? She's my daughter. I am so proud of her. She is simply awful. But she never quits. I love that determination.

She had never excelled at any one discipline, but she had mastered specific moves. Eventually she had combined the moves she was good at into an amalgamation of her own. But she had not practiced in many years, and though practitioners of the ancient arts employed all of their senses, she had not personally used the defensive tactics since losing her eyesight. Who knew if she would lose her balance or lash out aimlessly, connecting with nothing while her opponent danced around her, easily overpowering her defenses? The prospect was frightening.

During the Rosemary Finney case, and again at the recent hip-hop concert, she had been completely overwhelmed by the sense of helplessness that had been stalking her for years. Yoshi had begun to worry that she could no longer do her job alone. Perhaps her future lay not in direct, hands-on investigation, but rather in administrative support for her investigative team. She would give up the only job she had ever loved.

But tonight, tonight she was beginning to think otherwise. Perhaps Velvet's abandonment was a much-needed wake-up call to shake her out of her incessant reliance upon others. This could be the incentive she needed to reconnect with her self-reliance and shed the tedious role of the helpless disabled person.

She had heard about a new television program that featured a blind man who designed houses. If he could do that, why couldn't she continue investigating?

After traveling several blocks paralleling the through street, Yoshi realized that she had sensed neither an increase nor a decrease in altitude. If she was going neither uphill nor downhill, the street she was following must run perpendicular to the hills. If she continued along the road she was on, she would most certainly bypass the Castro neighborhood.

At the next intersection with a cross light, Yoshi continued striding away from the main road she had traveled on. It did not take long before her legs complained that they were marching *up*hill. This was good news. Most likely, she was following one of the numbered streets, and if she was correct about her location, Market Street would be the main thoroughfare at the crest of the first hill. On Market, she would find businesses, like the large Safeway grocery store. She would finally have a location to provide to the taxi dispatch.

Her fear having transformed into excitement, she eagerly blueprinted the remainder of her evening. She intended to—once and for all—reclaim her private investigator credentials and prove that Yoshi Yakamota did not *require* assistance to collect the evidence she needed to solve cases. Tonight would be the turning point in the Jeff Conant case. She could sense it. And she was determined to be the one who proved whether Jeff had truly taken his own life or if someone had simply made it look like he did. Jeff could have been murdered. Velvet was too hasty in her emotionally driven assumptions. Yoshi had not ruled out the possibility at all. Nothing could be ruled out until all the facts were in hand, and Yoshi intended to obtain them.

❖

The house at 585 Castro was a lime green Victorian. Bud drove past the address where Jeff Conant had lived with his drug-problem partner and turned the corner on Seventeenth Street. He parked his 1960 baby blue Chevy Impala in the first empty spot he found and hung his handicap-parking placard over the rearview mirror, so he wouldn't be ticketed for lacking a neighborhood sticker. It took him fifteen minutes to get out of the driver's seat, execute an ice-skating-like triple salchow while holding on to the top of the open back door, yank the wheelchair from behind his seat, fling his body around, and land his ass in the chair.

Tucker hung back and didn't offer help, even though she was terrified that Bud would hurt himself or end up rolling backward down the street straight into oncoming traffic. From the few times she'd ridden with him, she had come to recognize that Bud didn't want her assistance, even though she meant no harm in offering. After growing up with two disabled siblings, she'd gotten used to being the able-bodied assistant. She'd tried to help Bud on more than one occasion, but he never seemed to appreciate her thoughtfulness. In fact, he seemed to *resent* any move she made to offer support. It was as though he thought she was belittling him, like she didn't believe he was capable of doing things himself.

She wondered if her siblings had felt the same way, if they'd resented her help, too, but had just been too polite to mention it. The thought made her stomach hurt. She'd always felt kind of guilty about being the one healthy kid in the Shade household, having the life Hunter and Anastasia deserved. Not to mention her namesake, the firstborn son who died as an infant.

"Ready?" Bud asked, tipping back in his chair and popping a wheelie to get up on the sidewalk.

"Yeah." Tucker hadn't figured out how they were supposed to break into a second-floor apartment with all these people around.

The streets were well lit and the sidewalks crowded with men, their bulging muscles crammed into brightly colored skintight tees and ripped jeans. Thinking about how uncomfortable Bud must be with all the gay guys around, Tucker smirked. She didn't know if he was *really* homophobic or if he just thought he was supposed to act that way to prove he was still a virile heterosexual man, even if he was paralyzed below the waist.

The gated entrance with steps to the lime green Victorian was sandwiched between a liquor store and a Thai restaurant. Bud stopped at the restaurant and held the door for Tucker, even though his chair made it awkward for her to squeeze past.

"Why, Bud, how nice. You treating me to dinner? Is this a date?"

"Cram it." He glowered at her as though he was annoyed, but she saw a sparkle in the irises of his brown eyes. He was just playing.

They waited by the door for the waiter. When a young East Asian man came to seat them, Bud requested one of the small round tables at the front of the restaurant, next to the large window that looked out onto Castro. This didn't seem like his kind of restaurant.

Tucker glanced around at dimmed lights and flickering tea candles. Murmuring couples ate pad Thai and fancy curries. Her stomach rumbled at the thought of what was quickly becoming her favorite ethnic cuisine. Growing up on a small farm in southeastern Idaho, she'd never been exposed to ethnic cuisine, aside from Taco Bell. Velvet, on the other hand, was totally urbane and had taken it upon herself to educate the country bumpkin. Due to her coaching, Tucker could find her way around a Thai menu.

"How's this going to help us get into Tyrone's?" she asked, thinking about the curry options.

Bud lowered his menu and grinned at her. Something in his eyes made her nervous. She shifted in her seat.

"What?" she demanded.

He leaned forward and indicated for her to do the same. She scooted her straight-backed chair closer and leaned in.

"Their place is right next door, right?"

"Yeah?"

"These places are all the same. They've got little courtyards in the back."

"So?"

"So, this place probably has one."

"And?"

"And a bathroom."

"You asking permission to take a piss?"

He rolled his eyes like she was daft. "Restroom's always in the back."

She still didn't get the point.

He sighed. "You go to the bathroom. You climb out the window into the courtyard."

"*Me?*"

"You don't expect me to do it, do you?" He pointed at his withered legs.

"No, but—"

"I thought you wanted to be a PI. If you're too afraid—"

"Fine." Tucker ground her teeth. "So, let's say I manage to climb out the back window without getting caught. *Then* what?"

"There's probably stairs, leading from the back of the apartments down to the courtyard. You know, like some kind of shared backyard. You just go on up to the second floor...and there you are."

"There *I am*? How am I supposed to get inside? Did you think about that?"

"Oh for godssakes, Shade, haven't you learned *anything* yet? What are they teaching you at that detective school anyway?"

"Silly them, not teaching me how to get arrested committing a crime by breaking into someone's house."

"If you act like you belong, nobody's going to notice. If they do, just tell them you're Conant's little sister or something and you're staying there and got locked out. The neighbors would probably help you break in."

"How do you suggest I do that? It's not like I learned how to pick locks."

"One of the windows is probably unlocked. I doubt if they think someone's gonna break in from their private courtyard. But if not, then *improvise*. This is your chance to prove you've got what it takes to be a PI. Or should I just tell Yoshi you pussied out?"

Tucker imagined disappointment besmirching Yoshi's beautiful face. Damn. Bud was going to get her arrested.

"Fine," she said. "But you *owe* me."

A grin spread across his face.

"What am I looking for?" Tucker asked.

"Mostly a sense of who these guys are. Here." He shuffled through a pocket on the wheelchair's side and pushed something under the table at her.

It was a throwaway camera.

"Take photos. If you stumble on a diary, suicide note, or murder confession, bring them back with you. Oh yeah, and don't be gone too long."

Tucker stalked through the restaurant to the bathrooms, the camera tucked inside one of her jacket's many pockets. The women's restroom was not at the back of the building as Bud had suggested. She looked back at him, planning to make a nonverbal fuss about it, but he avoided her eyes as he ordered food.

She looked at the men's room, which *did* border the back wall, and sighed. *Improvise.* She knocked and when no one answered, she ducked inside and locked the door. The room reeked of urine. The burning ammonia smell seemed to have soaked into all four of the walls—and the ceilings. Boys were so gross.

Back home she'd caught the unneutered billy goats licking pee off each other. Their pheromones smelled almost as bad as the bathroom. Tucker's mom wiped a rag on the stud buck's head. The rag smelled as bad as the goat. She kept it in a glass jar, with the lid screwed tightly in place. When she wanted the does to come into heat, she'd take the lid off that jar and let the nanny goats sniff it. They'd be ready to breed within a week.

In the Thai restaurant's graffiti-brightened bathroom, Tucker looked around, hoping to quickly escape the stench. The one dust-encrusted window was about the size of the bamboo place mats out front. *You've got to be kidding.* She wondered if she would even fit through the damn thing. Only one way to be sure. She'd always been pretty good at getting through tight spaces. The lava field behind her childhood home had stretched for miles. It was crisscrossed with fissures that plunged fifteen feet or more to the ground. Some cracks were narrow enough to easily step over, but others dominated the landscape, spreading like wide canyons. Her mother made it clear that Tucker was to avoid those broad fissures.

As a teen, Tucker had ignored all warnings and advice. She used to clamber up and down the slick black rocks, slowly finding hand- and footholds like a free-form rock climber. She had no ropes, kneepads, or helmet to protect her if she fell. Once she reached the canyon floor, she'd follow it as far as possible. Above her, the crack would narrow progressively until it fused together over her head, becoming a cave. She had squeezed through a lot of narrow spaces in her time and she could probably get through this one, too. She stepped on the toilet seat, then up to the top of the tank. The porcelain lid shifted under her weight. She grabbed the top of the stall to keep her balance, and with one foot on the ceramic tank and the other hanging in the air over the toilet bowl, she reached for the window. It appeared to be painted shut. Still, she unlatched the metal hook from its donut eye and gave it a shove with the palm of her hand.

Tucker was surprised when it gave under pressure and swung outward. Her hand went with it. The motion reverberated through her body, pulling her toward the window. Her foot slipped off the toilet tank and she scrambled, grabbing at the lip of the windowsill and narrowly preventing her foot from a good soaking in foul toilet water. Clinging to the edge of the windowsill, she could not hold the dead weight of her legs for long. She jammed her sneakered feet into the corner and pushed off. Somehow she shoved her head through the open window. Cold air ruffled aside her short locks and blew a chill onto her scalp. It was no Idaho freeze, but winter was winter. Not her favorite season in any climate. Except maybe New Orleans. There it'd be a frickin' relief after the brutal tropical summers.

Tucker paused to assess her position. She was half in and half out of a men's bathroom window. She was probably going to get stuck here and have to be *cut* out by firefighters with huge saws that would slice right through the siding and sheet rock as though it were butter. Although her body muffled the restaurant's racket, she could hear someone banging hard on the restroom door. She wondered how long it would be before they called the manager. She hoped she wouldn't be trapped in the narrow window when the irate customer eventually got in.

The ground below her was littered with cement blocks. Not wanting to land on them headfirst, she slowly and painfully rotated her body. A few minutes later, her back was pressed against the windowsill and she was looking up at the night sky. The glow of the city hid the stars she remembered from back home. She hoped none of the neighbors would see her hanging there. After catching her breath, she squeezed her torso out until she was in a sitting position, facing the building, her nose brushing against the rough wood. She clung to the edges of the siding, her fingertips digging in. Preparing herself for a fall, she shuffled back so she could get one leg out, turned and sat awkwardly astride, then freed the other leg. Hunched forward with only her butt on the window ledge, hanging on with her hands behind her, she stared down into the courtyard, took a deep breath, and jumped.

The ground was hard. The courtyard had no lawn-quality turf. The wild grasses grew in clumps and their rough seeds scratched Tucker's legs and stuck in her socks as she shuffled toward the target Victorian. She was relieved to find the windows on the first floor dark. Above her head she could see the balconies that hung over the courtyard from the back. Buildings, all of which seemed to have residential apartments on their upper floors, surrounded the square yard. She could see the bright red glow of a cigarette as someone on the third floor across from her stood on the balcony and enjoyed his smoke.

Tucker had smoked as a teenager, ducking out into the darkness of the farm, not realizing how the strong odor clung to her clothes and even overwhelmed the corral's goat manure. She hadn't craved a cigarette for a long time but she wouldn't turn one down now, if it were offered.

Bud was wrong about the external stairway. The other building overlooking the courtyard had wooden steps, but not Jeff and Tyrone's converted Victorian. Tucker tried the windows on the first floor thinking that she maybe she could get access to the building's indoor stairwell and then figure out how to break into the apartment. The windows were shut tight and she looked up at the building again. As her eyes adjusted to the darkness, she finally noticed a fire escape above her. It was one of those where the last leg of the ladder remained a floor above the ground until it was released.

Tucker considered her options. There was no way she was going back through the bathroom window. Nor was she particularly thrilled with the idea of returning empty-handed and listening to Bud belittling her. Bracing herself against a drainpipe and using the door frame of the downstairs neighbors, Tucker reached the hanging ladder and climbed it to the second-floor balcony. She peered through the back window into Jeff's apartment and made sure there was no motion or noise coming from within. She tried the window. It was loose.

Tucker brushed slivers of peeled paint from her clothing and spent the next five minutes jimmying the window. She managed to pry it open it wide enough to slide a credit card through. Even she wasn't that thin, and she had to concede defeat. Frustrated, Tucker flopped against the back door.

It slid open behind her.

Muffling a scream, she scrambled to regain her footing, sure someone must have pulled the door open. But she heard no noises inside the apartment, and once she'd assured herself that she was alone, Tucker pulled the cell phone from her pocket and dashed off a quick test message: "I'm in."

The porch opened into the kitchen. She found a light switch and recoiled at the mess. Garbage overflowed the bin, and dirty dishes spilled from the sink and spread across the counters like a black cancer. The room reeked of spoiling food. She snapped a few photos and hurried into the hallway. The apartment was designed like a New Orleans shotgun, with a hallway on one side, rooms on the other. The long hall led straight from the kitchen to the front of the house. It was cluttered with a mishmash of discarded clothing, empty boxes, and what looked like several full garbage bags, tied off at the top.

She stepped over heaping pile of clothing discarded at the front door like a low-tech booby trap. She wondered if Jeff had been this messy or was Tyrone just a slob? Another possibility was that someone had trashed the apartment looking for something. Was that why the back door hadn't closed properly? She remembered when the police had searched Velvet's home in Bernal Heights, back during that frightening period when she was suspected of killing Rosemary Finney. That had also been a mess, but it had looked more...thorough than this.

The small bathroom was cluttered with expensive grooming products that held no interest to Tucker. She flicked off the light and moved to the next doorway down the hall. In the center of the room was, apparently, a bed. It was lost under several layers of strewn clothing. Tucker was about to commence a search through the bedroom drawers when the apartment door rattled.

Jesus. Tyrone. Bud was supposed to call and warn her if AJ reported he was on his way home. Tucker stuck her head out into the hallway and heard a key slide into the lock. He was at his front door and would soon discover her and think she was robbing the place. She glanced down the hallway toward the outside porch. There wasn't enough time to get to the kitchen's rear exit, let alone scramble down the fire escape. She would have to hide. *But where?*

Tucker ducked back into the bedroom, stumbling over piles of clothing on the floor. She felt under the bed for space. Her hand bumped against plastic storage containers. There was no room for her to squeeze in next to them. Panicking, she dove toward the open closet and frantically burrowed into discarded clothing. Out in the hall, the door swung open and closed.

Tucker froze. She held her breath. *Don't come in here,* she begged silently.

The hallway remained dark, as though Tyrone hadn't switched on the light. That struck Tucker as odd. Most people came into a dark house and wanted to light their way. What if it wasn't Tyrone at all? What if Jeff actually had been murdered and the perpetrator was here in the apartment because he had unfinished business?

From the hallway, she heard a loud crash and drew the obvious conclusion. It was Tyrone, but he had come home drunk or stoned and had fallen over the pile of clothing in front of the door. She pushed aside the clothes and heard a muffled moan followed by a string of curses. *Japanese* curses. In disbelief, she crept toward the door.

"I know you're in there," Yoshi called from the dark hallway. "Come out slowly. I am armed."

"Yoshi! Don't shoot, okay? It's Tucker."

"Tucker?" Yoshi groaned again. "What are you doing here?"

Tucker flicked on the hallway light and found Yoshi lying at her feet. She fought off a chuckle and quickly helped her boss up from the booby-trap clothing pile.

"Do you really have a gun?"

"What do you think, Tucker?" Yoshi raised her head, causing Tucker to gaze into shockingly blue irises that stared right through her. Yoshi didn't turn away. She seemed to be pointedly holding Tucker's gaze.

"Oh, *right*," Tucker said when she finally got it. Yoshi was making a point with her eyes. She couldn't have a gun. They wouldn't give her a permit, not when she was legally blind. "How'd you get a key?"

"From Velvet," Yoshi said, and then added, "Earlier today," as though answering some unspoken question. "I think a better question is, how did you gain entry *without* one?"

"The back door was open."

Yoshi raised an eyebrow.

"Bud made me do it," Tucker blurted.

"Well," Yoshi said, "we are both here now, so we may as well take advantage. Let us discover what we can ascertain about Jeff and his partner from elements in their domicile. If I may hazard a supposition, does it seem as though the apartment has not been tidied recently?"

"Yeah, it's a mess. How'd you know?"

"From the heap I stumbled over, for one thing. Jeff would *never* have tolerated that. When I called on him in the past, I always found his residences clean and sparse, with nothing out of place."

"Well, it certainly isn't that now. Looks more like a flophouse."

"Where is Bud?" Yoshi asked.

"Next door at the Thai restaurant."

"Eating dinner at my expense, no doubt."

Tucker did not even allow herself a grin. Yoshi seemed to know when she was chuckling. "The bedroom's right here. I was going to search it first."

"Correct," Yoshi said. "We are not searching for a specific item, so we must evaluate everything Jeff or the persons of interest wanted to keep private. These things are usually hidden in the most obvious places."

Tucker thought about her own most precious photographs and documents. She kept them in a business envelope at the bottom of a drawer full of socks. *Obvious?* She winced. She would find a better spot when she got home later. If she was going to be a PI, it was time she started thinking like one.

CHAPTER EIGHT

It took forever before Tyrone Hill finally stumbled out of Badlands. Parked across the street from the bar, AJ chilled in the leather driver's seat of her Escalade. She'd had to run the heater almost the whole damn time. It was motherfuckin' cold. It hadn't snowed, but San Francisco was only four hours from ski slopes, and that made it straight up the closest she'd *ever* been to snow. She knew she didn't want to get any closer.

It'd dipped down to thirty degrees *maybe* a dozen times when she was growing up in New Orleans. Each time it'd been an emergency and the city had run warnings about keeping your tap water flowing so the pipes wouldn't freeze. She'd like to be home right now. Or in bed kicking it with a hottie instead of freezing her ass off tailing some distraught brother. All so's the lady she'd last hit it with could decide whether or not to offer her a job.

The shit was messed up. AJ's gut told her Tyrone wasn't a murderer. He was just like a million other brothers who'd made some bad choices and let drugs destroy their lives. Same shit happened to her older brother, and now he was doing ten to twenty in Angola.

AJ watched Tyrone weave back and forth with his homies, one on either side of him, trying to keep him upright between them. She slid out her cell and dialed Bud as she'd agreed to do when she seen the bird fly the coop. With Tyrone moving as slow as the federal response to Katrina, she decided to follow on foot. She pulled on a black down jacket she'd bought when she'd figured out how frigid it was gonna get and yanked the hood tight over her head.

Tyrone didn't go to his apartment, though. Instead he stopped across from the Castro Muni between the Hot Cookie bakeshop and

Quicklys bubble tea. AJ ducked into Castro Smoke House and watched from just inside as Tyrone pushed on an intercom buzzer, then bent down to the box like he was conversing with it. A few seconds later he hitched open the metal door and disappeared inside, alone.

Keeping an eye on his homies, still on the sidewalk, AJ bought a pack of smokes, something she hadn't done in months. She stepped out and lit up, the perfect excuse for lurking around while she waited for Tyrone. Passing time, she watched men hanging around the Diesel Jeans store. Those that weren't ducking into the alley for a quick piss were smoking, and she could see glowing cherries rise and fall.

Keeping her head low so the hood shadowed her face, she shuffled closer to Tyrone's boys, who were lighting up on weed. She ducked into a doorway of a closed storefront. It stank. Probably some homeless brother's nighttime crib. With a roof and blocked from wind and rain on two sides, it was a top-of-the-line sidewalk hotel. Lighting up another smoke, AJ gave Tyrone's friends their own cherry light to watch.

She'd gotten through three cigarettes and lost feeling in her fingers before Tyrone stumbled down the steps and slapped one of his friend's palms. The guy stuffed a rolled-up baggie in his front pocket. A similar exchange happened when Tyrone high-fived the other homeboy, who furtively crammed his baggie inside his jacket. AJ didn't know if Tyrone was passing out pot or meth or something else, but she'd seen enough drug buys to recognize one when it went down in front of her. Whoever lived in the building was one of Tyrone's suppliers. That the homies hadn't gone in suggested that the slinger didn't know them. Drug dealers were a paranoid bunch and weren't about to sell to someone they didn't know.

Tyrone's two friends slugged him on the shoulder and walked away. He stood in front of his supplier's door as though trying to decide where to go. AJ hoped he'd go on home to his crib and get to bed alone. But she knew he wouldn't. He was like one of them crazy Cajun crackers living out on the bayou and wrestling gators. Some men are their own worst enemies, but some things aren't supposed to be trifled with.

Tyrone was no psychic and he didn't hear her warnings. He turned and hurried toward The Café on Market Street. His drunken stumbling was replaced by a quick shuffle. AJ would have arrested the homo homie by now if she was on the job; she ain't ever seen pot wake someone up. *He gotta be trippin' on uppers.* She followed him, hanging about ten paces back so as not to be seen. When Tyrone glanced over his shoulder at her a few seconds later, she turned down a side street, letting him get farther ahead. She knew where he was headed after all. There was a line of men outside of The Café.

AJ slowed her naturally long stride and was halfway down the block when she saw Tyrone bypass the line and keep going, scuttling past it with his head down. *Damn.* She sprinted across Market, passing the Escalade reluctantly. No time to get it without maybe losing him down a side street. She left the Escalade behind and shadowed Tyrone for ten minutes. He stopped at Club Eros, a beige stucco two-story industrial building across from Safeway, and entered below the green awning. From the line outside, AJ assumed it was maybe a dance club. She got in back of the line outside. The men in front of her all seemed to know each other. A bearded bouncer was checking IDs, collecting dead presidents from some and looking at a card others offered up.

When she got to the door he asked, "This your first time here?"

She nodded.

"I'll need to see your ID. Are you interested in one of our membership packages? As a member you'll only pay fifteen dollars a night instead of the usual twenty."

"No thanks." Twenty-dollar cover? *Fuck.* Good thing Yoshi was covering expenses. She handed him her driver's license and a Jackson from the wallet leashed to her back pocket and crossed her fingers.

"Angela Joy—?" He began reading her name aloud.

She felt the heat rise in her cheeks. "AJ," she corrected.

"Oh, I'm sorry. You're FTM?"

Until the homo-hop concert she'd never even heard the term. A tall sistah with big blond hair and a low-cut blouse had asked her the same question and AJ hadn't known how to reply. She'd wondered if it was some kind of West Coast lingo, like another way of saying NWA: nigga with attitude. Velvet had stepped in and introduced her, and she wanted to ask about the term then but she didn't get a chance, not with the music starting and Tucker hanging on Velvet all night.

Plus, then AJ and Yoshi went home and had make-up and break-up sex all in the same night. When she remembered the exchange a couple days later, she'd slipped onto one of the computers at East Palo Alto and punched the letters in a search engine. She clicked onto FTM

International and read maybe three lines before yanking the computer's plug from the wall to wipe the page from the screen. If the other cops seen that shit she'd never live it down.

Still, she'd been intrigued about the idea of there being guys who'd been born female. Like, how was that even possible? AJ finally found a local library and got online. An hour later she walked out with a better understanding of female to male transsexuals, but even more questions than she'd had when she'd gone in.

If this club's bouncer thought she was a trans guy that was cool, especially if it gained her entry to this boy's club. He was just a gatekeeper; she needed to get back to trailing her mark.

"That a problem?" she asked, sidestepping the question about her gender identity.

He shook his head. "No, of course not. We have a number of trans members, and we're working to make our space more trans-friendly. You might be interested in our Retool and Grind night."

"What's that?" AJ still pronounced it the N'awlins way, *What dat?*

"It's our special trans night, there's an open mic where we encourage transmen to share stories or whatever. Here…" He pulled a postcard from the bottom of his metal money box and shoved it AJ's way. "This has more information and our Web site's on it, too."

AJ took the card.

"Just follow the signs to the locker rooms," he directed as she stepped through the door.

Locker rooms? What kind of club was this?

❖

Most of the men were straight-up naked. Heat flushed AJ's face. Some guys had white towels wrapped around their waists. They reclined on red leather sofas in a lounge with dark carpeting and erotic drawings on walls the color of butter. A few of the homeboys wore nothing but underwear. She noticed one guy sauntering 'round the room wearing underwear and a white tank undershirt, with a towel draped over his shoulder. AJ was relieved. She might be able to pull *that* look off—at least long enough to find Tyrone in this two-floor sex club.

AJ stripped down to briefs and undershirt. Most of the homegirls back on the block in N'awlins favored bright colorful clothing, but AJ had always preferred the more muted gangsta uniform of low-slung jeans, white T-shirt, dope high-tops, and a zip-up hoodie.

Evaluating her appearance in the mirror, she nodded to herself. She liked the way the bright whites of her underwear contrasted with her rich chocolate coloring. Her breasts were small but still noticeable, so she pulled a towel from a stack of folded ones and hung it 'round her neck, the ends hanging down over her chest. She had strong thighs and wasn't one to shave the fine hairs on her legs, so they'd probably pass. And the packy in her molded briefs provided a realistic bulge.

Her stomach wasn't washboard flat, but flat enough. She had the round ass of a holler back girl, but her hips were slim. Her closely cropped hair coiled tightly against her head. The short hair, sharp lines of her face, and fuzzy upper-lip had gotten her mistaken as a man. Before tonight she'd never tired to pull it off intentionally, and here she was trying to do so in clothes that revealed her girliest features.

AJ took a deep breath to ready herself and stepped out from the locker room into the sex club. It was clearly a white club, so she figured Tyrone's skin tone would make him easy to find. In a tiled shower room, it was just white men doing what they called water sports. Must be a cracker thing. Like bondage. African Americans ain't into that shit. They'd too much history being chained up, degraded, and pissed on to make it seem hot. AJ checked the men in the sauna. Weren't none of them black.

A place like this where everyone stripped down, they'd probably all got to thinking it leveled the field and there was no difference between rich and poor. But that was bullshit. Even naked they weren't naked; AJ could see class. Strip down a homeboy and you see scars and tats. Addicts all skin n' bones. These guys had sculpted muscles and piercings and fancy tattoos—she ain't seen no prison tats crafted from soot or ballpoint ink, not here. No gang markings, neither.

AJ tried not to gawk at couples as she wove through the maze of upstairs playrooms colored with reds and blacks. Scanning the room, she noticed a Latino homie with ropey scars cupping his chest and tattoos wrapped around his biceps. His face was bearded in the style of her EPAPD coworkers, shaved but for circling the mouth. His eyes caught hers and he titled his head as though in a nod of acknowledgment. She didn't recognize him and wondered if she knew him from somewhere else. Not sure how gestures were coded in this place, AJ didn't return the nod in case it meant something, like colored handkerchiefs indicating different sexual proclivities.

It got darker farther into the maze and she had to look harder to determine skin tone. Finally, on one of the low red tables topped with black leather cushions, she noticed the ass of a black man draped over a white guy. It was hard to see his face without being forced to see more than she'd ever wanted of gay guys kicking it.

"Tyrone?" she whispered.

He didn't look up.

Though she was sort of relieved, she still had to know for sure it *wasn't* him. If it was her, it'd take lot more than some whispering to stop her from hitting it with a fly girl. Seemed like hours passed till the brother threw his head back, the veins bulging out. He wasn't Tyrone. *Fuck.* Where was that crazy-assed motherfucker? She was tripping. She had to get outta there quick.

AJ ducked into the shadows between a tangle of wooden bunk beds slathered in red paint and crammed together. She barely glanced at the guys coupling on it as she rushed past. She found Tyrone leaning against a bunk's ladder. His eyes were open but they didn't seem focused. What AJ saw next surprised her. Against good sense, and posted club regs, the white boy hitting Tyrone's ass wasn't wearing no glove. She was amazed at the intensity of her anger.

After a quick stop at the locker room to throw on clothes, she stomped into the office and demanded to see a manager. When she started ranting about one of their members barebacking and breaking their hard-and-fast safe-sex rules, he asked if she was with the health department or something. When she said no, she was an off-duty police officer, he told her to leave.

AJ went back to the Escalade and found a new parking spot at the Safeway across the street. She reclined in the driver's seat, but she still had a sharp eye on the door to the sex club. Even had time to check in with Yoshi. She didn't go into detail about her night, just gave Yoshi the short story and the address of Tyrone's dealer hoping maybe Yoshi would do something with it. Something more than ask the dealer for his whereabouts at the time of Jeff's death.

Her mind kept flashing on the club. It was like walking through a live porno. She wasn't turned on. She favored breasts and pussy, no question about it. And big-assed girls. Not that Yoshi was built that way. Now Velvet, there was a fine filly. AJ had no idea how a skinny little white child like Tucker managed a full-on woman like that. She must have some hidden depths, 'cause she sure as shit didn't exude the kind of strength and personality it seemed like Velvet would need.

AJ thought about the guys at the club. Some of them were butt ugly, but they still sauntered around naked, all comfortable with themselves like they were at home in their bodies. She didn't always feel that way about herself.

Gay men seemed to have this devotion to finding shit that felt good, just for the pleasure of it. She'd seen that kind of thing back on the block, people pursuing feel-good drugs without a care for their kids or food. That was wrong, no doubt about it, but the way these gay guys pursued pleasure kind of made her envious. Still, it seemed as if Tyrone Hill was all about pleasure, and it was killing him. It was like he wasn't even all there anymore. Least it seemed that way to AJ, even though she'd just met him. He had this aura like he was desperate for something to sooth his pain but all the things he tried didn't work no more. He was like a man who'd lost his taste for cake but kept trying to get back to the enjoyment he used to have. So he just kept on eating one after another till he was choking to death on frosting.

Still, you had to value the pleasures of life. They made the rest worth suffering through. Least that's what AJ had learnt growing up in N'awlins. The place was devoted to decadence: Mardi Gras parties, riverboat gambling, sensuous music, rich foods, heavy drinking, and lots of sex. Citizens knew how to enjoy themselves even through hurricanes, floods, poverty. And her people had been through even worse shit, but they still found joy in things. How else could they have survived?

❖

"Hold on, I see something."

They were checking under Tyrone's mattress for journals, private letters, compromising photos, or contraband. Everyone had secrets. After probing countless residential properties, Yoshi had concluded that those secrets would often be harbored betwixt mattress and box springs. More than anything, this suggested that Americans neither turned nor replaced their mattresses with any regularity.

Bedrooms were *the* site of personal and private items. After all, rooms that contained beds implied *sex*, and were therefore considered—in American culture—spaces removed from the public sphere. Yoshi could not conceive why anyone would chose to conceal their skeletons beneath where they slept, dreamt, and made love.

Convinced that what Jeff or Tyrone wanted most to hide from the world would undoubtedly be sequestered not just in the bedroom, but somewhere in or below the bed itself, she requested Tucker's assistance in peeking below the Conant-Hill mattress. But now, as she felt the weight of the mattress shift to her side, she worried that she had made a mistake. Obviously Tucker was retrieving whatever was hidden.

Yoshi called out a warning. "Tucker! Do not touch anything."

"Sorry. I'm touching it right now."

Of course you are. Yoshi sighed. "What is it?"

Hand grenades were too bulky to effectively hide in the space. She could picture Tucker standing there with a grenade in one hand and the pin in another. "Oops," Tucker would manage to intone, just before hot shrapnel tore through flesh and bone.

"I don't know."

Tucker's admission did not ease Yoshi's trepidation. "What does it look like?"

"Drugs," Tucker said, before hedging, "maybe." She described a baggie of white crystal-like substance that looked almost like broken shards of glass and a "weird" pipe with a big glass bowl.

"Put it down immediately!" Yoshi commanded. She had no desire to bear witness to an industrial injury.

"Why?" Tucker asked, fear in her voice.

Yoshi heard the methamphetamine crystals and freebase pipe bounce a little on the box springs as Tucker dropped them. She let the mattress fall, instructing Tucker, "You must cleanse your hand straight away. It is *essential* that you do so, right this minute."

"What was it?"

"Crystal meth. It can permeate layers of skin and gain access to your bloodstream. Wash your hands with soap and water. *Now.*"

"Okay, okay. I'm going."

A moment later Yoshi heard the sound of running water as Tucker rinsed her hands.

"What should we do?" Tucker asked when she returned. "Do we need to call the police or something?"

"It was just one baggie?"

"Yes."

"That is not enough to be distributing," Yoshi said. "It must be for personal use. *If* either of us had arrived with an evidence collection kit in hand, we could conceivably contain it and release it to the authorities for proper disposal. However—"

"Can't we just flush it?"

"No. The hazardous chemicals can attach to water molecules. Those are not removed fully from the sewage treatment process. The remainder eventually washes downstream to the ocean and contaminates fish."

With the mattress back in place, they returned the piles of clothing to the bed. Not that Tyrone would notice. Yoshi suggested that to more efficiently utilize their time, they split up and take different rooms. She would examine the remainder of the bedroom and then move to the bathroom while Tucker started with Jeff's office, searching the file drawers for financial and legal papers. Yoshi directed her to take digital photos of any papers of potential interest.

"I didn't bring a digital camera," Tucker admitted sheepishly. "Just this throwaway one."

"That's perfectly all right, I have mine in my purse. Here." Yoshi held out the small rectangular camera.

"You carry a camera?" Tucker asked.

Yoshi sighed. She got so tired of explaining that, just because she could not see, she was *not* incompetent. "It is a fully automated camera. It automatically focuses and adjusts the light. It allows me to take snapshots that I can relay to Bud or another investigator. Then the photographs can be carefully examined for clues I might have overlooked."

"Oh, cool. You are so smart, Yoshi. I would never have thought of that."

Thank Goodness. It would be time to hang up her skates if a PI-in-training receptionist outsmarted her.

Yoshi sorted through the clothes on the bedroom floor, sniffing the shirts. Some smelled like they had been drenched in sweat, maybe from nights of frenetic meth-fueled dance marathons. Sweat elicited by fear and anxiety smelled different from exercise sweat. Other garments reeked of cigarette smoke and hard alcohol, and she could distinguish nearly a dozen discrete fragrances, several of which coded "Jeff."

On the top of a dresser, under another layer of garment fabrics, was an assortment of glass cologne bottles. Spraying a sample from each into the air for a whiff, Yoshi slowly worked her way through the variously shaped containers. In doing so she was able to match up many of the clothing scents to cologne bottles. In fact, she found that the colognes accounted for half the shirt aromas.

Shirts with scents she could not identify, she set aside. After she'd finished in the bedroom, she walked down the hall, trailing her fingertips along the wall until she felt the bathroom door framing. Once in the small water closet, she bent down and felt around the bathtub until she located plastic bottles. She unscrewed each lid in turn and inhaled the content's bouquet before tightening the cap and turning to the next container. Paul Mitchell's distinct brand of shampoo and conditioner. A liquid soap using the purification power of citrus. A foaming facial cleanser with an olive oil base. Next Yoshi turned to the sink. She quickly ascertained that there was no cabinet below the freestanding porcelain bowl. A tube of toothpaste, shaving razor, hair pick, and a bar of hand soap shared the sink's broad lip.

Between the inset bathtub and the freestanding sink, she found a collection of bottles crowding the toilet's tank. Continuing to open and smell the products, she distinguished a few more scents from the bedroom's clothing—including something called Bold for Men's Dry Shave Gel, which elicited a fond smile when she discovered that its raised lettering could be read by her fingers.

With only a few scents remaining to identify, Yoshi tugged open the above-sink glass-fronted, aluminum-plated medicine cabinet. She whiffed shaving cream, aftershave, mouthwash, lube, hand lotion, face cream, and two cologne samples. Only one of the fragrances from the clothing eluded identification by the time she'd exhausted all options. Perhaps the one remaining clothing scent had belonged to someone other than Jeff and Tyrone. A visitor could have left the shirt. Or it could be trace. Someone wearing the scent could have come in contact with Jeff or Tyrone and transferred scent molecules to their clothing.

Yoshi called Tucker in and had her read aloud from labels on two rows of prescription medication vials. Although Tucker stumbled over pronunciations, Yoshi easily recognized several allergy and pain medications. Others described brand and drug names that were unfamiliar. Nearly all of these later medications were in Tyrone's name.

Yoshi asked Tucker to photograph the vials, taking care to include the medication names. Later they could do research to determine what ailments Tyrone might be receiving treatment for.

"Did you find anything interesting in the other rooms?" Yoshi asked Tucker.

"I don't know. I guess it's nothing,"

"What is nothing?"

"Well, Velvet says gay guys like a lot of porn. They've got a whole rack of it."

"Not surprising."

"She never said anything about Tyrone starring in his own."

"Excuse me?"

"There're two pornos in there with Tyrone's picture on the box. It's not his name or anything, but I swear it's him."

"Interesting. Did you photograph the boxes?"

"No, I can, though. There's also a stack of screeners for movies I've never heard of," Tucker said, using terminology she'd undoubtedly picked up from Velvet.

Velvet. So far, she had not answered Yoshi's many calls, not even after Yoshi left a rather extensive message explaining that she was no longer angry at being deserted after the memorial. After all, Yoshi had successfully rescued herself and safely returned to civilization on her own. In her self-congratulatory euphoria, she had easily abandoned her previous umbrage.

As if summoned psychically, Tucker's phone began to buzz on vibrate. Yoshi held her breath in expectation. She was disappointed when Tucker—rather than making the cooing noise that indicated she was speaking with Velvet—announced, "It's Bud."

Yoshi felt her letdown physically. It was as though a bird had leapt from her heart, springing into flight only to run smack into a glass window and plummet to the ground in a daze.

"He probably couldn't figure out how to text me," Tucker murmured, before answering, "Hey, what's up?" After a brief exchange, she ended the call and informed Yoshi, "Tyrone's on the move again. Sounds like he's going to another club."

"All right, then. Let's have you concentrate on taking the photographs we discussed. I would also like us to gather those screener films you mentioned seeing. I believe they may be the property of

Conant's employer, Frameline. We may as well return them when we drop in on their office tomorrow."

Yoshi was careful not to appear as though she was directing Tucker to *steal*. What with the country girl's moral code, Tucker would be reluctant to violate the letter of the law, even if requested to by Yoshi, whom she normally would do quite anything to please.

While Tucker was doing as directed, Yoshi stepped into the kitchen, not knowing what she was hoping to find. Near the stove, she discerned the faint scent of heavy chemicals hovering below the rank smell of spoiling food and rotting garbage. She wondered if Tyrone brewed his own methamphetamine at home. Thankfully, the scent was subtle and did not seem recent. Perish the thought that she and Tucker might have inadvertently stumbled into a hazardous environment.

This living space was so very different from how Yoshi recalled Jeff's prior apartment. When she had visited him—it was years ago, now—his place had been imbued with a combination of pleasant aromas. He had modern Scandinavian furnishings with clean lines, sprinkled with chic, handcrafted tchotchkes like a Jonathan Adler giraffe-shaped lamp, an Andy Warhol pillow, and an autographed vinyl 45 record of Jimmy Somerville's "Smalltown Boy" on the wall.

"Tucker?" Yoshi called. "We should leave now in case Hill decides to change his plan and come home."

Tucker joined her, and Yoshi could tell she was cramming items into her clothing. As they exited down the indoor stairs leading from Jeff's apartment, Yoshi considered Tyrone Hill's suitability as catalyst for his partner's suicide, and as a murder suspect.

From AJ's reports and from the state of the apartment, the man appeared to be losing a battle to control his drug use. His addiction could, undoubtedly, have taken a toll on his personal relationships. Had things gotten so dreadful that Jeff impulsively decided on suicide as a way out? That scenario did not mesh with what she knew of Jeff. He clearly cared deeply for Tyrone and had stood by his man, resisting the pressure of family and friends who had hoped to break up their relationship.

But then again, why had Jeff failed to obtain treatment for Tyrone? Had Tyrone hidden the extent of his addiction until he cracked, somehow killing Jeff in the process? Was Velvet right? Could Jeff have gotten into a fight with Tyrone over his drug use, infidelity, or porn appearances, and had Tyrone killed him? It was unlikely but possible, and there was one thing Yoshi felt sure of: if Tyrone had killed Jeff, he would have needed help to dispose of the body.

Even in the darkness of night, they would have had to contend with the post-9/11 bridge security that thwarted ninety percent of all would-be jumpers. Not to mention that it would have required more than one meth addict to haul Jeff's body up to the Golden Gate vista, drag him out on the pedestrian walkway, hoist him over the low fence, and shove him swan-diving over the edge.

❖

Tyrone never stopped moving. It was like his whole body was in a constant state of motion. He shifted from foot to foot, chewed nervously at his fingernails, talked real fast, and his eyes flitted from side to side. Sweat soaked through his tight tee. As soon as he walked out of Club Eros, AJ could tell straight away he was all revved up again. He'd probably taken another hit of meth. He pulled at a white dude's sleeve, and next thing they were heading toward the Castro with Tyrone rushing ahead and back like a little kid.

AJ followed them back to Badlands on Eighteenth Street. She avoided the dance floor, creeping in the shadows and using the cylinder support pillars as cover. Purple floodlights sent lavender beams bouncing off the mirrored disco ball rotating above. A large screen on the far wall played the music video image that repeated on smaller TVs dotting the bar. The club was dark, aside from the roving floods lighting up different groups. Gay guys packed the floor in jeans and tees. There were more brothers and homies here than there'd been at the sex club and the place was even more crowded than it had been earlier in the evening. From what she'd been learning about Tyrone, AJ would say the brother wasn't up for facing real life no more. Instead he was blotting it out and losing himself in drugs, sex, and dancing. What she ain't be knowing for sure was if the homo homeboy was drowning grief or *guilt*.

She watched him, dancing in close and then away like Muhammad Ali. His feet never stopped moving. Something about him reminded her of her older brother. She'd lost him to this. He wasn't gay, and his drug of choice was crack, not meth. He'd started using as part of a gang, and then he'd gone to slingin' to support his habit. He said he couldn't shake a drug that made him feel like he was in heaven. Until prison, that was. He'd gone cold turkey when they put him in solitary for shivving the inmate who'd been raping him.

AJ wiped her face with the back of her hand. She was hating the heat. At first she'd been thrilled to leave the Escalade after an hour or so of cold surveillance outside, but it didn't take long before the small club turned as hot as all those summers she'd spent in New Orleans with no air-conditioning. Even without grinding on the floor herself, she'd gotten thirsty enough to buy couple of forties. In three hours, she'd only seen Tyrone with one beer and after a few sips, he'd put it down and walked away.

While AJ kept him in sight, she was propositioned by more than one guy. She supposed she should be flattered; gay men had good taste. But she wanted to get out of this place. Tyrone might've been fucked up, high on uppers—but she wasn't and she was beat. Her head started dipping and her eyes drooped. The pounding bass reverberating through the floorboards, the walls, and her own internal organs was the only thing keeping her awake. Her watch said one thirty-seven, and she was expected back on the job in East Palo Alto at seven a.m. She wondered if she would make it.

When she looked up again she'd lost Tyrone in the crowd of a hundred dancing men. With more brown and black faces in the crowd it was harder to find him, but least there was only one room. Eventually she narrowed in on his now familiar face. Looked like he would be here for a while. AJ went outside for a slap in the face by the cold weather. She lit another smoke, telling herself she'd quit tomorrow. If it ever came.

She smoked and lost the feeling in her nose to the bitter cold. She was wide-awake but couldn't bring herself to go back into the club. She walked to her Escalade, moved into an eye view of the club. She jacked up the heater, rubbing her hands together while the engine slowly warmed. She hadn't been there long when she saw Tyrone exit the club, leaning on some dude's shoulder. AJ figured she'd let them get a head start and tail them in the comfort of the car. They were just a half block away when Tyrone kinda slumped to the side, slowly sliding down the white guy and crumpling at his feet.

AJ leaped from the Escalade and darted toward the two men. The white dude pulled Tyrone to his feet and they started walking again. AJ slowed from a sprint, relieved. Then she figured out that Tyrone wasn't doing any walking of his own. The white guy was half carrying, half dragging Tyrone down the street. He looked nervous. He lost his hold and Tyrone flopped to the ground again.

"Stop, police!" AJ hollered. It was a gut reaction. She wasn't really police, not right now, off-duty and working for Blind Eye. She wasn't sure if Tyrone really needed police right now. He needed an ambulance.

At her announcement, the white dude looked up at her gunning for them, a dark figure, face masked by a hoodie. He took off running fast as he could. She sprinted across the empty street at a kitty-corner. When she reached Tyrone he wasn't laying still. His body jerked madly like he was being electrocuted, like a wave started in his feet and rolled up his body till it got to his head, banging his melon against the cement sidewalk. He was seizing.

Like she'd smacked a ball outta the park, AJ slid home, dropping to her knees next to his jerking body. She yanked the chained wallet from her back pocket and jammed it between his teeth to keep him from biting off his tongue. She cradled his head in her lap, preventing it from striking the ground again. The back of his head was bleeding from abrasions.

"Call nine-one-one!" AJ shouted at the top of her lungs into the still night air. Ain't no one respond.

She struggled to get the cell from her front pocket without smacking Tyrone's head. Adrenaline surged through her as she fumbled with the dials. Her heart was racing, her hands shaking. She dialed nine-one-one. Waiting for her call to get routed to a local operator, she checked Tyrone's vitals. His skin was hot to the touch, but dry. The pulse was weak and his heartbeat was shallow—surprising for all the meth he'd had and the dancing he'd done. *That ain't a good sign.* Either he had overdosed or he was severely dehydrated. Either could kill him.

AJ provided the San Francisco dispatcher with location and Tyrone's condition. The dispatch said an ambulance was on its way, but they kept asking AJ one question after another. What'd Tyrone eaten? When did he last use the bathroom?

Suddenly, AJ realized Tyrone's body had stopped twitching. She lost her hold on the phone and it clattered against the pavement. He wasn't breathing. She swore at him and fought the urge to cry. Instead she started CPR. Just before she put her mouth over his, she remembered he was HIV positive. She didn't have a CPR mask on her, not even a plastic bag to improvise. He'd die for sure if she didn't breathe for him.

Ya gotta do what ya gotta do. She lowered her mouth to his and began the CPR count off in her head: one and two and three and…

CHAPTER NINE

Jeff clawed at her, his eyes wide and accusatory. A gash across his forehead bled profusely, covering the entire left side of his face in blood. A sutured chest wound fashioned a V-shaped zipper. His hands were wraithlike and nearly opaque, his fingernails were removed. The edges of every appendage seemed rounded as though he'd been in a rock tumbler. He leapt toward her, screaming. Suddenly he was tearing at a bag over his head.

All at once, Velvet couldn't breathe. She was screaming and crying but no sound came out. Choking, she dug her nails into the waxlike hands now around her throat. As she tore at his fingers, trying to peel them off her, the skin flayed, pulling away in her grasping claws.

She gasped for air, and her scream came out as only a whimper. Tears ran down her face, drowning her in guilt and shame. Just as she felt she was about to lose consciousness, she finally found her voice and began to scream loudly. A hand on her arm, not his but another, shook her. Faint voices murmured in the background. Why weren't they stopping this? Did they think she deserved it?

One voice grew louder and louder as though drawing closer. She finally heard what it was saying. "Velvet." The hand shook her.

She awoke with a start. Tucker was standing next to the bed, shaking her and calling her name. "Velvet, you're having a nightmare."

Just a dream? What a relief. "So Jeff's okay?"

"No baby, I'm sorry. Jeff's…gone." Tucker brushed the hair from Velvet's face and squeezed her into a tight hug.

Velvet rested her head on Tucker's shoulder and tried to remember falling asleep. She couldn't. The last thing she remembered was swilling her fourth—or was it her fifth?—triple X dirty martini: vodka dirtied with extra, extra, extra olive juice There had been no bartender to cut her off or slow her down by failing to get the mixture of ingredients just right. She had avoided that possibility by mixing her cocktails from her own well stocked bar. *When you want something done right…*

Tucker released her from the hug. "How are you feeling today, honey? You were really out of it last night."

Velvet rubbed her head, which seemed to have a train running through it. Her mouth was full of nasty-tasting cotton balls. "Did I invite you over?" She didn't remember doing so, but she'd clearly gotten…tipsy.

"No," Tucker said. "I came over on my own. You left your phone off the hook, silly. Nearly gave us a heart attack."

Us? Velvet had a sudden vision of Yoshi standing alone in the dark on a sidewalk. *Damn.* "Yoshi?"

Tucker smiled. "She said you guys had a fight."

"Is she—?"

"You know Yoshi. She's fine. She was worried about you. I'm glad you're awake now. She called a little while ago and wanted to know if you'd want to go with her when she talks with Theresa and Isabelle."

Velvet shook her head. She didn't think she could face her best friend, let alone the two women who'd stolen her only child.

Before she and Rosemary Finney had had their infamous falling-out—which eventually made her the primary suspect in Rosemary's murder—Velvet had thought the lesbian magazine they'd created together, *Womyn*, would be her legacy. When Rosemary's legal team stripped her of all the rights to the magazine, Velvet had felt as though she'd lost her only child. Now she was feeling something similar. She had never decided *not* to have children. She'd just assumed she had time. She'd been shagging her way through San Francisco's lesbians with the assumption that, in doing so, she'd stumble upon Ms. Right. They'd fall in love, get married, and in five years, when they were settled down and economically stable, she would get pregnant.

Now here she was in her mid-thirties and, according to the latest statistics in women's magazines, closing quickly on the end of her fertile years. While she wasn't paying attention, she'd allowed a sexual relationship with Tucker to morph into something more. Now she wondered if the twenty-two year old was coparenting material. She didn't think so.

Her baby daddy had gone and gotten himself killed, or worse.

If Yoshi was right, he'd *chosen* to kill himself, and to top it all off, the bastard had spilled his seed for some lesbian hussy who'd already found her co-mom. It wasn't fair.

Yoshi should have known Velvet would never want to talk with those two bitches, Theresa and Isabelle. She'd just invited her along to torture her, to pay her back for ditching her last night.

Well screw her.

"I'm going to hook up with Bud," Tucker was saying. "We're examining the evidence from a search."

So now Tucker was going to abandon her, too? Velvet liked her tricks and her one-night stands, but if she ever committed to somebody, she wanted to know that the commitment was mutual. Did she need any more proof that Tucker wasn't the caregiving type? *Screw her. Screw all of them.*

❖

Isabelle Cocitaux and Theresa Thompson resided in San Francisco's Noe Valley, a lesbian enclave in which the population was rising dramatically as couples rushed to acquire the *de rigueur* accessory of the moment, a baby.

Perhaps she was too cynical. Yoshi sometimes felt that she remained one of the few lesbians—or gay men for that matter—who was not succumbing to the compulsorily heteronormative and neo-conformative movement that had swept the LGBT nation. Suddenly gays and lesbians seemed to have forgotten about fighting for civil rights or changing the system. Instead, like the Boomer generation that had morphed from Vietnam protestors and sixties revolutionaries to crooked corporate CEOs and business-as-usual politicians, they were glorifying heterosexual marriage and raising children. Former Queer Nation advocates were settling blissfully into consumerism and family life.

She did not buy the argument that these LGBT parents were continuing their activism, changing the world by changing the diapers of the next generation. Not when the daughters of her generation's wonder women were forgoing careers to stay at home and raise babies. These children weren't the next LGBT generation; they would grow up heterosexual. If the queer community really wanted to impact the next generation, they should help raise their own youth instead of leaving that task to hetero parents who had no idea how to provide the skills or knowledge their children would need to survive as healthy adults in a homophobic world.

If everyone insisted on raising children, could they not have the decency to at least adopt? There were countless needy children in the system. Even Velvet, who had been raised by adoptive parents, wanted to bear biological children. Perhaps her adoption was actually *why* she wanted to share a bloodline and genetic heritage with her own children. When you've never seen your features or behaviors reflected in those of a relative, something was missing.

The shared sense of being severed from their own had been part of what had drawn Yoshi to Velvet. They were both cut off from their biological families and their ethnic and cultural heritages. At least Yoshi had always known she was Japanese. Velvet did not share that kind of certainty. Although she was fairly certain she had Native American and Latino heritage, she did not know for sure. That must be difficult.

Yoshi resolved to forgive Velvet for abandoning her the night before and to absolve her of anything else she would throw her way while she struggled with the ramifications of Jeff's death. She was, after all, the only family Yoshi had left.

The cabbie pulled over to the curb, indicating they were directly in front of Cocitaux and Thompson's address. He grudgingly accepted her credit card. Yoshi would rather sign her name on the bottom right than trust him with her cash. Unlike the currency of other countries, United States bills were not distinguishable to the touch. Due to a recent Supreme Court decision, the treasury would soon be required to change all that and make currency blind-friendly. Although they could do so by printing the various denominations on different-sized paper, or raising Braille letters, Yoshi had heard they would prefer to exchange dollar bills with coins—which would save the federal reserve millions. While coins were rugged, paper bills could not circulate for more than four or five years and therefore were more expensive to maintain.

Until the reserve instigated a solution, visually impaired individuals often relied on a core faith in humanity that Yoshi simply did not have. She was not comfortable allowing a stranger to rifle around in her wallet and confiscate whatever funds they elected. She had her bills carefully arranged together by denomination, with paper clips located at different intervals to indicate their value, a task she currently entrusted to Tucker. Bank tellers could shortchange you, too.

Credit cards offered more security and Yoshi provided a gratuity large enough to compensate for the inconvenience. She stepped out of the cab and prodded about with the telescoping cane until she located the steps. Nearly every home in San Francisco had stairs leading to the doorway. Yoshi wondered if this was an architectural side effect of San Francisco being built upon sand dunes and small hills. The doorbell was situated chest high on the door frame as though designed with only male occupants in mind. Yoshi pressed the small button and the door opened.

"Can I help you?"

"Isabelle Cocitaux?"

"No, I'm Theresa, her partner."

Yoshi hadn't expected Theresa to be home. It was a workday, after all. Yoshi's natural instinct was to schedule meetings, but this was an impromptu visit. Her father had taught her early that subjects were more forthright when they were caught off guard. Sometimes setting up meetings seemed to provide people with time to practice their lies. Or skip town.

"Theresa, I'm Yoshi Yakamota with Blind Eye Detective Agency. I wonder if I can have a moment of your time?"

"You're a detective?" Theresa did not invite her in.

"Yes, a private investigator. Charlene Conant hired me to look into her son's death."

"But…" the woman stammered, "you're blind."

For some reason people always felt it necessary to point this out, as though Yoshi would otherwise be unaware of her disability. *How could you be a private investigator? You are aware that you are blind, aren't you?* Perhaps she should hang a sign around her neck that proclaimed *Yes, I know I am blind.*

Ignoring the observation, she said, "I did not have a chance to speak with you and Isabelle at the memorial last night. Do you have a few moments to meet with me now or shall I come back?" Although they were almost as reluctant to speak with private investigators as police officers, most people did not want PIs following them around. Everyone had something they did not want caught on tape.

Once it was clear that she would not simply go away and not come back, Yoshi suspected Theresa would feel internal pressure to get the meeting over with. She had the polite tone New Englanders mastered, and would be gracious despite her misgivings and annoyance at the intrusion.

"We just got back from the doctor." Theresa raised her voice, as though now that Yoshi had acknowledged her blindness she had also gone deaf. She would have to add another line to her sandwich board sign: *I am blind, not deaf.* "I'm getting ready to leave for work, but I guess we have a few minutes."

She stepped back from the door.

"Doctor? Nothing too serious, I hope?"

"Just a checkup. Izzie?" Theresa called to her partner. "We've got company."

A faint smell of cinnamon and cardamom embraced Yoshi as she entered the house. Using her cane, she could ascertain that the pathway was clear of obstruction. She imagined it would not be so in several years, as children's toys cluttered the floor.

"Nice to meet you." Isabelle sounded like Oprah Winfrey with a faint Caribbean inflection. *First generation, perhaps.*

A groan escaped from Isabelle's direction, the sound of discomfort common to pregnant women negotiating the newly gained girth. Yoshi heard the sound of a lever being pulled and deduced that Isabelle had sat in a recliner and was extending the leg support.

"I apologize." Isabelle chuckled. "The doctor says I have to keep my feet up, to reduce the swelling. My ankles, actually. It's only my second trimester but they're the size of coconuts already."

Yoshi smiled but got directly to the point. "I understand the child was conceived with Jeff Conant's sperm, is that correct?"

"Yes," Isabelle answered without a hint of defense.

"Did you go through a local sperm bank?" Yoshi had done a little research when she first got into the office that morning and learned that most Bay Area sperm banks offered a service to women using outside donors. They could bring in the sample to be processed, tested, and inseminated on the premises or at their own residence.

"No, it was just between us. We've known Jeff for a year now. We met him at a meeting for queers who want kids, held at the community center. Afterward we hung out a few times, and when we were ready he just seemed like the perfect choice."

"What was the agreement?"

Theresa rushed to answer. "It was *just* a donation. He wasn't going to be involved. He was willing to be known and that was all."

"To be known?"

"We didn't want to go with an anonymous donor," Isabelle explained. "We want our child to know who his or her birth father is. Jeff was interested in passing on his genetic seed, so to speak, and was willing to meet when our child turns eighteen." Her voice trembled as though stumbling over the last sentence.

"Which is good," Theresa added. "Because we're moving and he wouldn't have been in our child's life anyway."

"You are moving far away?"

"Northampton, Massachusetts."

Yoshi nodded. Even she was familiar with the town *National Enquirer* dubbed "lesbianville."

"Do you have a copy of your legal agreement with Jeff? I would like to take a copy for my records if that's possible."

Yoshi heard shuffling feet. Neither woman responded quickly. Could Jeff have been so foolish as to not have legal paperwork drawn up clarifying his responsibilities regarding any offspring? Without an agreement, Isabelle could legally demand child support. But then again, Jeff could presumably challenge the couple for custody of their child.

"We just had a verbal agreement." Isabelle said. "We all trusted each other. Theresa realized how stupid that was once I got pregnant, so we've been working with a lawyer to draw something up."

"Can I ask who you hired?"

The couple was quiet again, as though carrying on a nonverbal conversation that she was not a part of. She could not compel them to reveal the name of their attorney, and nothing would prevent their attorney from claiming client-attorney confidentiality and refusing to reveal the details of the agreement. But Yoshi was interested in discovering exactly what it was about their arrangement with Jeff that had the couple so nervous. She would wager that things were not exactly as they claimed. Perhaps Jeff had wanted to play daddy and was not pleased with their pending cross-country move.

"Sorry, I don't think that's your business," Theresa said, standing abruptly. "I need to get to work. Can I show you out?"

"Of course. I just have one more question. Where were the two of you on the night Jeff died?"

"What are you implying?" Theresa growled. "Isabelle is pregnant, for God's sake. You can't think we would…"

"She's just doing her job," Isabelle soothed. "We were home that night, together. We've become homebodies since we got pregnant."

"Can anyone else verify that you were both here all night?" Yoshi asked, standing and collected her things.

"It's just the two of us," Theresa said.

That would be a no, then, Yoshi thought. She tried to imagine a pregnant woman pushing Jeff off the Golden Gate Bridge. It did seem a stretch. Still, mothers were known to have unusual strength, especially if they thought they were defending their young. Perhaps Jeff had had concerns or even a change of heart regarding the verbal agreement. If he had, he may well have hired a lawyer. There was one person who could tell her if Jeff had hired an attorney, and what his agreement with Isabelle and Theresa really entailed. That person also remained the most promising POI in a murder scenario—Jeff's partner, Tyrone Hill.

As Yoshi left Noe Valley, she wondered how Tyrone was this morning. When she'd spoken with AJ, the doctors were still stabilizing him. Yoshi hoped they'd been successful. She would be annoyed if he'd suffered some memory loss; she needed answers to questions.

❖

Bud laid his palm against the Impala's horn. That kid better not keep him waiting. Just because he took her out for a drink the night before didn't mean he'd gone soft or suddenly turned into her good buddy.

But boy, she sure showed him last night. He'd thought he was playing a smart trick on her, telling her to break into that apartment without any idea what she was doing. He figured his ploy would give him thirty minutes' peace and a chance to eat dinner on the clock. Instead, turned out the pup was more skilled than he'd given her credit for. He wasn't about to tell her, but he was fairly impressed. Who'd have known the country bumpkin was a fucking gymnast?

After that, he'd figured he owed the kid a beer. He would've treated Yoshi to a cold one, too, if she'd been interested. Not that he could see the Japanese princess swilling beer with him in some dive bar. Not her cup of tea. Instead she'd insisted that she had the perfect job for him;

he could watch a bunch of DVDs they'd found at Conant's place. Yoshi thought they might reveal something critical that would break open the case. Like there was a case. No one was pretending the vic *didn't* go over the bridge. And it seemed obvious that if the Conant guy took a header off the Golden Gate, then he meant to do it.

Watching those movies was probably some kind of ruse to get him to voluntarily expose himself to four hours of queer propaganda. Joke was on him. He was happy to have something he could do while sitting on his ass. 'Course, she hadn't warned him it was all gay shit. Probably knew he wouldn't have done the job if she had. He'd parked himself in front of the TV with a six-pack and a remote control. That was the only way he'd gotten through them—watching them on 6x. Bunch of disturbing queer flicks.

"Morning." Tucker slid in on the bench seat.

He watched her carefully out of the side of his eye, all but daring her to mention the black canvas bag that hung over the back of the seat between them. It had a large section for files, and big pockets on the sides where he stored his cameras and snacks. There was the slightest upturn of her lips, the same twitch he'd seen the last time she'd ridden with him. He knew what the brat was thinking. But they had an unspoken agreement. So long as she kept her trap shut about the bag, he didn't have to throw it out the window and drive back and forth over it for good measure.

He'd been a surprised when Tucker gave it to him for his birthday a couple of months ago. She'd only been working at Blind Eye a few weeks and he hadn't been nice to her once. He'd decided the kid had serious daddy issues. He wasn't about to accept that role, especially not for some needy little daddy's girl. He had his own problems. So he'd tossed the damn thing in his trunk and planned to forget about it. But the bag started haunting him. Like he kept thinking how useful it'd be. He'd fought the urge to cave; he didn't want to give the little sneak the satisfaction of thinking she knew him, even a little.

Then Yoshi had insisted he had to start letting the kid tag along with him and he'd had to make space for her on the front seat. That was the reason, the *only* reason, he'd started using the gift. He'd *stop* doing so in an instant if she mentioned it. He couldn't let that kind of thing rest.

"Your old lady get pissed about you coming home late?" He used the euphemism even though he knew Velvet would kick his ass if she heard him. She was one hot mama, with curves in all the right places and a spicy temper to match. Probably a hellcat in bed. He wouldn't mind knocking boots with her.

That didn't mean he envied Tucker. Velvet had that girl whipped. He didn't get it. He'd thought these so-called "butch-femme" couples made more sense, because you could see which one was the chick and which the guy. Leave it to girls to go and fuck it up. They were so far from normal that even when they tried to mimic *normal* couples they got it all wrong. Velvet might look all feminine and everything with those curves and the provocative clothes she wore, but she was one bossy bitch. It was clear who wore the pants in her and Tucker's relationship.

He snuck a furtive glance at Tucker. She was a little too dykey for his taste but not a bad-looking chick. Velvet was a babe, but surely Tucker could find a lesbo who wouldn't insist on setting all the rules. Unless she liked it that way. He narrowed his eyes and tried to read her mind.

"Nope." Tucker answered the question he'd already forgotten. "She was, like, totally out of it when I got in. Apparently she went on a bender." Tucker shook her head. "She's pissed this morning, though, going on about how she never invited me over in the first place. That's the thanks I get for checking on her and putting her to bed."

"That's broads for you."

"Yeah, I guess. So, did you find anything useful on those DVDs?"

"You tell me. There was one called *Tour de Pants* that was some kind of weird bicycle porno flick, and a way-too-long film about this transsexual broad in the Ozarks running for state senate as a Republican. They just kept getting wackier. Something about sex slaves—international trafficking and shit. Oh yeah, and there was one disc that wouldn't work at all, kept giving me an error message. Waste of my time, if you ask me."

Chapter Ten

Tyrone Hill's dark eyes tracked across the hospital's tiled ceiling, as though he was trying to figure out where he was.

AJ popped up from the uncomfortable straight-back chair where she'd been trying to chill for hours, watching Tyrone drift through unconsciousness, and waiting, *prayin'* for this moment. "Hey dawg, am I glad to see you wake your ass up."

He blinked at her. She wondered if he even remembered her from last night. He'd been through hell. And the worst was to come. He opened his mouth and licked his dry lips. He'd had an IV of fluids in his arm for six hours, and still he was dehydrated. On breakfast round, a nurse had left Tyrone a box of apple juice and told AJ he could drink it, slow, when he woke up. She reached for the juice box now and stuck the straw in his mouth. He sucked out enough to wet his mouth.

"I remember you," he croaked. "From The Café." He winced as he turned his head to scan the room. "What happened?"

"You were totally fucked up on meth and dehydrated. Just about bit it and that's a fact. Your body shut down and you was passed out on the sidewalk." She didn't tell him if she hadn't given him CPR he would've died for sure.

"Maybe I should have," he mumbled.

"Bullshit. Don't pull that crap. You ain't no use to anyone dead."

"You don't know me."

"I know more'n you think. I ain't some dumbass shortie you just met last night. I'm police."

"Shit." He drew the word out.

"I ain't here to bust your ass."

"So what, then?"

"I'm working with the Blind Eye Detective Agency investigating your boy Jeff's death."

"What for?" He narrowed his eyes.

"We got reason to think it ain't suicide." Least she hoped they would, and soon.

When she got on the phone and told Yoshi about the shit that went down last night, Yoshi'd gone, "I ain't convinced one way or another about murder or suicide."

But Yoshi still wanted to press forward. For her part, AJ hoped Jeff's death *was* a homicide. Guilt was breaking Tyrone and she didn't want to attend *his* funeral.

A funeral was still way better than what her homies had gotten after Katrina. They'd been swept away in floodwaters or left in a rotting pile of corpses at the convention center. Funeral pyres going all day and no funerals; she'd never go on about being sick of funerals again.

"You think I killed him?" Tyrone lashed out at her.

AJ didn't step back far enough for his fist to miss. The blow caught her arm but didn't hurt. Tyrone was still weak.

"I ain't thinking you had a thing to do with it," she said. "But there's some questions I gotta ask."

"Do I have a choice?"

"Nope. I'm gonna stay right here till I get answers."

"Whatever." He acted like a man who'd given up. "Just go ahead, then."

"Ya know anybody who'd wanna hurt your guy?"

"No, everybody loved Jeff."

"Folks say that, but it ain't never the truth."

Tyrone's eyes focused on her face like that got him thinking.

"Who'd benefit if he was gone?"

"Those bitches," he answered right away. "The *girls*, he called them. His baby mommas."

"He was gonna be a baby daddy?"

"Yeah, *we* was."

"Go on about it."

"Jeff always wanted kids. He thought he'd end up coparenting with his friend Velvet, but…"

Tyrone shrugged, as though he didn't know what had changed.

AJ could guess. Velvet probably thought Jeff was too good for Tyrone. She sure as shit wouldn't want a brother with a drug problem around *her* baby.

"It just kept not happening," Tyrone said. "So we went to this meeting to learn more about adoption, surrogates, foster parenting. That's where we met them. We had sperm and no womb and they had a womb and no sperm. We started having coffee. Most of the time was just Jeff and the girls, 'cause that's not my scene. Anyway, I guess they tried sperm banks, but fresh sperm is supposed to be more effective."

AJ nodded. She'd heard that from lesbian friends. The frozen stuff didn't work as well: the little guys were too sluggish or something.

"So they asked Jeff. He was excited about pairing up 'cause he and Isabelle would make a mix-race kid like the two of us would, you know, if we could. They wanted to look after the baby most of the time. We were going to have rotating weekends and take the baby when they needed a break."

"Did y'all work this out on paper, like with a lawyer?"

"No, it was informal. Which I guess was stupid, since sure enough, when Isabelle got pregnant, everything changed."

"Like what?" AJ stopped herself from grinning. She was getting somewhere. Yoshi was going to find this information very interesting.

"Like suddenly they didn't want Jeff to have any parental rights. We thought it was 'cause they found out about my bad habits and didn't want me around *their* kid."

"Y'all ask them about that?"

"No, we weren't having coffee anymore," Tyrone said. "A friend of ours, a lawyer, said we needed to get everything in writing before the baby came. Especially since they started saying they were going to fight Jeff for full custody. That would bring up all my problems, and with Jeff's job, we didn't need the publicity."

"Damn, he must've been totally buggin'. Do you know if he confronted them?"

Tyrone nodded. "He came home one day really angry. He'd just found out they were planning a move out east without even telling him. That was a week before he…died. He had a meeting scheduled to talk with their lawyer that week." Tyrone got quiet. "When can I get out of here?"

"Ya trippin'? Honey, you ain't goin' nowhere."

"I thought you said—"

"Don't be a hater, dawg. You can't just *go*. Got to get over your addictions first. I'm gonna get you in a bitchin' program, but for now, they think you're a flight risk and they keeping you locked down."

❖

Once inside suite 300 at 145 Ninth Street, Tucker immediately knew they were in the right place. Queer movie memorabilia and quirky, spectacle-sporting girls were everywhere. She and Bud stopped in front of the desk with a hanging plastic lanyard with a photo of a cinema reel overlaid with the heading DAVINA SINGLETON, FRAMELINE FILM FESTIVAL STAFF.

"Hi," Tucker said. "We're from Blind Eye Detective Agency. We were told you'd be expecting us. We're looking into Jeff Conant's death."

An expression formed slowly on the woman's face. It gave Tucker the feeling that Davina had expected someone else.

"We'd like to speak with Jennifer Morris," Bud added, as though that would elicit a different response than Tucker could alone.

"Please have a seat." Davina's face went red and, glancing swiftly away from Bud and his wheelchair, she stammered, "I mean, please wait."

Her reaction made Tucker want to laugh, but she hid her snicker by brushing her hand across her face as though wiping crumbs from her upper lip. She sat down on one of the straight-back metal seats with pleather padding. There wasn't really space for Bud to park his chair next to her, so he simply stopped in front, leaving her with an excellent view of the back of his slightly balding head.

"What is Frameline, anyway?" Bud never had much tact.

Davina looked up from her desk. "Well, sir, we're producers of an annual, international LGBT film festival. In fact, Frameline is the largest and best known of these events in the world. We've been an organization since 1977, and our festival has become one of the most prominent and well-attended LGBT arts event in North America. Nearly seventy thousand people attend each year." Davina spoke as though reciting words directly from a promotional brochure.

Tucker wondered if the answer came even close to what Bud was hoping for. Or maybe he didn't care what she said or what Jennifer Morris said or whether they learned anything at all. He didn't seem to believe that a crime had even been committed, and he didn't accept the typical judicial argument that suicide was a crime against the state's interests. Tucker thought Bud could probably understand why someone would end it all, so he too easily accepted the suicide concept. Or maybe not. She had no reason to believe Bud was more suicidal than anyone else. Just because he was disabled didn't mean he'd thought about suicide. Neither did the fact that *she*'d thought about it in the past mean he had, too.

They sat in silence for ten minutes before Jennifer Morris opened her door. The acting executive director of Frameline was a short and stocky butch who immediately reminded Tucker of Drew Carey because of her buzz-cut blond hair and, admittedly smaller, black glasses. Velvet had once insisted that the Carey was a lesbian icon in a man's body. Tucker didn't get the analogy, which was a common occurrence when Velvet theorized about lesbian iconography, but it made her feel better about comparing Morris to Carey now. Velvet found lesbians in odd places, and it was kind of nice reading popular culture that way because then you didn't feel so much like dykes were invisible. Morris's choice of professional attire was not unlike Tucker's, jeans topped by a striped shirt, black suit coat, and skinny black tie.

Tucker stood to greet Morris and tried to catch a glimpse of Bud's reaction. His chair came to her waist. All she could see now was the crown of his head. She was getting really familiar with his bald spot. He would undoubtedly call Morris a mannish dyke after they left the building, but she wasn't able to. "I'd be happy to speak with you now," Morris said in a calm, confident manner that Velvet would have called swagger.

Tucker hurried after the woman, excited about tagging along for her first real interview with a person of interest. She could feel the weight of the recording device in the inside pocket of her suit jacket and practiced asking permission to use it in her head. By the time Bud rolled through the doorway, she had already shaken hands, introduced herself, and was sitting opposite Jennifer Morris's desk with her left leg bent and her foot resting below her right knee.

"What do you do here?" Bud asked without any pleasantries.

Morris explained that as the acting executive director she had taken over the fiscal responsibilities but her primary job, as programming director, was to solicit, review, and select the films to be shown at the festival.

"Do you mind if I record our conversation?" Tucker asked quickly before Bud could lob another question. "It makes things easier for our boss." This was only one reason for using the microrecorder, but she thought the rationale sounded convincing. Anyway, if people thought overt evidence gathering was happening, they might decline.

"Yes, of course." Morris took a seat behind a neat and tidy desk.

"Where were you the night Jeff went missing?" Bud asked.

"I had a meeting with our marketing director, then I was with some friends at Mecca for cocktails and then...I don't know...It was probably around midnight, I guess, when I left and went home."

"Could you spell the names of the people you were with and provide us with their phone numbers for verification purposes?" Tucker asked.

Morris hesitated only briefly before doing so. She looked up most of the information on her cell phone, but it seemed that one required a glimpse at her computer. Or she was looking at something else. Curious.

"What's your security like?" Tucker asked.

"We've always felt pretty safe here. The building has its own twenty-four/seven security. A guard does rounds every hour and the outer door is locked between six p.m. and eight a.m., so you need a key to get in during those hours. Our office has its own separate alarm system—but, to be truthful, we don't arm it very often anymore, since the building's security is so good. We're open nine to five but I often stay late, and Jeff did, too."

"Yeah, actually, we stopped and talked with the building security on the way up," Tucker said. "We kind of hoped they might have surveillance video, but I guess they don't. Your computers, how secure are they? Are they all password protected? Does everyone know each other's passwords? That kind of thing."

"Well we're just a nonprofit arts organization. We're not protecting state secrets here or anything." Morris smiled at her own joke. "We end up using each other's computers far too frequently to tolerate sophisticated encryption programs or secret passwords. Staff members can access each other's files on the server and can open hard drives on each other's computers manually. Jeff maintains...*maintained* a few administrative files that were password protected. Mostly individual documents containing confidential human resources information. We're rather transparent. The people in this organization trust one another."

Bud asked, "Did you notice anything out of the ordinary around the time Mr. Conant first went missing?"

A look crossed Morris's features. She cleared it away by shaking her head, like a human Etch-a-Sketch.

"There was *something*, wasn't there?" Tucker asked more sensitively.

"Possibly. I don't know."

"*Whatever* it is…" Tucker began.

"This is going to sound crazy. There was something going on. I just can't put my finger on what."

"That *is* crazy," Bud muttered under his breath.

Tucker squinted at him in warning. "Go on," she prompted.

"Okay. I don't know if you knew Jeff, but he was incredibly fastidious. He had a specific spot for everything. He kept all his books and films—even the ones that had just been submitted—in alphabetical order."

"So he was anal," Bud concluded.

"Yeah, in a good way. And that first morning, before I even knew he was missing, I stepped into his office and something felt…" She struggled for the appropriate word. "Something felt *off*."

"Off?" Bud asked.

Tucker heard mockery in his tone. She could imagine his thoughts about how that would never hold up in court: the witness felt *off*.

"I had a feeling something wasn't in its proper place, as though things had been messed with and put back neatly, just not as fastidiously as Jeff would have arranged things. I told this to the detectives…" Morris sighed. "Not that they cared."

"How much have you changed his office since?" Tucker asked.

"Not a lot, I haven't been able to bring myself to go through it. I need to do that soon in preparation for his permanent replacement. I sent a box of his personal items to the memorial with Davina. Photos, clothes, knickknacks, that kind of thing. She gave them to Jeff's mother."

"Do you mind if we have a look around before we go?" Bud asked.

"No, not at all."

"And could you hold off from altering it further, until we complete our investigation? It should only be another week or two."

Morris nodded. "Certainly. We can do that. Aside from accessing his computer files and the film screeners, that is."

"So you haven't been through all the films that have been submitted?" Tucker asked.

"Not yet, no. We're accepting submissions for another three months."

"But Jeff had taken some screeners home," Tucker said. "Was that...how..."

"Was that unusual?" Bud finished her sentence while she was still trying to avoid sounding accusatory.

"No, Jeff liked to keep abreast of what had come in, and he'd let me know what he thought, even though the decision was always mine on whether to include a film or not."

"Do people get mad when you reject their films?" Tucker asked.

"We try to keep the process a friendly one. Filmmakers usually understand that a film just isn't right for us or doesn't fit in this year."

"Some must be disappointed," Bud said.

Morris conceded that likelihood with a wry nod. "Fortunately, I don't have to deal with any of that for another three months."

"I was thinking." Tucker hesitated, wondering if her idea made any sense. "It might be good if you'd watch this year's screeners just to see if there's anything strange in them, anything that might have to do with Jeff's death..." Bud was looking at her, and it made her nervous. "It's not important. I guess we're really just pursuing every line of inquiry."

She ignored the sharp look from Bud at her use of detective-speak.

"I have a particular system I like to use," Morris said. "But I'll give it some thought."

"Was there anything in Jeff's behavior to indicate he might be depressed or thinking about taking his own life?" Bud asked.

"No." Morris shook her head adamantly. "In fact, it's just so unlikely Jeff would do something like this. You know, we started a home DVD line earlier this year and our second release was Jenni Olson's *The Joy of Life*, which is partly about the death of a friend of hers, Mark Finch. Ironically, he held Jeff's position here at Frameline ten years ago."

"Our boss mentioned something about that." Tucker tried to recall Yoshi's comments about the Bridge Authority meeting she'd attended with Velvet. The exercise had sounded like a waste of time. What did those bureaucrats care about saving lives when there was money at stake? "Mark Finch jumped off the Golden Gate Bridge," Morris said.

Tucker was incredulous. "Are you saying this guy was in Jeff's job and he jumped off the bridge and now ten years later the *exact* same thing happens? Can that be a coincidence? Really, I mean, what are the odds?"

"I know," Morris acknowledged. "But it wasn't *exactly* the same, I mean I believe Mark had several prior suicide attempts. But my point here is that Jenni's film was just heart wrenching. It was an incredibly powerful film and Jeff was one of its greatest proponents. He really pushed for us to pick it up for distribution. I just don't see how he could do something like that after he'd seen just how devastating suicide is on family and friends."

When people kill themselves, Tucker thought, *they don't do it to cause other people pain. They do it to end their own.* She wondered if Jeff might have confided in a woman who must know a lot about suicide.

"Did Jenni and Jeff know each other personally?"

"They were good friends," Morris said. "Jenni's just as mystified by this as we all are."

So, maybe he hadn't said anything. Secrecy made sense. If someone really intended to take their own life, they probably avoided dropping hints to friends who would stop them. She kept her thoughts to herself as Bud closed their conversation, offered thanks, and asked if they could see Jeff's office now.

Morris led them to a small, refined office with a black lacquer desk and white oversized square chairs with huge pillows emblazoned with black-and-white prints. Tucker recognized the design as Pucci-style from a magazine she'd flipped through at Velvet's. On one wall was a series of photos of Jeff with celebrities, filmmakers, and what Tucker assumed were friends and staff. On the other, a small window overlooked the concrete cityscape. Giant stained-wood bookcases, the kind with glass on three sides, were filled with DVDs, CDs, books, and binders. Each shelf was labeled with a small leather-framed tag that read "Submitted," "Viewed," "Accepted," Rejected."

The whole office shone, in stark contrast to the messiness of the Conant/Hill apartment. Yoshi was right. Jeff's home no longer bore his fastidious stamp. She wondered if that had happened before or after his death. It seemed like there were still a lot of questions that Tyrone Hill would have to answer.

Bud pulled the digital camera from the side pocket of his wheelchair and began snapping photos. Once he'd gotten the room from every achievable direction, he focused on smaller details. Jeff's desk was as large as Yoshi's and almost as sparse, even though more of his was dedicated to objects like metal stacking trays marked "In," "Out," "File," and "Read." There was a black waist-high countertop and, parked below it, a mesh metal rolling cart with an all-in-one printer. Next to this stood a steely gray two-drawer filing cabinet.

Tucker did not know what Bud was searching for, and she was too embarrassed by Morris's presence to ask. She hadn't learned enough from her PI course to know what to look for besides the obvious: blood, fingerprints, trace. She'd gotten that much from episodes of *CSI*. Not wanting to be outed as just a receptionist with PI dreams, Tucker affected her best serious-detective air and carefully examined areas she thought might be important.

She looked at the office door and saw no evidence that it had been jimmied or tampered with.

"Did Jeff lock his door at nights?" she asked Morris.

"No, he wasn't the paranoid type."

Drawing on her understanding of TV detective work, Tucker viewed the uncluttered areas of the bookshelves and counters. These surfaces looked like they could hold a good print. She wondered why they weren't dusting; didn't PIs do that kind of thing? Carefully, she eyed the walls and carpeting for small rust-colored drops that might indicate blood, or even the residual chemical odor of spot cleaning. Regular cleaning staff had long ago sucked up and disposed of any evidence like soils, hairs, or clothing fibers that could have been left by an *unsub*. Tucker kind of preferred the terminology from *Criminal Minds* to Blind Eye's POI—person of interest—even though "unidentified subject" was probably less relevant to Blind Eye's approach. Most of the time someone was hiring them to investigate *identifiable* subjects.

Bud was opening the drawers of Jeff's desk, snapping photos of objects within. Tucker was about to suggest he rummage through them to see if anything was hidden, but a quick peek over his shoulder proved the idea pointless. Everything was so intricately organized, all in its place, that anything unusual would be in plain view. There was no convenient little black address book of potential murder suspects sitting open with a Post-it next to the name of the culprit.

Tucker wandered back over to the wooden bookshelf where the screener films were divided into "Received," "Watch," "Chosen," and "Denied." They were arranged in alphabetical order with A on the left and Z on the right. Tucker wondered if that meant Jeff was right-handed or whether everyone ordered things in the same way. Some were in tall DVD cases with their titles printed on the spine so they could be easily identifiable. Others were in the small square CD cases like those Yoshi had sent home with Bud and didn't want her to mention to Frameline just yet, the ones that didn't have names printed on the spine. She took a few CD jewel cases from the shelf and flipped through them like a deck of cards.

Most were the kind of nondescript DVD discs that you could buy at any office supply or drug store, with titles printed in black marker across the front of the discs themselves or typed on white address labels and stuck to the front of the cases. She put the small stack of screeners back up, careful to keep them in their original order.

As Bud was still taking photos of who knew what, Tucker looked around the room again, hoping she'd see something important, something she wouldn't even think to look for until she saw it, but that would impress Yoshi. She did not see anything like that, but what she did see sent a shiver down her back. With Jeff's personal items already packed up and returned to his mother, the room seemed antiseptic and bore no sign of the personality who had worked there only a few weeks ago. Tucker found it disturbing that someone could so quickly be erased from one of the most important places in his life.

She thought of how unpredictable life was, how death hid around corners, and what it said about her as a person that she had escaped her mother's fortress but left her little brother behind, locked in the dungeon of his own mind. His condition dramatically reduced his life expectancy. Even if Hunter died, Tucker vowed she wouldn't let him disappear like that.

"So you don't know what seemed to be different?" she asked Jennifer Morris again as they walked to the door.

With her brow in a small knot, Morris halted and stared back into the room. Her glasses couldn't hide the sorrow in her eyes. "Maybe it's just that Jeff has gone. So nothing will ever look right again."

On their way out, Davina stopped Tucker. "I put together a list of filmmakers and producers who'd been mad their film didn't show or their 'donation' wasn't accepted."

Davina made quote marks with her fingers when she said the word "donation," Tucker wasn't really sure why. She took the list, rolled it up, and stuck it in her back pocket. Walking down the hallway away from Frameline, Tucker couldn't shake the feeling that, like Morris, she too felt *something* was amiss in Jeff's office. Something she just couldn't put her finger on.

❖

"You didn't bring Velvet, did you?" Tyrone sounded nervous as Yoshi made her way to his bedside.

"No."

"Good. I thought she was going to deck me the other night. Thanks for pulling her back."

"So, you do remember me from the memorial."

"Yes."

"I am a private investigator with Blind Eye Detective Agency. We're investigating Jeff's death."

"You work with AJ?"

"She works for me, yes."

"You have more questions?"

The truth was, Yoshi respected AJ's investigative skills. She *had* assigned AJ surveillance duty, after all. But not to ask questions. When AJ spoke with her earlier, she mentioned the rapport she'd developed with Tyrone Hill and what she'd learned of Jeff's arrangement with Isabelle and Theresa. However, AJ was neither a private investigator nor a detective. There were things she might not have thought to ask Tyrone, and methods of questioning that were more likely to elicit truthful responses.

"I spoke with Theresa Thompson and Isabelle Cocitaux this morning. They tell me Jeff never intended to coparent."

"Bullshit! That's a lie."

"Did you two work with a lawyer?"

"No. Like I told AJ, we arranged things informally. Big mistake."

"Yes. Can anyone else verify the nature of your arrangements with Isabelle and Theresa?"

"Jeff talked to his mom every week. He also called a lawyer, you know, after Isabelle got pregnant. They were drawing up some papers."

"What's the lawyer's name?"

"I don't remember."

Yoshi heard the sound of Tyrone's head moving back and forth on the pillow. Then he moaned. The shaking of his head must have hurt.

"Where would Jeff have kept a record of his communication with this lawyer?"

"Probably in the office at our apartment."

Yoshi nodded. She did not inform him that she had been in his apartment the previous evening. She did wonder if Tucker had taken photos of a notepad beside the phone or anything else that would show the lawyer's information. After she finished up here, Yoshi would drop into the Blind Eye Office and have her go through the digital images taken at Jeff's apartment.

"Would you happen to know if Jeff had a will or life insurance?"

"No, man. We didn't talk about that kind of shit. You know, he was only in his mid-thirties. Who knew he was going to *die*?" He was silent for a moment and then added, "Except him, I guess."

If he was telling the truth, a financial motive could probably be ruled out. Yoshi needed to be sure. "I understand the two of you were having financial difficulties," she said, recalling what Charlene Conant had told her.

"So?"

"Why was that?"

"'Cause I'm a loser…that's what you want me to say, right? You think my drug habit didn't just cost Jeff custody of his kid and his financial stability, but his life, too, don't you?"

"Did it?"

"Maybe a little," he muttered. "But it was more than that."

"Your HIV meds?"

"You know about that?"

"Yes." Yoshi had discovered Tyrone's HIV status when she looked up the medications from his bathroom cabinet. As a potential suspect in this investigation, he might be less than thrilled by her subterfuge, so she hoped he would not ask how she came to know that confidential information.

"Yeah, my meds. They're fucking expensive. But he also just hired a lawyer and started putting aside some money for the kid."

"Is that why he asked his parents for money?"

"He asked Charlie-squared?"

"Charlie-squared?" Yoshi frowned, not sure what he meant.

"Yeah, his parents? You know, since his mom and dad both go by Charlie, we called them Charlie-squared. It was our private joke." His voice trailed off and he was quiet again, thinking. When he spoke next, there was a tightness in his voice as though he was physically restraining emotions. "He was trying to get me into a rehab program. They're very expensive." As though he really wanted her to understand, he said, "It's hard to quit crystal meth. You can't just take methadone or something. None of that works."

"AJ has taken it upon herself to get you help," Yoshi reminded him.

"That's great. She's gonna get me arrested, confined to a program, and force me to go cold turkey while they hold me here."

"Give her a break. She saved your life."

"You mean she will have, once I get clean."

"No. Last night. You almost died. She was the one who performed CPR and saved your life."

"I didn't know." He sounded embarrassed. As he should. "Sorry."

"I have to ask, where were you the night Jeff died?"

"Screw you."

"It is a simple, routine question. I need to isolate anyone known to Jeff who does not have an alibi for the night of his disappearance."

He still didn't answer.

"Maybe you simply cannot recall. Is that it? Were you too high to know *where* you were?" She had it. "You were with another man, weren't you?" She wished she could see the truth on his face. She could not. When she listened carefully, it sounded like his breathing had changed. She would bet his heart rate had gone up as well. "Do you even know his name?"

"I only knew his screen name," he growled and spelled it out: "hard4u."

"Where did you meet?"

"Online." She could almost hear his eyes rolling at her obtuseness.

"I meant IRL." Yoshi used instant-messaging terminology. "In real life? Did you go to your place?"

"No! I never brought men to our apartment. His place."

"The address?"

"On Seventeenth Street."

"You can do better than that, Tyrone."

"Something like 1420 or 1430."

"Wouldn't Jeff wonder where you were?"

"No, our arrangement was I just had to be home by eight p.m. on weeknights."

"Is there anyone besides Theresa and Isabelle that you can think of who might have reason to harm Jeff?" Yoshi lobbed another question before he could have time to prepare, hoping to get his gut reaction.

"No."

"Tell me about Chase Devlin," Yoshi requested. "I heard the two of you had an affair."

Tyrone flinched, physically, as though she had threatened him. "It wasn't an *affair*." He spat the word out.

"All right, what was it, then?"

"You wouldn't understand."

"Try me."

"Chase Devlin does not have affairs," Tyrone replied. "He has acquisitions."

"Can you explain what you mean by that? Acquisitions?"

"When Chase wants something he doesn't just get it, he *acquires* it. He *owns* it in this incredibly intrinsic way. The way he talks about it is bizarre, as if he chases down whatever he wants like he's some kind of lion." He made a sound Yoshi took for a snort. "Guess that makes me that one stupid gazelle that wandered off from the herd, huh. More like I walked right up to him thinking, 'Aw, what a cute little kitty cat,' then 'Roar,' and I'm down with my neck broken and my guts hanging out, wondering what the hell just happened."

"In what manner did he acquire you?"

Tyrone sighed. He seemed to be tiring of their conversation. "Let's just say that my 'participation' was not voluntary." He waved a hand, the movement of it sending a light breeze toward Yoshi's face.

"In a manner of speaking, he raped me. In another it might be more appropriate to say I was acting. I *am* an actor, you know."

Before Yoshi had a chance to delve further into his enigmatic answer, a nurse came in from the hall and informed her that Tyrone needed his rest. Yoshi wondered if he had summoned the nurse by prayer or the touch of a silent panic alarm. Whichever it was, she was sure Tyrone was relieved to see her depart.

Chapter Eleven

Just as soon as AJ sauntered into the Blind Eye Detective Office, she could tell Yoshi wasn't in. Rock music blared from small computer speakers. Bud was chillin', flipping the pages of a *Guns & Jugs*. Tucker was grooving to the music, swaying and bouncing her booty in her chair like some sorta white girl sit'n dance move.

"What up?" AJ asked.

"It's Wild Strawberries," Tucker said like she thought AJ had asked about the band.

"Can y'all turn that down?" AJ hollered, illustrating her request with a knob-turning motion.

Tucker replied with a few mouse clicks. "Hey, AJ, how's it going?"

"Yoshi ain't in?"

"Nope."

Bud put down his girlie mag. "So, you like that Tyrone fellow for this so-called murder?"

"Naw, I think he's clean."

"Really?" Bud sneered. "I heard he's a user."

"That's right," Tucker piped in. "We found meth at his apartment, and he's been in *porn*."

"So *what*? Y'all think anybody who does drugs or pornos is a murderer? Maybe Tyrone ain't a totally stand-up guy, but my gut says he ain't no murderer, neither."

"Your gut, huh? Is that all you got?"

Bud was still butting heads with her like one of them young buck shorties up on the block trying to prove they's the Mac Daddy instead of a punk-assed bitch.

"You got any proof he's guilty?" AJ asked.

"Maybe. What's your *evidence* that he's innocent?" Bud's face lit up like a bulb, like he'd just got a golden idea. "Is this because he's black?"

AJ shot him a hateful look.

Oblivious, Bud said, "I don't get it. If it wasn't a drive-by, it *couldn't* be this guy?"

Tucker, her cheeks flushed rosy, ignored Bud and addressed AJ. "You're the one who spent all that time with him. If you say he didn't do it, I believe *you*."

Like a shortie screaming for attention, Bud jumped. "You girls go have a love fest if you want to, but I'm a *detective* and I'm waiting till I *detect* some evidence before I buy that the SO wasn't involved."

Although Bud used the shorthand for "significant other," something about the way he said it suggested a sneer.

"Wait," Tucker protested. "You said you don't even think it *was* a murder."

"Yeah, I still think Conant just took a header off the bridge. But his *boyfriend* was probably the extenuating circumstances." Bud smirked at AJ like he hoped to egg her on.

While she was glaring at him, the smirk just fell away and he ran his finger straight across his throat. Next he jammed his girlie mag under the cushion of his wheelchair and sat up straight while Tucker muted the music and got busy with the papers on her desk.

Just as AJ added the clues together, Yoshi entered the office.

"AJ?" She hung up her coat and telescoping cane. "I am quite surprised to find you here. I thought you had to be at your place of employment hours ago?"

"I...I..." AJ stammered like she just got caught ditching school by her mama, and her ass was gonna get a big ol' whuppin'. "I called in sick."

A look of concern crossed Yoshi's face. Damn. Ain't no way to make a good impression with the lady she wanted to get with, employment-wise. AJ was no good at fibbing. Her mama and her Grandma Latisha had a bullshit detector that could read a fib at twenty paces. And forgiveness? Lordy, child, a vengeful God was more forgivin' than Mama.

"Have you gotten checked out by a medical professional?"

"Naw."

"Why not?" Yoshi asked, steppin' in front of her.

When that fly girl got so close, AJ could remember why she'd wanted to hit it with her in the first place. Her face stung with embarrassment—from her sinful thoughts so soon after recalling the wrath of Mama, and from getting caught up in a lie.

"I ain't sick," she admitted.

"Now you've done it," Bud muttered gleefully.

"May I see you in my office? Privately."

Tucker scrunched her eyebrows and Bud mimed laughter. AJ flipped him off before following Yoshi inside the private office; she could see one advantage of a blind boss.

Yoshi pointed in the general direction of the plush leather seat in front of her desk and slid into her own executive chair. AJ sat and thought about being called to the principal's office.

"It is very important that you get proper medical attention, AJ."

"Yo, I'm sorry I lied but it ain't no biggie. I was just plain busted from the all-nighter tailing Tyrone. But I straight up swear on the mass grave of Katrina victims that I wouldn't never do that working for y'all."

"AJ, this is quite serious. You must make arrangements to be examined by a medical professional."

"Honest, I'm fit as a fiddle. There ain't nothing wrong with me."

"Tucker and I searched Tyrone's apartment..." Yoshi let the sentence hang there like she was waiting for AJ to add something. AJ wasn't sure *what* she oughta be confessing.

Yoshi sighed. "We stumbled on Tyrone's HIV medication."

AJ didn't wanna think about *that*. Thinking about it felt like rats gnawin' on her insides.

"The nurses tell me that Tyrone Hill owes you his life."

AJ didn't say nothing. Whatever Tyrone owed, it wasn't to her.

"You performed live-saving CPR for, what was it—" Yoshi broke off again. "*Ten* minutes?"

AJ shrugged. If Yoshi or Tyrone wanted to thank someone, they should go directly to the Mac Daddy himself, our savior, Jesus Christ.

"That is quite a long time. You must have been exhausted." Yoshi sounded impressed. "However, you failed to utilize a protective mouth guard."

"I didn't have one on me."

"I do not like my employees taking that level of risk."

Good thing I ain't your employee yet, AJ thought, a little taken back. Yoshi might be one fly grrl detective, but if this shit was her way of saying "good job," she *sucked* at it. Big-time.

Yoshi leaned forward across the broad desk. "AJ, I am simply attempting to convey, with some level of urgency, that it is absolutely essential that you undergo an HIV test. Posthaste. Now, I have spoken with my attorney—"

"Ya talkin' to a lawyer about me?"

"No. I asked a hypothetical question. I have already filed paperwork to cover any on-the-job injury you may sustain while you volunteer here, even if you never become a full-time employee."

"You don't got to do that."

"Perhaps not. However, it could be critical to your care if..." Apparently, Yoshi didn't want to give voice to the idea neither.

"Ain't nothing gonna happen. I'm fine."

Yoshi opened her mouth to protest.

"Yo, okay, here the four-one-one. I already *got* my blood take when I was there. I totally get that HIV is serious, Yosh, but like ya said, that boy woulda died without the CPR. So I got tested."

Yoshi bit her lip and nodded. Her translucent blue eyes seem misted with water.

"It's gonna be okay." AJ spoke low but with assurance. She refused to have it any other way.

❖

Tucker pulled her chair into Yoshi's office, joining the circle around the long dark-cherry desk. The high-gloss finish reflected the Blind Eye team gathered there. It was so cool to be part of a group like this. Just a month ago she didn't feel like she was really even a part of the team, and now here she was in the staff meeting, and not just to take notes.

Carefully arranged on the desktop were three low-profile brunette platters, one chocolate leather velvet-inlaid tray, a clean black phone, a recorder with microphone, and a slim iMac computer. It was never more cluttered than at this moment.

"All right," Yoshi said. Her voice was all it took to gain their attention and call the meeting to order. "Bud, why don't you tell us what you have uncovered on the film festival angle?"

"Sure. I think that line of investigation is dead in the water, no pun intended. I mean, maybe somebody could be driven to suicide by the weird shit in those films, but I can't imagine anybody killing over them. We did talk to the broad in charge since Conant bit it. Name's Jennifer Morris. Seems she's the power broker in the place, makes all the decisions about which films make it to the festival and all that. We got this list of disgruntled individuals from the assistant, but I don't see that panning out. Nobody's even been turned down yet this year, so it doesn't seem like anyone would have a motive for being mad at the vic, 'specially not with Morris calling all the shots. There was one thing…"

Bud caught Tucker's eye and tipped his head to her. He'd just thrown her a pass and told her to run with it. She smiled her acknowledgment and thanks. When his face soured in response, she quickly dropped the grin and played serious professional.

"Jennifer Morris said that when Jeff first went missing, she noticed something about his office. It hadn't been trashed or anything, but…" She tried to draw out the suspense. "She said she felt like something was *off*."

Yoshi drew her naturally thin eyebrows together in perplexity. "In what way, exactly?"

"That's the thing. She couldn't say, exactly. Just had this feeling like things weren't in their right places. I think I did, too."

"You think you what?" Bud asked.

"I don't know, like I also had this sense something wasn't where it should be, but I just couldn't pinpoint *what* it was."

"Maybe you've got a magic gut like AJ here," Bud opined. "One that can tell if a guy's a murderer just by looking at him."

Tucker made a face at him, screwing her features into a glare that hopefully conveyed *Stop that!* She went on, "I downloaded the digital images we got from Jeff and Tyrone's place. You looked up those prescriptions, didn't you, Yoshi?"

"Yes, I located the information I needed."

"Bud and I were looking at the photos of the legal papers I found. He says they look like…what was it, Bud?"

"Power of Attorney." Bud grunted. "And one of them Domestic Partnership Agreements. Between the boys."

"Right, and I also got a photo of this business card, I think it's for Jeff's attorney."

"Excellent." Yoshi said. Her smile warmed the fire in Tucker's gut.

"Oh, yeah, and Bud?" Tucker added.

"Hmm."

"I was thinking maybe you could let me look at that screener you had that didn't play, just in case I can get it to run."

"Sure."

"Cool."

"So we heard AJ doesn't think Tyrone could've offed our DB," Bud said snarkily. "Maybe she'd like to share her wisdom with us."

AJ glared at him. "I already done my reportin' to Yoshi."

"True," Yoshi said. "Can you summarize, for their benefit?"

"Okay. Tyrone's a meth junkie. I tipped SF Narcotics off to his supplier, who turned out to be just a low-level player. Tyrone, he gets around a lot with other guys, but he says it ain't on the down low, 'cause he and Conant had an arrangement so it ain't *cheating*. But he didn't always wear a glove, and he's got HIV-plus." AJ glanced at Yoshi. "I don't know about whether he told his boy or not. But it so clear he loved Jeff and he's totally buggin' over Jeff's death. So, yeah, I don't think he coulda killed him."

Bud mumbled something, but no one asked him to speak up.

"Another thing." AJ barely paused long enough to take a breath. "Tyrone swears Jeff was pumped about the baby and he picked a sistah so it'd be like the baby he and Tyrone would have if they could make one. Tyrone thinks them females was ditching 'cause they knew about his drug problem. DB was supposed to have a meeting with their lawyer right around the time he went off the bridge."

Yoshi didn't give Bud time to add any rude comments. "That is correct, Hill maintains that Thompson and Cocitaux were lying when they claimed Jeff had never intended to coparent. He thinks they had planned to move all along. I am hoping we will be able to get to the bottom of that disagreement. I also obtained Tyrone's alibi. Which," Yoshi concluded, "we must locate and confirm."

"What is it?" Bud asked.

"That he was with someone he met online."

"So," Bud snorted. "Let's say Tyrone's alibi checks out, who've we got left for suspects? Guess we better hope this Chase Devlin individual is a bad bad man, 'cause it's hard to pin this one on a preggo lady, even if she is a dyke."

The way he glanced about after pronouncing the last word made it clear to Tucker that he was hoping to get a rise from AJ or Yoshi. Neither took the bait.

"If there even was a murder," Bud muttered under his breath so Tucker could barely hear.

Yoshi ignored his final remark. "I gather that Devlin is indeed a shady character. Tomorrow I intend to speak with him directly. I am hoping he will clear up a few things, for instance, what would lead Tyrone to term their sexual relationship as alternately rape and performance?"

The look that darted across AJ's face like a figure skulking in the shadows struck Tucker as one of pain and anger.

"I wanna be there for that."

"Do you think you will still be under the weather tomorrow?" Yoshi asked, and, Tucker could have sworn, winked at AJ.

AJ, who didn't appear to be ill, had a slight grin on her pouty lips. "Ain't no telling," she said. "I'll let ya know in the a.m."

Tucker wasn't sure she liked what she was seeing. Apparently Yoshi and AJ had some kind of code or they felt so close they didn't need to express what they were thinking because the other one already knew it. They'd only been on two dates, as far as Tucker could tell. And now AJ was moving in on Tucker's territory at Blind Eye, which just wasn't fair. Not when AJ had the advantage of already being a police officer whose investigative skills Yoshi clearly respected. How could Tucker compete with that? She was already playing catch-up.

The whole time they'd been together, Velvet had been saying that Yoshi could use another investigator at Blind Eye. Tucker was working as hard as she could to fill that role, but at only 40 hours a week, her remaining 5,000 hours still seemed like an eternity. Especially when AJ could probably just pass an exam and then march into Blind Eye, and Yoshi would notice Tucker even less than she did now.

It seemed like having AJ on board was a test to decide about offering her a job. Tucker might have had a chance to outshine *Bud*, but she couldn't compete with AJ, and if AJ and Yoshi just kept getting closer they'd never ever break up. So much for Tucker's plans to become a PI to get Yoshi's attention—and so much more. *Damn.*

Why did she keep thinking this way about her boss? Especially when she was lucky enough to have a hottie like Velvet waiting at home in bed for her? Tucker conjured up a visual and visceral vision of Velvet with a sexy black and purple bustier cinched around her waist, her DD breasts barely restrained by the lacy fabric and silk ribbon ties. Maybe that's how the garment got its name, because a woman endowed like Velvet nearly busted out of the contraption.

"Tucker!"

The vision of Velvet vanished. Bud and AJ were staring at her. *God.* She'd spaced off again. Still, she was a little embarrassed, as if they had all read her thoughts just by looking at her face. "Yes?"

"I asked if you would accompany Bud tomorrow."

"Uh, sure. Where we going?"

AJ hid a grin. Bud did not. Tucker could feel the heat in her cheeks and she was glad Yoshi couldn't see her blush. She wondered if Yoshi could *feel* her embarrassment. Dogs could sense fear. Yoshi could probably sense humiliation.

"I would appreciate," Yoshi spoke as though this were the first time she'd addressed the subject, "if you and Bud could interview Jeff's attorney, Vincent Broadwell. I want to know if Jeff had a will or life insurance, and who the beneficiaries are. I want to know what was going on, legally, about the baby."

"Okay, boss."

"Let me just make this clear. I am *not* requesting that any of you break any laws, practice any advanced investigation techniques, climb up any drainpipes, or snoop in confidential files."

"Okay?" Tucker heard the question in her answer even before she saw Yoshi grimace. *Shoot.* She'd been working so hard on breaking that habit ever since Yoshi had first expressed her disdain for the tendency. She said it made Tucker sound unsure of herself. Tucker didn't want Yoshio to think less of her just because she *sounded* insecure.

Fake it till you make it. She couldn't remember who said that. But it was Velvet who showed a study that proved if you forced a smile, eventually you would actually feel better. Maybe that could work with confidence, too.

Still, Tucker *was* worried. Yoshi's unusual lecture seemed evidence of her displeasure at the one thing Tucker had been proud of, her totally cool *Mission Impossible* break-in of Jeff Conant's apartment. If that had not only failed to impress Yoshi but actually *displeased* her, Tucker was even worse at this whole private investigator thing than she originally thought. *One step forward, two steps back.* Would she ever look like more than a fuckup in Yoshi's eyes?

As the meeting broke up, Yoshi asked Bud to stay behind. Tucker thought the look on her face warned that a tongue-lashing was in the works.

❖

"What was *that* about?" Tucker whispered to Bud as soon as he left Yoshi's office.

He nodded toward the main door. "Walk me to the john?" he said loud enough to be heard by anyone eavesdropping.

When they were several wheelchair lengths down the hall, and presumably out of hearing distance of the closed Blind Eye door, Bud reduced the speed at which he spun his wheels. He muttered, "Yoshi's got a hair up her ass. She read me the riot act about last night."

"What's up with that?"

"Fuck if I know." He rolled his eyes skyward as if he'd find the answer on the ceiling tiles.

"What's she steamed about?" The kid'd gotten all worked up, her face pinched in concern. It didn't take a lot for the kid to buy someone else's opinion that she'd fucked up. She was going to have to learn to let shit roll off her back if she was going to make it as a PI.

"She's mad 'cause I had you break into Jeff's apartment."

Yoshi had stayed mad, too, even after he let her in on the joke about how he'd never expected Tucker to succeed. How the break-in was supposed to be a practical joke in which Tucker failed at a task she'd never been trained to do. He'd get a break from babysitting, have some alone time to eat a nice dinner charged off as a work expense, and all while he showed the kid how difficult the job could be. Plus, as an added benefit, he'd have a good laugh at her expense when a restaurant patron caught her trying to crawl out the bathroom window.

Yoshi hadn't found any of it funny. Women did have senses of humor worth shit.

"I thought that was the kind of thing you guys do all the time." The poor girl was confused. He didn't blame her. Yoshi's reasoning had seemed fucked up to him, too.

"Yeah."

"So, what's the problem?"

"She was just pissed we broke in when she already had a key. She says she wants us to explore all options before resorting to *dangerous, criminal activities*."

Bud didn't see that kind of fieldwork as *criminal* activity, that's for sure. It was just part of the job and Yoshi should've been impressed, not pissed, by the kid's natural skills.

"Don't take it personal, kid," Bud said. "She's just jealous 'cause you got there before her." That didn't change the look on her face, and he was starting to feel sorry for her. *Goddamn*. He sighed. He hated her for what she was making him do. "The truth is, she was worried about you."

This perked her up. "Really?"

"Yeah. She was mad that I put you in a position where you might've gotten hurt or arrested. She said I didn't do a good job babysitting you."

He made it sound like a joke, masking what he really felt about getting his ass handed to him like that. Against his better judgment, he was growing fond of the kid and didn't want her to feel bad. If he wasn't in his chair, he'd have tousled her hair like she was a child. Instead he punched her in the arm for good measure.

She rewarded him with a crooked smile. "You'd better keep a close eye on me later in case I get the urge to draw on the big man's important papers."

Bud played along with the mock baby talk. "Now be a good girl and bring your dolly along to play with while Daddy talks to the big man."

"Dolly?" Tucker reverted to her normal voice and affected indignation. "For your information, I played with action figures, *not* dollies."

Her eyes thanked him. He was relieved she didn't verbalize her appreciation.

With a grin and a slight swagger, she went back to the Blind Eye office.

CHAPTER TWELVE

Chase Devlin's office was in the forty-two-story Spear Tower, part of the One Market Plaza that included a giant retail pavilion. As she entered the lobby, Yoshi almost wished she could see what she had read about, the eleven-story glass atrium pavilion with its giant hexagonal metal sculpture floating on water in the middle.

In the material that Tucker had provided, Chase Devlin was described as a fairly established film producer who'd recently moved from L.A. to San Francisco and formed a production company with Jeff Conant, purportedly to apply Devlin's skill in producing mainstream films to the gay film market. His ability to pay almost twenty grand a month for rent for only 1,500 square feet could indicate he was either extremely proficient at what he did, or obsessively concerned with his image and the suggestion of wealth, or he was a drug baron who needed to launder cash.

Like many producers, Devlin had apparently gotten involved in the entertainment world initially as a financial resource. He was said to possess a unparalleled gift for wrangling money from traditional studio heads and unlikely financiers. He often secured nonconventional investments to finance the films he was involved in, such as those from Silicon Valley that had funded his last film, a thriller about nanotechnology. This box-office smash was surprisingly intelligent for what was, essentially an extended product-placement advertisement.

The instant Yoshi shook Chase Devlin's manicured but clammy hand, she knew she'd smelled his rather overpowering cologne before. It was the combination of spicy scents, cedar, pepper, and ginger that she had not been able to place on a clothing item at Jeff and Tyrone's apartment.

After the professional introductions and some polite conversation about Devlin's office, his latest film, and the chance meeting with Jeff that eventually led to their partnership, but before Yoshi and AJ could even begin their interrogation, Devlin confessed.

"I'm fairly certain what brings a private investigator by. I understand you've been speaking with Tyrone Hill."

Yoshi wondered if Hill had spoken directly with Devlin or how the financier came by the knowledge. It was a little creepy to think she or AJ might have been the target of surveillance.

Without pause, Devlin continued, "In which case he may well have revealed the nature of our relationship and, perhaps, other information of a more sensitive nature. Rather than beat around the bush, I'd prefer to deal with this directly and confess my complicity in Jeff Conant's death."

Yoshi's mouth involuntarily fell ajar and hung open. AJ, too, was completely silent. Yoshi could not even hear her breathing in the museumlike stillness of the room. She had to admit in all of her time as a private investigator, nothing of this kind had ever occurred, and she was at somewhat of a loss as to how to proceed. Yoshi discovered herself wondering if they were to leave the room alive.

"I am not sure that I understand," she said, hoping he could not hear the tremor in her voice, like she could.

Devlin made no attempt to explain himself or clarify in a manner that made sense. "To truly understand, I'm afraid, requires a bit of backstory, if you'll indulge me?"

"Of course."

"As you may know, I have made quite a name for myself in the film business. But what you may not know is that I recently began a foray into the adult entertainment industry."

Devlin was full of so many shocking twists that Yoshi was beginning to wonder if this was a scripted interaction intended to completely invalidate the words he'd spoken just seconds ago, casually, as if murder was of no concern.

"I'm expanding, in fact," Devlin continued. "I've capitalized on Kink-dot-com's recent purchase of the old armory building in the Mission."

It was difficult to avoid the media frenzy surrounding Kink.com's new headquarters. The porn company had bought the armory, built in

1912 and listed on the National Register of Historic Places but vacant since 1970, for nearly $15 million. A small coalition of community groups had protested the sale, but since Kink was planning to use the place as a dungeon and not make any structural changes, and the location had been vacant so long, there was little ammunition for the city to prevent the acquisition.

Kink.com had widespread support, too, although many proponents kept their involvement low key and avoided public identification. Yoshi had been one of them. It was not that she supported the adult entertainment industry per se, but she did feel that Kink's architectural plans for the space, which relied on restoring and maintaining the historic armory, was one of the more intelligent designs to sidestep the often unsuitable gentrification that had been occurring in the Mission.

Devlin continued, "I've acquired the New Mission Theater and four neighboring buildings, and I'm currently working with an architectural team to create the largest adult-entertainment complex and porn playground in America."

The New Mission Theater was the grand dame of famed San Francisco theaters. Much like the armory, the theater had not been an active film house since the early '90s, but had been saved from demolition more than once by inclusion on the National Register and fierce protest from neighbors. Yoshi could not imagine turning the theater, which could seat several thousand moviegoers, into a porn playground. Nor could she conceive of what exactly a porn playground might entail.

Yoshi couldn't imagine that such ambitions reflected Jeff Conant's interests and she wondered how they meshed with the production company he was developing with Devlin. Still, there was nothing to preclude Devlin from pursuing divergent paths.

AJ spoke before Yoshi could. "Jeff was dope to this?"

"No, no," Devlin said with a hint of condescension. "That's the thing. Conant-Devlin Productions is an entirely separate venture. Jeff wanted to develop big-budget, big-market, gay-themed films, and producing adult-entertainment films held no interest for him. In fact, he was troubled by my plans for the Mission Theater district, and was talking about pulling out of our venture. He was concerned that being even incidentally connected to the project might hurt our production company's image."

"So ya killed him 'cause he backed outta it?" AJ deduced.

"Oh, no. Of course not. But then Jeff discovered another element of my adult-entertainment company that he found impossible to ignore."

"That ya messin' with his lover?" AJ suggested.

"Yeah, he really didn't like that one bit, despite their open relationship." Devlin paused long enough for Yoshi to hear the flick of a lighter and inhale the pungent aroma of cigar smoke.

She wondered if he was not required to follow state regulations against smoking in public buildings because this was a private office, or whether he had simply bribed a government official to grant him immunity. She would not be surprised. Not about bribery, at any rate, but certainly Devlin's morphing confession had her attention. She wondered if he was so quick to share these details with other people.

"Jeff did nothing about it. However, he was less fettered in other areas." Devlin puffed happily at his cigar as though they were out at a social event.

Yoshi was getting impatient with Devlin's epic-style storytelling. She could already tell he was a fairly classic narcissist, but she wanted to get to the punch. "When was the last time you saw Jeff?"

"The night he was killed, of course," Devlin said with such nonchalance it surprised even Yoshi, who considered herself fairly unflappable. He sighed. "Please allow me to continue, and all of your questions will be answered presently."

"Fine." Yoshi agreed through tightened teeth.

"Although Jeff had begun looking for an investor willing to buy out his shares in our partnership, we were moving forward with development, meeting to discuss developing one of the screenplays that came our way. Then things really heated up when Jeff learned that I had imagined Tyrone playing a central role in my new porn empire. That's what we were discussing at his office the evening of the night in question. Jeff made a rather generous offer if I would relinquish Tyrone from his contractual obligations."

"I had been led to believe that Jeff was having financial problems," Yoshi said.

"That could be. I did not inquire as to where he intended to get the funds. To put it mildly, I was not interested. Though the offer was generous, it paled in comparison to what Tyrone is worth to my company."

"So then what?" AJ asked. "How'd it happen?"

"Then I left."

"And ya came back later? Or did y'all wait for him outside?"

"No, quite the contrary, I went straight home. I never saw Jeff again."

"What the fuck? Are ya trippin'?" AJ sounded angry.

"As I recall, I said I was complicit in his death, which I'm afraid I was. Clearly my conflict with him weighed heavily enough that it led directly to his decision to take his own life." Devlin paused. "I'm sure there's no one reason for suicide, but explanations seem important to loved ones, and in good faith, I'm attempting to provide one."

Yoshi did not like his tone. Despite the appearance of plausibility and the implication that Devlin was speaking from his conscience, his speech seemed too rehearsed. Chase Devlin had far too many plausible responses for her taste and she was certain of one thing: he would not have been so direct about his relationship with Tyrone and his presence at Jeff's office that night unless he believed they could already place him there.

Devlin thought he was very smart, but he had just placed himself with a dead man only hours before his disappearance. He had also provided them with Jeff's whereabouts immediately prior to his death. There must have been something, something they hadn't yet realized that would tie Devlin to the Frameline office. He was being very clever, keeping one step in front of their investigation. It would be difficult to trip him up. Still, she would attempt to do just that.

"Tyrone does not have a bank account." Yoshi remembered this from Tucker's credit bureau research. "How do you pay him? In cash?" If Devlin was paying in cash, it might be to avoid paying taxes.

"No, Ms. Yakamoto. I see that you're unfamiliar with adult entertainment, but it's a business like any other. We have payroll every other Thursday just like other companies. I don't know much about payroll, as I obviously don't do the company's accounting. Simon?"

Devlin raised his voice toward what was probably an adjoining room. Yoshi felt someone move through the office.

AJ leaned in and whispered in Yoshi's ear. "That's one scary motherfucker."

Yoshi couldn't see the man who'd just entered but she could smell him. It was a faint smell before—perhaps he was listening in just behind the partition—but now Simon's strangely odd combination of scents was almost overwhelming. He smelled like diesel fuel, fish oil, and Mr. Clean. It was a very un-accountant-like smell. Yoshi wondered if the others felt like gagging.

Chase Devlin didn't bother to introduce this lackey. "Can you obtain some records for me?"

Simon did not speak, but apparently assented in another fashion because Devlin thanked him and the smell drifted toward the door and became less toxic.

"He might be a minute. Do you ladies have other questions?"

Yoshi felt AJ tense beside her as though he'd just issued an edict.

"How'd y'all work 'round Tyrone's HIV status?" AJ was blunt.

"I'm sure you know that the industry instigated strict safe-sex and testing policies years ago."

"I would have thought testing HIV positive ends an actor's career," Yoshi said.

"Certainly not, although there has to be full disclosure, of course. We collect signatures from any negative actors or actresses prior to doing a scene with a positive actor, and positive actors are precluded from certain scenes, like some money shots. Otherwise we simply employ the same safe-sex requirements that we have for all of our other actors and actresses."

"How about drugs?"

"We're employers, not parents. We can't control what our actors chose to do in their off hours, but when they're on set they're required to stay clean."

Yoshi didn't respond. She was aware that some people employed in sex work felt the need to alter their consciousness through drug use in order to do their jobs. She could also imagine that actors were expendable; there seemed to be an infinite supply.

"Can you think of any reason why Tyrone would say that he was not a voluntary participant in your relationship?" she asked.

Devlin laughed. "That's my Tyrone. He's always had a twisted sense of humor."

I think you are the twisted one, Yoshi thought. *I cannot prove it—yet—but eventually, I will.*

"You could say I *acquired* him, I suppose. I bought out his contract with Phantasm Video and I now have him on an exclusive contract. But involuntary? I can't imagine what he could mean by that. You can clearly see that he's certainly not starring in any of my productions against his will, if that's what you mean."

"Maybe y'all blackmailing him, or keeping him fucked up, sniffin' Tina," AJ said.

Devlin did not answer immediately. When he did, he seemed to be speaking through clenched teeth. "I agreed to speak to you out of respect for my Tyrone and regret at Jeff Conant's untimely demise. I've been more than forthright, and despite my courtesy, you have the gall to accuse me of dealing drugs. *Really*. I think we're done here."

Irritated, Yoshi felt AJ rise to her feet. She did the same. On the way down in the elevator, she examined her reasons for bringing AJ along to the meeting. She wanted the security of a police officer, and one who looked sufficiently frightening that Yoshi felt safe in her company. She also wanted to see how AJ conducted herself in an interview. She had a lot to learn about when to apply pressure and when to sit back and listen. Even being fed phony information could reveal something about the truth it was designed to hide. They might have gotten that far with Devlin if they'd handled the meeting more delicately.

AJ said what Yoshi was already thinking. "He played us."

Yoshi nodded. Devlin had learned exactly what he had hoped to by agreeing to their interview, and more to the point, he had fed them exactly the information he had intended to. What was he hiding? She was almost positive he was afflicted with hidden perversions that drove him to devote so much energy to his new porn company. Had Jeff somehow threatened Devlin's dream of a porn empire and paid for it with his life? Did Devlin kill Jeff in order to have Tyrone to himself? It was certainly creepy how Devlin referred to Tyrone as "my Tyrone." That spoke to just the kind of controlling relationship Tyrone had alluded to.

Yoshi did not know what flavor Devlin's perversions were and whether they, or his obsessive relationship with Tyrone, lay behind Jeff's death. This meeting, however, more than anything else they'd learned so far, suggested that Jeff had died under suspicious circumstances. And those circumstances had Chase Devlin prints all over them.

❖

At the Blind Eye Detective Agency, Tucker stared at her cell phone, urging it to ring. Three luminescent bars taunted her, proving the problem wasn't a lack of service. She dialed her mailbox. Still no new messages. Just like the last time she checked, five minutes ago. Maybe she should call and leave another message. Just because Velvet didn't want to be bothered didn't necessarily mean that she wouldn't appreciate Tucker checking in, did it?

They hadn't gone this long without speaking since before the Rosemary Finney case. They always called each other at work at least once during the day, just to say hi or leave a message full of innuendo.

Tucker punched in seven numbers and hit Send. A moment later she heard the phone in Yoshi's office ringing, and the light for the extension throbbed red. She ended her call and Yoshi's phone went silent. *That proves it. There's nothing wrong with my phone.* So why hadn't Velvet called?

Tucker could tell Velvet's home phone was still working because she'd gotten Velvet's answering machine each of the fifty times she'd dialed. That probably just meant Velvet wasn't home. But not being home didn't explain why Velvet hadn't answered her work line or her cell phone, nor called Tucker back in response to the many messages. Tucker was beginning to get really worried. But she was in a bind. Was it better to give Velvet the space she said she wanted or invade that space to ensure she was okay? Maybe she should she call the police. She could pretend Velvet was her frail grandmother who might have fallen and ask them to do a welfare check by driving over to the house.

But what if Velvet wasn't home and was lying in a ditch someplace? Should she pretend Velvet's car got stolen so the police would go out looking for it? That option seemed to be the kind of thing that would land Tucker in hot water. With Velvet *and* the police. She put away her phone, reasoning with herself that Velvet would be fine. This was Velvet Erickson, intrepid grrl reporter, after all, not some anxious country girl afraid of the city's dark corners. Velvet was just taking time to grieve in her own way. Her not answering the phone didn't mean anything.

Later, when Tucker got off work, she could catch BART to Sixteenth Street and flatfoot it to Bernal Heights. If she came bearing gifts, Velvet would be glad to see her. Tucker would just pop in, make sure she was okay and didn't need anything, and then go spend the night at her basement apartment in Oakland and let Velvet sleep alone.

Tucker forced thoughts of Velvet out of her mind and focused on the digital photographs Bud had taken of Jeff's office. They didn't seem to tell her anything more than being *in* Jeff's office had. Just the same meticulously organized desk and alphabetized books on the big bookshelves.

Tucker opened another image of two gray file cabinets. The Drew Carey–like Jennifer Morris had said one held paperwork about each of the films that had played Frameline's festival over the years. The other cabinet, which was locked, apparently held more sensitive material like employee files, fiscal records, and information about Frameline's financial supporters. Tucker had thought the contents of that cabinet would be of most interest to an intruder, but Morris assured them that the file lock had not been tampered with and nothing was missing.

Tucker wasn't sure if that was really *proof* of anything. Couldn't someone have forced Jeff to open the file cabinet and photocopy material they were interested in? Bud hadn't insisted on Morris opening the locked drawers, so Tucker couldn't even look at file names on the chance one would be a clue. In her PI course, she'd learned that the odds of solving a crime reduce dramatically after the first forty-eight hours. She could see why. The more time passed, the more evidence would be lost and people forgot things. Even now, the POIs they were interviewing had to think back more than a month, and it wasn't as if Yoshi even knew what information they were looking for.

Pulling up another image, Tucker focused on the shelves that held film screeners. She zoomed in to different places and back out again. She stared at the photo for a long time. Whatever had been troubling her about Jeff's office started yelling, "Hot, hot, hot," like she was narrowing in on the problem. She looked at the rows of DVD and CD cases and didn't get it. Damn. She was never going to make private eye. She was just too stupid.

She sighed and moved on to the next image, higher up on the towering cherry shelves where the fastidiously organized books replaced films. Tucker got the hot feeling again before she looked away. She chased her mouse until the cursor hovered over a row of books. Tucker clicked the zoom in three times. As she suspected, the books were carefully arranged in alphabetical order based on title. Jeff was as anal as Velvet was with her collection of films.

Tucker remembered helping Velvet put her house together after the cops ransacked it executing a search warrant in the Rosemary Finney case. They'd knocked all of the movies—each and every one—off their shelves. Hundreds of DVDs were scattered on the floor. Tucker had volunteered to help put them back up on their floor-to-ceiling shelves, but it wasn't that simple. Velvet demanded that not only must every thing be shelved, but in its *specific* spot on the shelf. Every film had a correct location. Like Jeff's books, Velvet's DVD collection was carefully alphabetized. Velvet had been really strict about that system, too, making Tucker redo everything when she put something in the wrong place.

Tucker froze with her mouse over books with titles beginning with *T*'s and zoomed in. Her heart pounded and she wanted to run out in the hallway and announce, *Eureka!* Feeling a little foolish, she stared at the titles more closely. It wasn't like she'd *solved* the case or anything, was it? Probably not, but it would still be totally cool, if she was right.

She decided not to share her enthusiasm with Yoshi or Bud without verifying her find first. Lord knows, she didn't want to give either of them fuel for teasing, or another reason to roll their eyes. Nothing like telling folks you grew up on a small Idaho farm to get them thinking you're nothing but a rube. From her back pocket, she pulled the business card she'd gotten from Jennifer Morris and dialed the number.

After Jennifer greeted her politely, she said, "Hey, Jennifer, I don't know if you remember me, but I'm Tucker Shade, from Blind Eye Detective Agency?" Although Yoshi weren't in the room, Tucker immediately flinched at her questioning tone. Yet again she'd sounded uncertain and unprofessional.

"Of course, Tucker, what can I do for you?"

"You remember saying how most of Jeff's office hadn't been messed with?"

"Yes."

"What about the screeners, on the shelves?" The words came out in a rush. Tucker held her breath and crossed her fingers.

"No, you're right. The screener shelves aren't the way he left them."

"Oh," Disappointment washed over her. Of course she hadn't been right.

"That wasn't the answer you hoped for?" Jennifer asked astutely.

"I guess not. See, I've been looking through these photos we took of the office and I just thought I'd found something important, but I guess I was wrong."

"Really?" Jennifer sounded hopeful. "What's that?"

There was no reason not to tell her now. "You know how Jeff liked things alphabetized?"

Morris chuckled. "It was hard not to. He would pitch a fit if anyone put things back in the wrong order. Why?"

"When we were there, I was flipping through some of the screener films? At first I couldn't put my finger on what it was that bothered me about them. You know, I was starting to think I was crazy."

"Yes?" Jennifer's voice sounded like Yoshi's when she was saying, "Get to the point."

"Anyway, so then I'm looking at the photos Bud took? And then I totally saw it."

"Saw what?"

"That whoever last organized the films messed them up. See, everything's in alphabetical order until you get to titles that started with *The*, you know, like *The Last Supper*?" Tucker didn't pause for Morris to answer the rhetorical question. "Well, someone filed those titles in the *T* section. Now I don't know about Jeff, but my girlfriend, Velvet—"

"No, you're right. Jeff would *never* have tolerated that."

"He treated beginning *A* and *The* as silent?" Tucker clarified.

"Absolutely. So what does this mean? Oh, my God, you think someone was here in his office looking for something?" Her voice cracked. "You think it was something to do with what happened?"

"Wait." Now Tucker was confused. "You just said the screeners had been messed with since Jeff went missing. Couldn't it just been someone in the office?"

"No." Jennifer was adamant. "Everyone here knows better. We're all *extremely* careful about returning things in Jeff's office to their proper order. All I meant earlier was that *I*'ve added new screeners to the 'Submitted' shelf. I've also viewed several films and moved them to the 'Screened' section. I don't think anyone else has—"

"Really?" Tucker was excited again. Maybe she *was* right after all. "Would you mind checking them again? Don't touch them or anything, and leave them in the order they're in now, okay?"

"Of course. I'll just put you on hold."

"That's awesome, thanks!"

Tucker was put on a silent hold. She wondered if it cost a great deal extra to entertain callers with music while they waited. Music was better, because then you didn't wonder if you'd gotten cut off somehow. But you'd have to be really careful about choosing which kind of music to use, making sure it fit with your audience. She thought back to the hip-hop concert at El Rio before any of this had happened and tried to imagine if Blind Eye greeted callers with Katastrophe's "Let's F*ck and Then Talk about My Problems." She hummed a couple of lines and was having a good chuckle when Jennifer came back on the line, breathing hard.

"Tucker?"

"I'm still here."

"You're right!" Jennifer exclaimed. "*The Jammed* and *The Estrogen Files* are *both* filed under *T*. I would never have done something like that. I can't believe this. What should we do? Should I call the police?"

No, no. Don't steal my thunder. "We don't have anything to tell the police," Tucker said. "We need to know a lot more about who might have been in Jeff's office before we can jump to any conclusions. Why don't you give me a little while to confer with Yoshi, my boss, and get back to you?"

"But if they didn't find what they were looking for and there is a connection to Jeff's death? Is my staff in danger?"

I don't know. Maybe. Tucker tried to still the tremor in her voice before answering. She wasn't sure how to soothe Jennifer's fears.

"I'm sure it's all going to be okay," she said. It was the kind of thing she used to say to her sister, who'd been so sick as a kid. Over the years she'd repeated, "It's going to be okay," over and over like a prayer. She hadn't believed it then and she wasn't sure about it now, but she said it anyway.

It seemed to work. Jennifer gave Tucker until the next morning to talk with Yoshi and call back.

❖

Before she had even hung up the office phone, Tucker punched Yoshi's number into her cell. Her boss was going to be so proud of her. She was disappointed when the call went straight to voice mail. She didn't want to share her good news with an automated system, so she just asked Yoshi to call the office ASAP.

   She wanted to call Velvet next, shout into the answering machine that she'd proven Jeff didn't kill himself, but she didn't want to give her girlfriend false hope. Right now all they had were two screener DVDs out of alphabetical order. It was hardly a smoking gun.

   Instead she called Bud. She was surprised when she landed in voice mail again. Maybe he'd turned it off to interview hard4u, Tyrone's alibi for the Saturday night Jeff died. Tucker had insisted he handle that important interview partly out of spite to pay him back for making her crawl through that bathroom window.

   They'd met with Jeff's lawyer, Vincent Broadwell, that morning, and Bud was pretty confident they could rule out anyone offing the vic for financial gain. The DB didn't have any life insurance—in fact, Jeff didn't have a lot of paperwork on file. Maybe he shared Bud's less-than-positive view of lawyers: nothing but a bunch of shysters, if you asked him.

   Broadwell said he was an acquaintance of Jeff's, which probably meant fuck-buddy. The lawyer said he'd only come to represent Jeff recently, but it wasn't like in the movies where the guy's saying, if I get killed, look at so-and-so for it. They were just putting together a batch of standard material to do with the baby. Broadwell said they hadn't finished hashing out the new will, so an earlier version would stand. In that five-year-old document, Tyrone Hill stood to receive mostly sentimental objects while any funds reverted to Jeff's parents.

   After the discussion Bud told Tucker his money was on the Cocitaux broad. Broadwell had insisted that Jeff planned to play daddy, and way more than just in name. The lawyer happened to have both sides' paperwork. Cocitaux and Thompson's proposal would've significantly restricted Jeff's involvement with the child and barred Tyrone from *any* unsupervised contact. Neither side had managed to con the other into signing, but with Jeff out of the picture, it looked like everything worked out best for the two mommies. Even if Conant's parents sued for custody, the best they'd probably get was visitation rights. Judges hated taking kids away from the biological mother, even if she was a dyke.

   Tucker left a message that would make Bud grind his teeth. "While you were out, getting to know hard4u *really well*, I solved the case.

Call me." That ought to get his attention. Or maybe she should have mentioned beer and naked women.

Tucker hung up and wondered what someone would have hoped to find in Jeff's office. Why they would have searched the screeners. Maybe it was completely innocent. Some clueless new film director might have sent in a wrong version and wanted to get it back and swap it for the right one without admitting to his mistake. There could be a boring, logical explanation for the disorder. She closed her eyes conjured up the inside of Jeff and Tyrone's apartment. The *screeners*. He'd taken some of the screeners home to watch.

Tucker yanked open her top desk drawer. Damn, Bud had given her the disc he couldn't play on his DVD player. Where had she put that? She wasn't as organized as Jeff or Yoshi, or even Velvet, and some of the drawers of her desk were crammed with an assortment of music CDs, notes she scrawled down about Blind Eye procedure, sandwich bags she'd forgotten to take home, loose tampons, lip balm, a family picture of her, Hunter, and Anastasia, newspaper clippings of things she found interesting, and dried ramen packets.

Finally, she found the disc she was looking for tucked into Rose Beecham's *Grave Silence*, the book she'd gotten to read on BART trips *under* San Francisco Bay. The topic of a polygamous Mormon sect distracted her from the fact that she was in a train shaped like a metal hot dog that was rocketing through a tunnel like one of those vacuum message delivery systems, and if that tunnel sprung a leak they could all drown 135 feet underground. Tucker knew enough about cultish religions to totally forget, during those BART rides, about being sandwiched between the combined pressure of the Bay waters and its muddy bottom.

She popped the disc into her Mac. When it showed up on the screen, she left clicked and scrolled down to Get Info, hoping to find the name of the person who created it, the way Microsoft Word documents had this information listed. It didn't.

She closed the window and double clicked on the disc to see the menu of its contents. It wasn't a film at all.

❖

hard4u was a bearded white guy tripped out in jeans and a leather vest open across his hairy chest. Spiked pronglike bling glittered from his nipples, looking like Texas longhorns piercing his skin. AJ threw a stare back at Bud sitting on his ass in his Impala. When he up and smiled at her, she flipped him off and turned back to hard4u. Motherfuckin' Bud had gotten straight up giddy when he got here before and found stairs leading to hard4u's basement crib. That sure 'nough gave his punk ass an excuse to sit in the car.

She shoulda known straight off that he wouldn't go into no gay guy's crib and talk about sex. That's why she was here. Bud called Yoshi and said ain't no way his chair gonna make it. AJ was getting a damn good idea about why Yoshi wanted to bring her on. She needed someone pulling their own weight round here.

Even though AJ was far from her jurisdiction, she flashed her badge, slapping the leather closed before the POI noticed East Palo Alto PD. Dude gave his name as Peter Colt. He tried to shake her hand but she brushed him off and followed him into the dark and dirty living room. He flopped down into a La-Z-Boy and poked his finger toward a tattered couch piled with magazines.

When AJ knocked some aside, their slick covers slid right off each other and fell to the floor, falling open and revealing naked homeboys. Seemed like the guy was fond of brothers.

"Ya been kickin' it with Tyrone Hill?" she asked, not wasting any time.

He shrugged. "I kick it with a lot of guys."

AJ pulled out a snapshot of Tyrone.

Colt glanced at it. "Yeah, him I know. He was a good fuck."

"Ya get with him the night of November eighteenth?"

"What's this about? He say I do something?"

"No. I just got to establish his whereabouts the night in question. Was he here or not?"

"That was, like, a whole month ago. How the fuck am I supposed to remember?"

"Y'all hook up online?" That was Tyrone's story.

He consulted the photograph as though it would tell him. "Yeah, sounds right."

"Ya have some kinda archive on your computer?"

"Yeah, right. Totally. Hold on a minute, I can tell you." Colt got up and shuffled over to a computer in the corner of the room. He clicked a few keys and pushed the mouse around. AJ followed him and took a look over his shoulder. There was his handle, hard4u, and a November time stamp.

"That him?" she asked, pointin' at the screen name "HungNHorny."

"Yeah that's him. I remember. Said his old man was working late. He was looking to PNP with a top who'd ride him hard."

AJ read some of the text.

"Here it is. See, this is where I invited him over to my place. I stayed online till he showed. He must have got here around 6:26, since that's when I signed off. He was here maybe three hours. I got back online when he left." Colt pointed at the screen. The login time noted was 9:14 p.m.

Chapter Thirteen

"D amn it!"

Yoshi heard the muttered cursing while she was still in the hallway outside the Blind Eye entrance. It was disappointing to hear. Was this the kind of language her receptionist used when Yoshi was not supervising in person? It was utterly inappropriate. If a potential client were to step off the elevator and be accosted with gutter vocabulary, she would not blame them if they turned right around and left without ever making it all the way to Blind Eye's front desk. That would certainly be her response. Yoshi fretted that this irresponsible behavior might require some sort of reprimand. Perhaps if Tucker was contrite and offered a sincere apology, she could get away with a warning. This time.

Yoshi pushed the door open, stepped inside, and without a word to Tucker, removed her soft suede jacket, and hung it on the coat rack. She intended to go out again shortly to strike up another conversation with Tyrone Hill, but in the meantime it would be too hot in the radiator-heated office to remain bundled in winter garments.

"Hi, Yoshi," Tucker said, bouncing out of her chair on legs made of springs. The young receptionist oozed with exuberance.

"Good evening, Tucker. Am I to conclude that your colorful outburst was in celebration of a notable discovery?"

"Oh yeah it's fu—I mean *totally* awesome."

At least the girl was learning to avoid such language in Yoshi's presence. Obscenity was the crutch of the lazy or those with poor vocabularies. There were plenty of colorful phrases someone could use that more clearly conveyed the message they intended to relay.

"I think it is really significant." Tucker made another attempt at proper English. It was the least the descendant of British immigrants could do.

"What is it that you have found?" Yoshi asked.

"I don't know."

"Pardon me?" Perhaps Tucker intended to be funny. If so, it had not translated appropriately in her voice. Some jokers made their intentions known with body language—a wink, glimmer in their eye, or whatever—that might not be apparent to the blind.

"I mean, I don't know exactly what it *is*, but I do know what it's *not*. It's not a film screener."

"What, pray tell, is not a screener?" Yoshi was starting to feel exasperated.

"This disc that we got from Jeff's apartment, the one Bud couldn't get to play? It's not a DVD, it's a CD, and it's got data burned on it."

"Interesting. What manner of data?"

"Yeah, that's where I'm stuck. I haven't been able to tell. See, the whole thing is password protected, and I'm not a hacker or anything. I've tried a few things, but they're the kind of things people use when they want to make things easy. Passwords like one-two-three-four or a simple return."

Yoshi pulled a chair next to Tucker's desk, sat down, and began brainstorming possible passwords. She soon realized that not knowing the disc's owner made it far from likely they would correctly guess the proper code. Still, she ticked off a few. Each time, Tucker's fingers flew over the keys and then she verbally discounted the offering. Twenty minutes later Yoshi had run dry of ideas and the disc's security system still resisted entry.

"Without knowing more about the person who created the disc, our efforts are liable to remain futile," Yoshi said.

"True, but the one good thing is that most people use something fairly familiar. You know, because they have to *remember* it." Tucker sounded hopeful. "But at the same time they don't want it *so* familiar that anybody could figure it out. Like birth dates are way too easy, but another date might mean something."

"Would you mind playing a brainstorming game with me?"

"Sure."

"Let us pretend that the disc belonged to one of our POIs—say, Chase Devlin."

"You think it does? You think he killed Jeff?" Tucker jumped to conclusions.

"I would not presume so much. In our interview with Devlin I sensed there was something more, something he was withholding. It may be worth our time to attempt a few key words or dates that would be likely suspects for possible passwords. I will provide the code and you type it in, all right?"

"Cool."

"Let's start with his birthday. It is June 15, 1959."

Tucker typed it in as six keystrokes. "That's not it. Let me try it in different formats."

Yoshi listened as Tucker typed in various configurations of Devlin's birthday, and muttered, "Nope," as she discarded each in turn. "How about other important dates?" she asked. "Like when he started his company or got married or had kids."

"I do not believe he had either of the later two, but we can look up when he filed for a fictitious name."

When that bore no fruit, Yoshi paused for a moment, mulling the puzzle over in her mind. "Okay, try a bunch of things: money, Hollywood, erotica, all of the less dignified words for female anatomy."

"Nope," Tucker said to the last suggestion Yoshi had made. She had mentioned everything about Chase Devlin that she could think of and none of them had worked.

Tucker had also offered a few suggestions, like Devlin's astrological sign of Gemini.

"I think we should call it a night," Yoshi said, not admitting defeat but willing to retreat and regroup in the morning. "I have a friend with the SFPD who might be able to help. Still, I think this may be a significant discovery. Kudos, Tucker."

"Oh, snap! I almost forgot," Tucker babbled. "There's something else, too, something that might prove Jeff was murdered. Or at least that there are suspicious circumstances."

How someone in her employ could simply forget to mention a discovery of that stated magnitude, Yoshi did not know.

Tucker scrambled through mouse clicks until she had found what she wanted. "Right here," she announced as though Yoshi could see the evidence for herself. "Jeff was a stickler for order, right? His books are all alphabetized, but the titles that begin with *The* are arranged in order of the word that comes after."

"Yes, that is quite a standard practice, Tucker. I do not see the relevance."

"Okay, well, the screener films in his office? They *aren't* ordered that way. Someone put the ones with *The* next to the other *T* titles." Tucker made it sound like she had discovered the Holy Grail, but Yoshi still was not convinced of the significance.

"Granted, it might not have been Conant who placed them in that order, but surely, any number of people could have. You have no evidence of when that may have occurred or who may have done it."

"Maybe." Tucker sounded crestfallen. "But Jennifer Morris says the staff knew to put things back in the same order. Plus, don't you see how it ties in with this CD? What if Jeff accidentally got a hold of this disc? And then what if someone went to his office to get it back? And they went through all his DVDs, trying to find what they were looking for and they tried to put everything back the way it was, so nobody would know? Only they made a mistake."

"That, my dear Tucker, is rather a lot of conjecture," Yoshi said, pushing back her chair, standing, and stretching out her arms.

She barely heard Tucker's dejected "Oh."

"But it is a reasonable working hypothesis. One of the best we've had so far in this case."

"Really?" Tucker bounced back quickly.

"Yes. But remember that a hypothesis is not proof. We need more evidence before we can adequately evaluate its eloquence in explaining the details of the case. You have done well, Tucker. Why don't you call it a night and go home? I will get this disc to Ari Fleischman and we'll regroup in the morning."

Yoshi sensed Tucker move from behind the desk. She was surprised when Tucker bounded up to her and wrapped her in an impulsive hug. "Thanks," she whispered in her ear.

Tucker's warm breath unexpectedly excited her and sent a shiver down Yoshi's spine. Her whole body tensed. Then as quickly as Tucker had invaded her space, she let her go and went back to her desk as though nothing had happened. *What was that about*, Yoshi pondered.

Suddenly Yoshi felt certain she knew what Devlin's password was. "Wait," she said, dancing toward Tucker's desk. "I want to try one last thing. Try Tyrone."

Tucker typed in the name.

Yoshi held her breath, crossing her fingers.

"I'm sorry. I tried it without caps and all caps and backward. It was an awesome idea. Maybe it just isn't something that obvious."

"Captain Blackdong," Yoshi said.

Tucker burst into laughter. "It sounded like you said Black*dong*."

"I did. That was the name of the first adult film that Tyrone starred in. Just try it."

"Aye aye, my captain!" Tucker clattered at the keyboard. "Oh, my God."

"What?"

Tucker pushed back her chair and jumped up. "You did it, matey. We're in."

Yoshi was delighted. She just did not need to jump up and dance around like Tucker, doing the field-goal two-step. She allowed her trainee sixty seconds of jubilation before killing the mood. "Okay, enough already. I want to know what is on this disc. You know, the whole point of this exercise."

"Oh, right." Tucker collapsed back down in her chair, breathing hard from the exuberance, ignoring Yoshi's sarcasm. She rolled forward and focused in on the screen.

"Okay, let's start by going to Documents." Tucker quoted a batch of file names. "BrightS, Mailan, Tress, Kisser."

"Kisser?" Yoshi repeated. "Try that."

Yoshi waited with bated breath, hoping that whatever came up would be worth all the trouble they had gone to.

"That's weird."

"What is it?"

"It's Greek to me."

"Excuse me?"

"Yeah. The words have all been Greeked or something. It's not English."

"Is it a conversion issue or is it really another language? Try another file."

To their immense disappointment, they soon discovered that all of the documents had been encrypted. There was also a database file, but it required another password to enter and it was not the title of any Tyrone Hill adult film. Another forty-five frustrating minutes later, Yoshi convinced Tucker to call it a night and go home.

When the receptionist finally left at a little after six, Yoshi called Ari Fleishman.

"We need to meet," she said.

❖

It was only a phone call.

Velvet had not been to work since she'd accompanied Yoshi to
see the Marin County medical examiner. Her boss at the *San Francisco
Chronicle*, Stanley Wozlawski, thought she was wrapping up a piece
he'd assigned her, investigating a Bay Area residential de-gaying
program from which several troubled teens had gone missing. She had
pictures of the wayward kids and had initially planned to canvass the
Haight Street neighborhood, one of the first places queer runaways
congregated in San Francisco.

She wasn't doing that either. She'd turned her cell phone off days
ago. If friends wanted to reach her they could call her home number.
She hadn't been up for checking e-mail, either. By now there were
probably thousands of unread e-mails, and it would be easier just to
sign up for a brand-new address and start from scratch.

Velvet was lying in bed. Again. Or was it still? Unable to
concentrate on anything since they'd found Jeff's swollen corpse, she'd
barely dragged herself up in the evenings to be civil to Tucker. Her
"girlfriend," or whatever it was that Tucker had become in the last six
months, didn't seem to notice. In fact, Tucker seemed nearly phobic
about discussing death or even mentioning Jeff's demise. In the end
Velvet had said she needed some space.

Tucker kept calling and leaving messages. Most of them were
along the lines of *Hope you're feeling better,* as though the death of
a close friend was akin to a passing stomach flu and she should have
recovered by now.

No one seemed to understand why she was so insistent that Jeff's
death was something other than suicide. She'd gotten so fucking mad
at Yoshi for refusing to accept that she might know Jeff well enough to
know he would never have taken his own life. Why couldn't Yoshi just
trust her? That hurt. She was especially angry about Yoshi discounting
her instincts as clouded by emotion. Wasn't that what sexist men always
said about women?

So, yeah, she'd lashed out, admittedly. But only momentarily.
She'd driven toward home alone that evening after the memorial, but
before reaching her Bernal Heights residence she'd turned around and
sped back to where she left Yoshi, only to discover that Yoshi had,
once again, failed to have faith in her. She wondered how long Yoshi
had waited before calling a cab. Had she even waited for Velvet to

turn the corner? Or had she decided before she'd even gotten out of the car, before they'd even left the memorial, or sometime even before then—maybe when Velvet felt sick and had to leave Yoshi alone with the Marin County ME—that she could no longer trust Velvet…not her judgment, not her friendship, nothing?

After all these years of Velvet's loyal friendship, how could Yoshi do that to her? Yoshi had probably only called her that night so she wouldn't have to pay for a cab. Besides that first phone call in which Yoshi hadn't even apologized, she hadn't bothered checking in to make sure Velvet was okay since. For all she knew, Velvet could have gotten in an accident on the way home and be lying in a gutter somewhere.

If things were the other way around, Velvet was sure she'd be calling Yoshi every few minutes begging for forgiveness. She'd picked up the receiver a dozen times today, ready to break down and ask Yoshi to forgive her, even though it should rightly be the other way around. But had Yoshi tried calling *her* even once? No.

It was only because Yoshi and Tucker had abandoned her in her time of need that Velvet had even replied to yesterday's sympathetic message from Davina. Screw the both of them. They deserved each other. There were plenty of other girls out there, girls who thought she was hot and smart and accepted on faith that when she said Jeff didn't kill himself, she would be proven right in the end. Someone who would help her feel better *now*. Someone like Davina, who understood the depth of her pain and who actually seemed to care that Velvet was still terribly upset, grieving the loss of her friend.

She and Davina had eventually talked for hours last night, recalling those little moments with Jeff that had taken on greater meaning now that he was gone. They fantasized about what things would be like if Jeff hadn't died. The amazing queer films he'd produce, the children he'd parent. They bemoaned the fact that Isabelle and Theresa's child would grow up without knowing Jeff, a fact made worse because those two women seemed to prefer it that way.

Davina had agreed that Velvet should encourage Jeff's parents to fight for custody of their grandkid. She *wanted* to hear the stories about the childhood Velvet had shared with Jeff, the kind of stories Tucker had started wincing at because she'd already heard them once or twice before.

Tucker had never appreciated her. Meanwhile, Davina was a huge fan of Velvet's writing. She was not only aware of Velvet's impact on lesbian history, she had experienced and could recall the good old days when Velvet used to edit *Woymn*, the magazine she'd founded with Rosemary Finney. She had actually *read* and could both reference Velvet's work and place it within the context of other lesbian writers. None of which were things Tucker could do.

Unlike Tucker, Davina was closer to Velvet's own age, and she'd been a lesbian for over a decade. It had been kind of fun, at first, to introduce Tucker to lesbian history and culture. But Velvet was growing weary of being a tutor, as anyone would. It was just a relief to speak with someone who understood Lesbian 101, to whom she didn't have to give a crash course in LGBT history every time she dropped a name or phrase like "Joan Nestle," "Queer Nation," or "Stonewall Riots."

Perhaps most important of all, Davina Singleton understood the importance of *film*. She was a University of California film school graduate and had cultivated an addiction to the medium that rivaled Velvet's own appreciation of cult B-movie favorites, highbrow independents, lowest-common-denominator blockbusters, Oscar winners, and obtuse foreign flicks.

Velvet experienced her motion-picture obsession as a brand of collector's madness. Like fanatical PEZ dispenser owners the world over, her passion spilled from one room to the next until it threatened to engulf her entire home. Her living room housed three floor-to-ceiling shelves packed tight with DVDs carefully arranged in alphabetical order by title.

Davina had asked if she owned a particularly obscure Polish film, *Nothing*. Velvet did. After they shared a good laugh, Davina mentioned that she'd enjoy viewing the flick again. Perhaps sometime soon.

"Yes," Velvet had said. "That would be nice."

They'd moved on to other subjects. Davina mentioned she was dropping by Blue Plate, Velvet's favorite restaurant for comfort food, and before she knew it, Velvet was accepting Davina's offer to bring by an uplifting pot of handmade chicken noodle soup and fresh cornbread.

It's just dinner, Velvet had told herself. Weren't friends supposed to bring meals to their grieving pals so they wouldn't have to cook?

Tucker had called earlier and left a rather curt message saying that if Velvet wanted to see her, all she had to do was call. It seemed like a lot of work, calling. If Tucker really cared about her, wouldn't she have come by and talked to her in person? *Especially* since Velvet hadn't answered her messages? She could be lying dead on the floor and her so-called friends would just let her lie there, rotting, with rats nibbling at her toes. Or wild dogs. She imagined the scene from *Bridget Jones's Diary* with the heroine lying on the floor with dogs circling her corpse, part of her envisioned scenario of dying alone. If British Bridget could use that image as an excuse to hook up with a wanker, certainly it was reason enough for Velvet to accept a friendly dinner from another dyke.

After all, it used to be when someone close to you died, your neighbors took turns bringing over pots of food, picking up your mail, and checking to be sure the rats weren't chewing off your fingertips. But lately, in the city, Velvet had felt so alone, so distant from any sense of community that she'd felt a shot of adrenaline when Davina arrived. First, because the woman looked way too sexy to be schlepping soup across town. Plus, she oohed and ahed her way through Velvet's apartment, delighted by the movie posters receiving fine-art treatment in framed and lighted displays that lined the hallway of her shotgun house. Culled from Velvet's private reserve, currently showing were seventies sexploitation films with teasingly kitschy titles like *The Devil's Playground, Chained Heat,* and *Barbed Wire Dolls*.

Davina shared witty comments about the directors, actors, and sometimes even stunt doubles from nearly each and every film. Velvet had felt a kinship right away, but in Davina's presence felt something else, something more urgent. Desire.

When they'd ended up in Velvet's bedroom, both women knew what was going to happen. Velvet deactivated her guilt mechanisms. Surprisingly, this time she had to work at it a way she'd never done previously, assuaging her conscience with rationalizations: *It's only a one-night stand. Another notch in the belt. Meaningless. I don't just want this, damn it, I need it.*

Velvet had been hungry for an experience that would take her beyond her current circumstance. Her need felt so base, so primal, and Davina was clearly eager to acquiesce. The strange coincidence that Davina looked slightly reminiscent of a high-school classmate Velvet had desperately desired once upon a time only intensified Velvet's craving. She was under Davina's skirt, and between her legs, and out of her mind in no time.

Velvet checked the time and dialed Davina's number. They'd talked about meeting after Davina finished work today, if Velvet was in the mood. Scoring with Davina had lifted her feelings, and today she actually felt up for leaving her house. Velvet figured they'd have one more tumble in the sheets before she sent the girl packing. Then she knew she would have to face up to her life and figure out what she was doing with Tucker and how to make amends with Yoshi.

Meantime, she deserved one more night for herself. And she was going to enjoy it in the way only possible with a new playmate. For the first time in weeks she wasn't thinking about Jeff Conant at all.

❖

Tucker pulled crumpled bills from her front jeans pocket, paid the cashier, and accepted the plastic bag of square Styrofoam containers. She smiled to herself as she exited the Thai Restaurant onto Mission Street. Velvet was going to be surprised. The bag contained her favorite Thai dishes, pad Thai and panang curry. In her other hand Tucker carried a bouquet of yellow roses and a bottle of Napa Valley Chardonnay that the liquor store owner said would go well with Thai food. Her well-worn backpack bounced against her spine as she walked.

She was sure Velvet would be too tired to cook when she got home from the *San Francisco Chronicle*. Obviously she'd been swamped with work and that was why hadn't been able to call Tucker back during the day. When she came home to find her favorite meal waiting for her, Velvet would be so relieved she'd forget she wanted space. She shouldn't be alone right now, anyway, not while she was still so depressed about Jeff's death. Besides, Velvet had accused Tucker of not being spontaneous.

It could be true. Growing up with an autistic brother made her whole family a little compulsive about maintaining structure. Hunter demanded routines. They ate at exactly the same time every day. Hunter always used the same utensils. He dressed in the same order. It might have had rubbed off. But here she was, planning this dinner at the last minute. That should show Velvet how spontaneous she could be.

The winter evening was already dark and the cold nipped at her bare hands and exposed ears. Still, it wasn't anything like Idaho's winters. Here it never seemed to even dip below freezing. Where they'd have snowstorms from October to April back home, in San Francisco there'd be a cold rain. Although it didn't get as cold as Idaho, there was something about the humidity that made 45 degrees feel a lot colder than it should.

The darkness made Tucker a little nervous about walking through the Mission District alone. Back home she'd never been afraid of the dark, but here— There was something about the presence of people that made her nervous. She wasn't afraid of the dark itself, but the people who could hide in it. The kind of people who'd throw your baby off the Golden Gate Bridge if something went wrong. People were scary.

Was there something on that CD that had cost Jeff his life, whether or not someone else actually did the deed? Tucker wondered what Yoshi was going to do now that they could open the file. They were halfway there. Maybe they could find a nerd who knew encryption or had some software to unlock it.

At Cortland Avenue, Tucker turned left. In doing so she moved away from the businesses that previously lit her path. Here there were no businesses and the streetlights were scattered a block apart. A block up the hill, she glanced behind her. There was no one there. Passing the darkened store windows, she skirted their murky doorways and stepped off the sidewalk.

At the sound of distant footsteps behind her, she felt her heart catch. A surge of adrenaline made her walk faster. Doing so, she could only hear her own footsteps. She stopped briefly and could still hear the footsteps. They were closer. She glanced around and saw a shrouded figure coming up behind her. She rushed around the corner and crouched down next behind the wheel of a tall SUV, next to a white picket fence. Her heart pounded so loudly, she was afraid the man could hear it and pinpoint where she was hiding. She breathed in and out deeply trying to calm herself.

Was this how Yoshi felt, being blind? It must be like walking in the dark all the time. Tucker pressed herself down by the tire, clutching her flowers, and silently prayed the heavy footsteps would pass her by.

They did. Without pause.

She stayed still until the sound faded away, then stood and shook out the kinks that had formed in her legs. She was glad she hadn't set off the car alarm and hoped the Neighborhood Watch hadn't called the cops on her. With her heartbeat returning to normal, she continued on her way.

Five minutes later she was on the steps of Velvet's shotgun-style

Victorian. The windows were dark and Velvet's Toyota Celica was not in the driveway. She had beaten Velvet home. Tucker was happy. She could set up a romantic dinner with candles and the works. She retrieved the hidden door key from its hiding place tucked under the ledge of the cement stairway, pulled open the squeaky screen door, and rattled the key in the sticky lock. The heavy door opened inward.

Tucker pulled the key out, picked up the bag of takeout, stuck the flowers under her arm and held the wine bottle in her right. She stepped inside and swung the door closed behind her. The hall was dark, but a faint light shined in the kitchen. Tucker felt for the light switch with the back of her right hand, the wine bottle bouncing lightly against the sheetrock. She thought she heard something move in the back office. Maybe Velvet had parked inside the garage.

"It's me, Tuck!" she called loudly, not wanting to frighten her lover if Velvet hadn't heard her come in.

She paused. The noise didn't repeat. Of course Velvet wasn't home. It was just Tucker's mind playing tricks on her. She stepped forward. Her knuckles found the edge of the light switch plate. A floorboard squeaked behind her. Her heart in her throat, Tucker swung around, in time to see the blur of motion. Someone had been hiding in the space behind the door.

Choking on fear, Tucker opened her mouth to scream. Before she could force a sound past the lump in her throat, a meaty hand blocked its escape and she was grabbed roughly. The hand pressed hard against her mouth, bruising her lips against her teeth. She tasted blood. The Thai food slid from her hand. The flowers fluttered down after it. The wine bottle slipped from her fingers, hit the floor with a thud, bounced off the wood and clattered against the closed door. Tucker yanked at the hand at her mouth. She couldn't pry it away. She scratched her short nails against his skin.

"Goddamn," a deep, raspy voice swore.

Another hand wrapped around her throat and pressed on her windpipe. She gagged and kicked frantically.

"Stop struggling, bitch."

She dropped her hands. Tried to breathe through her nose but it didn't seem enough. The grip on her throat loosened.

Down the hall a shadowy figure stepped out of Velvet's office.

"It's not here," the second man said, disappointed. "Is that her?"

"The girl from the office, yeah," the man holding her said. "You want me to search her?"

Tucker tried to shake her head. She didn't want to be pawed at.

The man in front of her stepped forward. With all the light behind him, she could not make out his features. He seemed to be less than four inches taller than her. He reached behind his back and produced something dark, which he pointed at her stomach. Light reflected off the weapon. A knife? A gun? She wasn't sure.

"Scream or try anything stupid and you're dead. Got it?"

Tucker made a nod. The hand moved away from her mouth. She took deep gasping breaths.

The man behind her smelled of sweat and Old Spice. He roughly yanked off her knapsack and kicked it down the hallway to his friend like it was a soccer ball.

He wrenched one of her arms behind her and twisted it until she thought it would break. She cried out and bent away from the pain. He ran his free hand across her shoulders.

She flinched. "Please stop. I don't have any money, I swear."

They ignored her. Old Spice pressed his palm against her back and slid it down toward her butt. The other man crouched down and unzipped her knapsack, dumping out its contents. Her change of clothes and forensic books fell to the floor with a thump, while loose papers drifted slowly feathers on the wind.

"What are you looking for?" Tucker asked, afraid she knew already. If she didn't give them what they wanted, would they kill her and dump her body off the bridge? Was that what had happened to Jeff? Why didn't he just tell them he had some screeners at his home? Had he been worried about them hurting Tyrone? Did he know what they wanted and where it was because he'd hidden it? What would be so important that he would rather die than tell? Or maybe he had told them and they'd killed him anyway.

The man searching her bag opened the smaller pocket in front. Her keys clattered to the floor followed by her wallet and a handful of pens. At each item he pulled from the bag, the man down the hall seemed to get angrier. He shook the empty bag, threw it angrily to the floor, and kicked it. When he stopped and stared in their direction, Old Spice tensed again, as though he was afraid of his partner.

"Where's the goddamn disc?" he snarled at Tucker.

If she told them where it was, would they let her go? They would probably kill her anyway. As long as she knew where it was and they didn't, they wouldn't kill her, would they?

"What disc?" Tucker feigned ignorance.

"You know damn well what disc." He waved the weapon and moved menacingly toward her. "The one you took from that dead fag's place."

How did they know that? Had they been watching her? Following her around?

"Where's Velvet?"

"Shut up." He was almost in her face now. Up close she could tell he was wearing a dark ski mask. She was relieved not to see his features. Maybe they wouldn't kill her if she couldn't identify them.

"I don't have any disc, I swear."

"Hurry up," he commanded the guy frisking Tucker. "The other one could be home any minute."

She sighed in relief, then immediately tensed again when Old Spice cupped her ass. She jerked away from him with a force that surprised her and kicked backward, connecting with his shin. Suddenly she was out of his grip and pressing her back against the wall, yelling, "Leave me the fuck alone!"

The masked man rushed her. She cowered against the wall. He lifted the thing in his hand and pressed it against her temple, the cold of the metal proving it to be a handgun. He caught her eyes with his and his breath came out hot and sour on her face.

"Where's the disc?" he demanded, dimpling her skin with the barrel of the gun.

Time seemed to slow. Tucker wondered if she was going to die. She'd heard that when people face death, they are suddenly struck by an overwhelming feeling of wanting to live. The survivor who Velvet had interviewed for the Bridge suicide piece said he felt that, on the way down. Her life wasn't flashing in front of her eyes, but somehow that didn't seem to prove anything. She'd always felt sort of guilty for the life she'd had, being healthy when her siblings weren't, so she wouldn't have minded if the cold bite of the barrel in her temple had given her an epiphany. It did not.

"Stop wasting our time, bitch. Where is it?"

She heard the sharp click. Tucker knew that sound. It was the safety switch being turned off. Her legs shook beneath her, her stomach fell like a lead weight, and she could feel the cold sweat on the back of her neck. She opened her mouth. It was so dry she could barely speak the words.

"Everything we got from the apartment is at the office. The Blind Eye Office."

She had to tell, and she still made her answer vague, refusing to concede that she knew about "a disc." It would be okay. The Flood Building had security and they would probably be caught breaking into the Blind Eye Offices. Except she had the keys.

Tucker barely heard the sound of a car door slam from the street. Everything suddenly moved in high speed. Old Spice stepped toward her. A small shadow followed him. Tucker registered the wine bottle flying like a bird toward the ceiling. Then, as though it had been shot, the bird plunged toward her head and everything went black.

CHAPTER FOURTEEN

W hat's up?" Ari Fleishman asked when Yoshi slid into her seat at Dolores Park Café. She opened her purse, found the encrypted disc, and passed it across the table to the detective.

"What is this? Your YouTube party videos?"

Ari liked to joke. Yoshi didn't get small talk, so she often skipped the useless chatter that passed for courtesy these days.

"This disc is password protected and it seems to be encrypted. I need it broken into. And I need it done quick and quietly. I don't want it to get out that you have this."

"Damn, what is it?" Ari grabbed the disc. "Proof of weapons of mass destruction in Iraq? Hillary's game plan for winning the election?"

"I don't know. It may or may not have anything to do with national security."

"Intriguing." Ari whistled.

Yoshi ignored his antics. "I hear you have a genius hacker working for the department. Could you get him to take a crack at it?"

"Maybe. Dare I ask where you got it?"

"Jeff Conant's residence. But I did not break in, if that is what you are implying." No point in mentioning that PI wannabe Tucker *had* crossed that line. "I had a key." She also did not tell him the key was *not* from Tyrone. What he did not know would not hurt him.

"So, the disc is his or the boyfriend's?"

"I don't think so. It was with some film screeners Conant had brought home to review. It is possible that it came into his possession by accident. Which reminds me—" She took a deep breath and went for broke. "Can you send a CSI team over to Conant's office and dust for prints?"

"A month after the fact? What's the *point*? Anything they found would just be thrown out because the scene hasn't been secure."

Yoshi sighed. "Sometimes I forget how you cops work. I guess we'll do it ourselves. It's just that we have reason to believe that someone who was looking for this disc thought it was at Conant's office and searched for it. They may have left their prints on the jewel cases. If the prints were collected and run through IBIS, and there was a hit, we just might be able to identify a potential suspect."

"You really think Conant was *murdered*?" Ari pushed his black curls away from his forehead.

"I am not sure, but I *am* starting to think there is more to the story than a simple suicide. Whoever owns the disc went to great lengths to make sure it was not easily readable, and that intrigues me. What are they hiding? And why was it in Conant's possession? If someone did rifle through his office trying to find it, I want to know who and why and whether it has anything to do with his death. You knew him. Don't you want to know what happened? Don't you think we owe him that?"

"Okay, fine," Ari said. "I'll send someone over. But you better hope there's something there and that I get a collar off all this."

"You are the one who will get all the glory," Yoshi teased. "So, can I count on you to forward this disc to your tech or not?"

"Yes, but I think this means you owe me."

"Not unless he actually gets something. Now, if you are done with me, I need to get to the hospital and visit a certain patient. I have a few more questions to ask him." Yoshi stood up and slung her purse over her shoulder.

Ari stopped her with a gentle hand on her arm. "Tyrone Hill? He's not there."

"He is no longer at the hospital? Have they already transferred him to the detox program?"

"No, he's no longer in our custody."

"You *released* him?" Yoshi was incredulous. She knew overcrowding at the residential treatment centers could lead to premature release dates, but this was ridiculous. It had only been four hours since she last spoke with Tyrone, and she was sure it would take longer than that for him to break his methamphetamine addiction.

"We had no choice. Somehow he managed to get a high-priced

lawyer to spring him. The guy marches into the DA's office demanding that Hill be released immediately. He's with some schmancy-pants law firm—don't ask me how an unemployed crankhead ranks that kind of legal bling, but apparently, Hill does."

"What about the plea deal?" Yoshi asked. AJ had arranged for Hill to plead no contest to drug charges in exchange for a sentence confining him to a residential treatment center.

"They rejected it. Next thing you know, Hill's poured into an Armani suit and standing in front of a judge pleading not guilty. I was sitting in the courtroom on another matter and I swear I could see the lawyer's lips move, but it was a damn good show, him pulling the strings and throwing his voice like that. The prosecutor got bail set at fifty thousand, and fancy-pants announces that Chase Devlin himself is fronting the capital. Sure as hell, there was Devlin sitting there pleased as punch. I guess that guy at the memorial was right—Devlin and Hill *are* a couple."

Yoshi was silent, thinking.

"What, you don't think so?"

"They both told me otherwise. You didn't put a tail on Tyrone, did you?" she asked hopefully.

"He's not a suspect as far the force is concerned. He's just a small time user out on bail."

As Ari walked her out to the curb and flagged down a taxi, Yoshi wondered why Devlin had chosen to spring Tyrone. Did he just want to spend time with him or was he hoping to keep Tyrone quiet about something? Did Tyrone have information connecting Devlin to Conant's death? Or was this evidence of Tyrone's claim that Devlin owned and controlled him? She did not think Tyrone had killed Jeff, but she did think Tyrone had information he had not yet shared with the Blind Eye staff. Now, with him under Devlin's control, she wondered if she would ever get a chance to learn the truth.

"Let me know as soon as you have something on the CD," she said as Ari opened the taxi door for her. Was there information on there worth killing for? If so, what? And who was trying to get it back?

❖

Velvet laughed at something Davina had just said. They were driving back from dinner at the Rickshaw Stop, a Hayes Valley bar-restaurant-club combo that was so cool the *SF Weekly* had likened it to "being in Katie Holmes's vagina." That was before the indie star of *Pieces of April* married Tom Cruise and went all Scientology. Velvet had never eaten there before, but it seemed safe to bet that she wouldn't run into Tucker or Yoshi.

They stopped to wait for a light to change when refrains of the *Law & Order* theme song informed Velvet that she had a phone call. She glanced at the number, didn't recognize it, and sent the call to voice mail. She turned onto Cortland Avenue and heard the tone that marked her messages. Then the phone rang again. This time Davina picked it up and read the number out loud. It was the same as last time. Probably some telemarketer.

Davina hit the End button and started in on a story about an annoying telemarketer in her past. There was another message beep.

"This one's a text message," Davina said. "Want me to read it?"

"Sure."

Davina pressed the appropriate keys. At the sharp inhalation of her breath, Velvet glanced over and found the color drained from Davina's face.

"What?"

The phone began to ring again. Davina shoved it at her. "You'd better answer."

"Why? What's going on?"

"It said if you didn't answer your phone, Tucker Shade would be sorry."

As soon as the words registered, Velvet snatched up the phone and hit Send. "Hello."

"Velvet Erickson?" The masculine voice sounded like it had been altered.

"Yes?"

"We have your friend Tucker Shade."

"Who the hell is this? What do you mean, you *have* her?"

"Shut up, bitch. If you want to see her alive, you need to listen carefully."

She felt the air suck from her lungs and she teared up. "Don't hurt her. What do you want?"

"Your friends at Blind Eye have something that doesn't belong to them. We want it back. We have something you want and we're willing to make a trade."

"Of course, anything, just tell me what you want."

"Tell that blind gal pal of yours that we want the disc back. We'll give you one hour to get it and then we will call you back."

"No, wait." Velvet needed more information.

"We sent you a photo you might enjoy," the caller menaced, then hung up.

Velvet pulled into her driveway, and killed the engine. Davina started to ask a question. Velvet held up a hand to cut her off and punched in numbers for her voice mail and password. Holding her breath, her heart banging against her ribs like a bird caught in a cage, she clicked on the message photo, and gasped. The image was of Tucker, her hair disheveled, her head sagging to one side, a blindfold covering her eyes. Had they already hurt her? Velvet was suddenly overwhelmed with the desire to lash out, to make them pay for harming her sweet girl.

She darted from the Celica and up her front steps with Davina trailing behind her. The front door slipped open under her hand, before she could get the key in the lock. She immediately thought back to the night when the police tore her place apart, when they thought she'd killed her ex-lover and arch nemesis Rosemary Finney. The hallway floor was a mess. Pad Thai spilled from an open Styrofoam box, pieces of broken glass and the remains of a wine bottle were scattered across papers, a pair of Tucker's jeans lay jumbled near a small puddle.

Velvet felt sick to her stomach. Davina put an arm on her back and Velvet jerked away. She wanted the other woman to go away, to never have been here. If Velvet hadn't just been out at dinner with a distraction, Tucker wouldn't have gotten hurt.

"You need to go," she said, not looking at Davina. She was suddenly awash in guilt and anger and panic.

"Are you sure? Don't you want—"

Velvet looked the woman right in the eyes so she'd understand. "I want you to leave. Now."

Davina blanched. Perhaps she'd seen the anger and hatred in Velvet's eyes.

Velvet slid down the wall until she was sitting next to Tucker's things. Her hands were shaking and when she tried to dial the speed dial number for Yoshi, her fingers slipped and she had to start over. Tears were pooling in her eyes when Yoshi answered.

"Yosh?" Velvet's voice cracked.

"Velvet? Is that you? I'm so glad to hear from you. Since the other night—"

"Yoshi." Velvet cut her off. "This is an emergency. Tucker's been kidnapped."

"Kidnapped?" Yoshi obviously found the idea was preposterous. "Are you sure this isn't some kind of joke?"

"Yes, I'm *sure*. They sent me a photo. She's tied up and blindfolded, what if she's been hurt? I couldn't live with myself." Velvet began to sob.

"Velvet, please, get a hold of yourself so I can understand. Who sent you photos?"

"I don't know who they are. They just called my cell phone and told me they wanted to trade Tucker for some CD they say you have. And they sent a photo to prove they had her. They took her from my house, Yoshi. They were in my *house*."

"Where are you now?" Yoshi's concern came through the phone.

"Home."

"Have you been through the house?"

"No."

"Called the police?"

"No."

"Okay, I want you to leave the house right now. This instant. Get in your car and lock the doors. Then call the police and tell them you had a break-in."

"All right." Velvet pushed herself up off the floor, casting a suspicious look toward the back of her dark house. She sure hoped the intruder wasn't still there, but Yoshi was right, better safe than sorry.

"They'll kill Tucker if they don't get this CD."

"I promise you, we will *not* let that happen. Did they give you instructions for the exchange?"

"They said they would call back in an hour."

"All right, Velvet, I'm going to take care of a few things on this end and then call you back."

❖

Yoshi leaned forward in the seat and directed the cab driver to turn around and head back to the Mission. She needed to get that disc back. Immediately. And she needed reinforcements.

Who would have done this? Who could connect Velvet to the mysterious CD? Had someone been following Tucker and seen her all but living at Velvet's place? What about the other Blind Eye staff? The idea that she might have been under surveillance since the night of the memorial made her skin crawl. Who would be willing to go to these lengths to get back a computer disc?

A man's voice sounded in her head and a picture formed in her mind's eye. *Chase Devlin.* The image probably wasn't accurate, but she though her instincts might be. Unless she had terribly misjudged someone, like the lesbian moms-to-be, Devlin was the only figure who had emerged from her investigation as someone with the connections and determination to instigate a crime like this. She could not imagine why a man with so much to lose would get involved in kidnapping and possibly murder, but Devlin seemed arrogant enough to think he could do as he pleased with impunity. If Devlin had Tucker, she would not be anywhere near his estate. He would not muck up his manicure by getting his hands dirty. Some underlings would be doing his dirty work for him, perhaps the heavy-booted presence she had felt in Devlin's office, hulking behind his desk. AJ had described the two as thick-necked muscle men. Had the same two thugs tried to get the disc from Jeff? What was he doing with it in the first place? Yoshi wondered if he'd even known what he had. He could have had possession of it by some kind of fluke. She wondered whether Tyrone was working with Devlin somehow. She hoped not. Yoshi's thought returned to Tucker, who would assume the disc was still at the office. What would Devlin's boys do to her if they thought she had lied to them?

Yoshi tried to purge the ghastly images from her imagination and quickly dialed detective Chico Hernandez. In one breath she told him everything she knew about the case—at least the parts he needed to know, such as Velvet's break in. She neglected to mention the kidnap. Too many cooks in the kitchen could screw up everything. Yoshi prodded him to send a couple of uniforms over to Blind Eye's office, and another past her house. If these perps had raided Velvet's house looking for the disc, they might try the same tactic at other locations as well.

Still, Yoshi did not want to send Bud or even AJ to check for further break-ins, not when she was certain that now that they had a hostage, they wouldn't waste their time getting caught in a simple B&E. Let the uniforms deal with that possibility.

She called Bud next, wanting to give him some extra time to mobilize. He exploded with a string of expletives when she told him about Tucker. He was apparently still with AJ. The duo had gone for a drink after their interview with Tyrone's sex buddy, but they were immediately ready to spring into action.

"I'm entrusting you with Chase Devlin," Yoshi said. "I think we may find that the two goons we met at his office are facilitating the exchange, but use caution. He is bound to have other security. Do not make your move until I give you authorization, is that clear?"

Bud had handed the phone over to AJ, whose breathless answer assured Yoshi that she was pushing Bud's chair and racing to his car as they spoke. After warning AJ that they might find Tyrone at Devlin's, Yoshi hung up and called Ari Fleishman.

"Miss me already?" he asked.

"I need to get that disc back, immediately," Yoshi said, no time for pleasantries.

"Good evening to you, too, Yoshi. I told you I'd call you the minute our tech has anything."

"Damn it, Ari, I can't afford to wait. I need it now."

Ari sounded stunned. No doubt since Yoshi was always so proper, he had never heard her swear in all their years as colleagues. "Why? What's going on?"

"Whatever is on that disc apparently means an awful lot to someone, and they have kidnapped Tucker Shade. If the kidnappers don't get the CD, she could be killed. I need it back."

"Wait. Someone *kidnapped* her? Yoshi, this is serious, I have to call this in."

"Please don't." San Francisco did not often invite the FBI to get involved in high-profile kidnapping cases. In Yoshi's experience, the Bureau could easily lose sight of the captive in their zeal to catch the perpetrator. In this instance, she was more interested in getting Tucker back safely than in closing a case.

"You know I have to."

"Fine, at least give me a half an hour before you do."

"Do you have a drop location?"

"Not yet. Ari, I *need* that disc."

"If someone is going to all this trouble to reclaim it, doesn't that imply it's somehow damning? What if the information on that disc implicates someone in Jeff Conant's death?"

"I'm willing to run that risk. Plus, I am relatively certain that our kidnappers will help us access the CD."

"Really? What do you know that I don't?"

"You'll see."

"Take a blank disc instead," Fleishman insisted. "And let me know where the drop is so I can bring in a team."

"I will let you in on it *only* if I have the *real* disc at the drop. I can't make a copy because of the encryption."

Ari knew she was like a pit bull and when she got something in her maw she would not let go. "You can have access to it, but I'll need it as evidence as well," he said. "Meet me at the Mission precinct. I'll be out front."

"I am on my way there now, then I have to pick Velvet up. The kidnappers are calling on her cell phone."

Yoshi heard him swear under his breath and knew he was probably feeling played since she'd left for the Mission station before she got his go-ahead. She hoped she was not pushing him too far, but Tucker Shade's life meant more than Ari's friendship at this point.

❖

It was a smart move on the kidnappers' part, choosing Fisherman's Wharf, where patrons could take a sightseeing trip to Alcatraz, buy tacky tourist tchotchkes, and indulge in fresh-out-of-the-sea crab and the city's special sourdough bread. Because of the design of the pier as a shopping magnet, it wasn't as linear as the name would suggest. Some stores and cafés jutted out in strange angles, creating the kind of architectural nooks and crannies someone needing a hiding spot would love. The cacophony of noises would also consume the sound of gunshots, and there were plenty of befuddled out-of-towners to get in the way of a real chase.

This close to Christmas, the pier would be packed with holiday shoppers joining the regular tourists. No vehicles were allowed, which meant that everyone was on foot. The police would not be able to evacuate a large crowd of people quickly without starting a panic, and in all of the pedestrian chaos, the kidnappers could easily disappear into the crowd. If that failed, they were guaranteed their pick of civilian hostages and the assurance that the police would not risk endangering Wharf visitors through a shoot-out.

Still, the Wharf was bounded on three sides by water. Unless the kidnappers had a boat at their disposal, they would have to go out the way they came in. The police could set up a line there and effectively trap them on the pier.

The voice on the phone had insisted—as voices were wont to do in kidnap cases—that if the cops showed up, harm would befall the kidnap victim. Yoshi had been instructed to take a Yellow Cab, and when the car pulled up outside Velvet's Bernal Heights home, the Pakistani driver was swarmed by Fleishman's hastily organized team. Velvet said he went quite ashen and insisted he was not involved in a kidnapping scheme. Still, the SFPD commandeered his cab, swept it for bombs and bugs, and installed one of their own—an elite sharpshooter—as the driver. Another officer wedged herself in the front passenger foot space and was covered by a blanket.

The holiday rush meant parking was even more intense than usual. Yoshi was thankful they were in a cab. The kidnappers hadn't provided an explicit location for the exchange and she feared it would be all too easy to lose what Velvet called their pigtail, the police officer who would be trailing them into the thick of the crowd. Yoshi felt apprehensive, all the more so because her experience at the hip-hop concert the previous month had crystallized just how frightening crowds could be for her. She could not afford missteps, not while Tucker's life was on the line.

Velvet dragged Yoshi by one arm past the aerial acrobatics of tourists on the bungee-trampoline near the entrance to the pier. As they plowed into the wall of holiday shoppers, the crowd parted around them like water off a boat's bow. Yoshi's senses were quickly overwhelmed, accosted by a multitude of converging voices, sweating bodies, bad perfume and grooming products, marijuana smoke, the barking of the Pier's renowned sea lions, the subtle movement of the wooden planks under the weight of a hundred tromping feet, the distant sound of waves beating against wooden pillars, and an incessant jangle of Christmas music piping through the loudspeakers.

Pedestrians pressed against them, dragging them down. Bodies knocked against hers. Though different cultures had varying needs for personal space, during holiday shopping frenzies there seemed to be an unspoken consensus that skin-on-skin contact, stepping on toes, and knocking shoulders was unavoidable. This was why Yoshi did her shopping online.

Years ago, she had braved the pier's fabricated aura in order to purchase movie paraphernalia for Velvet at Pier 39's Hollywood USA. It was her last trip there. There were over a hundred shops on Pier 39 and even if she wasn't blind, navigating around all of them was difficult. Velvet stopped suddenly and Yoshi barreled into her cushiony backside. Velvet's phone was barely audible over the noise.

"Hello?" she shouted to be heard. "Where?" She pressing her face to Yoshi's ear and yelled, "The carousel."

Yoshi tucked her right hand into her jacket pocket and typed a text message to Fleishman. One advantage of her new cell phone was that the keys provided tactual differentiation, so placing a call or sending a text message did not require her to look at the phone. Even if they were being watched, no one could see her sending the message.

The carousel was located on the first level near the Bay end of the pier. It was a brilliant choice for a handoff. The spot was always packed to the gills with freely spending tourists juggling bags and binoculars while their candy-faced children ran around and screamed in delight. Cops and shamuses alike wouldn't want to endanger the kids on the carousel.

Yoshi remembered from childhood that this famed antique attraction was hand-painted with scenes of famous San Francisco landmarks, including the Golden Gate Bridge, Lombard Street, and Alcatraz. It also had moving horses, rocking chariots, spinning tubs and swings, all illuminated by twinkling lights and accompanied by traditional organ music.

She could judge their progression by the carousal tune, which got louder as they approached. "Do you see anything?" she asked.

She hoped Velvet would not see police officers. She wanted them to be there, certainly, but to remain invisible until they were needed.

"No." Velvet sounded slightly alarmed. "What if they don't show?"

Yoshi's reply was cut off when yet another person knocked into her. She stepped aside to let them pass. The person didn't move on. Instead something hard and cold was jammed into her back. She froze. Hot breath, reeking of salami and stale coffee, gave her a wholly unwelcome shiver.

"You got the disc?" the man snarled. The accent was Mid-Atlantic, hard to place but definitely not native Californian.

She shook her head, then tilted up her chin to indicate Velvet in front of her.

"Tell your friend not to turn around. Just get the disc."

Yoshi slid up to Velvet. "Don't turn around," she whispered.

"Did you hear them? Are they here?"

"There's a gun at my back." Yoshi enunciated her words carefully.

Velvet stiffened. "Fuck."

"It's all right. Give me the disc without looking back."

Yoshi heard Velvet rustling in her clothes, pulling the disc from her favorite hiding pace under her shirt. Yoshi felt the pressure of the disc against her outstretched hand, accepted the still-warm contraband, and quickly stuffed it down the front of her own trousers.

Suddenly she was yanked backward. She lost her hold on Velvet and bounced off other bodies as she was hauled in reverse through the crowd. Then just as suddenly the noise of the crowd reduced and she no longer could feel people around her. She guessed her abductor had pulled her into one of the wooden-plank little alleys between the pier buildings. She thought they were on the north side of the pier but it was hard to keep a sense of direction sometimes. The sea lions were louder. She was pulled around and pressed back against the wooden facade of the building. It occurred to her that she herself might not make it out of this encounter unscathed.

"Give me the disc."

"That's not how it works," Yoshi said, hoping her voice did not betray the fear she felt climbing up her mouth. "I need assurances that Tucker is unharmed."

"Your friend is fine. She's right there."

"You *know* I'm blind. I will not give you the disc until I hear Tucker say she's okay." Yoshi believed the kidnappers had chosen her for the exchange because she was blind. They would not have been able to walk through the pier with their visages obscured by masks, but they thought their identity would be safe with Yoshi. She would find some way to take advantage of their assumptions.

"I bet I can make you."

"I'll scream rape," Yoshi bluffed.

"I'll shoot you," he growled.

She shook her head. "You won't risk the noise. You better hurry. My friend will find us soon, or someone will see us."

He swore and pulled her to where a breeze peppered her with salty spritz from the Bay. He spoke urgently in a hushed voice. "Bring her out."

Thirty seconds ticked by very slowly before she heard "Yoshi!" It was Tucker's unmistakable voice.

"Are you all right?" Yoshi asked.

"Yeah. I'm okay." Tucker was relieved; Yoshi could hear it in her voice.

Yoshi retrieved the disc and held it out. Her guard snatched it away. "Try anything and we hurt the kid."

He backed away from her. She heard the click of something opening and a popping noise that reminded her of her own laptop. Yoshi was expecting this. She was even counting on it. *They are going to play the disc.*

"Okay," he said. "I'm ready."

His co-conspirator, the man Yoshi assumed was restraining Tucker, did not answer. As she hoped, her man was on the phone and soon he would have the password to access the material on the disc. Whoever was on the other end of the line—Chase Devlin, she suspected—wanted to be sure that the disc they had was the correct one. The only way for his henchmen to authenticate it would be for them to access a file.

He typed the password on the keyboard.

"Yeah," he said. "I'm in."

Now he would receive instructions to decipher an encoded file.

He typed something. The seconds drew out like the endless days of Alaskan summers. As they drew nearer to the critical moment, Yoshi felt the blood pounding in her ears. In her jacket pocket her cell phone vibrated quietly, the signal that Fleishman's team was ready to go. Any second now they would burst around corners and yell, "Drop your weapons, we have you surrounded."

Everything was going as planned. And then, instead of hearing her abductor verifying the material on the disc, Yoshi heard something heavy crash to the pier—was that the laptop? Scuffling feet. A rough hand grabbed her arm and spun her around. Cold steel kissed her temple.

The man behind her yelled, "Back off or the blind chick gets it."

He must have made one of Fleishman's team. She should never have agreed to bring them in on this. They were probably thinking more about making the arrest than Tucker's safety. She would *never* let Ari live this down. Now *she* was a goddamn hostage. And if one more person called her a blind chick, she was going to turn to violence herself.

Someone was pulling her backward again, toward the edge of the pier. Yoshi suddenly imagined what would happen if he threw her into the choppy waters. Everyone would immediately focus on rescuing her and in the commotion the kidnappers would slip away. *Not today*, she thought, *not interested in playing the damsel in distress, buddy.*

She waited three seconds, like a coiled rattler, and then threw herself into kinetic ferocity. Using a trick her father taught her, she jerked her head back with all her might. Before her captor could recover, the motion pitched her head away from the gun barrel and her head crunched into cartilage. She'd broken his nose. He cried out in pain and instinctively dropped the gun to raise his hand to his battered face.

She immediately kicked at the spot where she heard the gun drop and was rewarded with bruised toes when she connected with something hard and sent it scuttling across the wooden pier.

"Bitch," he yelled, alerting her to his approach. She sidestepped and stuck out her throbbing foot, hoping to trip him. She had not moved far enough and he made contact with a force that hit her shoulder like an earthquake. Successive waves of pain rolled through her bones and exited her feet. She stumbled backward, then used the motion, pivoting on her right heel and converting the momentum to her defensive move that sent him charging past her.

Just as she sensed him passing her, she aimed a succession of kicks his way. He grabbed at her as he fell, catching her leg and yanking it back over him. She couldn't get away and landed atop the guy hard enough to force the air from his lungs. He let out a "woof" sound but recovered quickly and got his hands around her throat. She could smell the iron in his blood and punched him square in the face. Her hand came away damp. The grip on her neck loosened. With the edge of her straight hand she chopped at what she hoped was an arm. She had never been one to break bricks with this method, or anything much thicker than a wooden ruler. Still, it seemed to do the trick. A few well-placed knee jabs to the back and she pushed him off her chest and struggled to her feet.

Yoshi had only taken two steps when he slammed into her hip, tackling her. She tumbled sideways and braced herself for the splintery landing that never came. She kept falling. At first she could feel him at her waist, falling with her, then he seemed to twist away. She hit hard enough to cause pain but it seemed only to slow, not stop her descent. She kept falling. He was gone. Everything went quiet, and her body dipped into water so cold it felt like liquid nitrogen on her skin. She screamed and inhaled a mouthful of brackish water. She flailed at the water as if trying to climb it like a ladder.

Yoshi fought at the panic that was washing over her like a wave. *So this is how it feels to drown.* She'd fallen into the Bay. The icy water quickly soaked through her clothing. Her boots hung on her like lead weights. She needed to break the surface and get air in her lungs or she would die. Her lungs were burning when her head finally came out of the water. If she did not drown, she would die of hypothermia. How long before she started losing her cognitive abilities?

Yoshi dog-paddled to keep afloat while trying to figure out what to do. These moments were crucial. By now many others would have gone into cardiac arrest. Perhaps she was as strong as her father always assumed she would be.

A few slow breaths and Yoshi regained some of her wits. She searched her memory bank for the rescue training she'd had as a teenager. First, calm down. Even in December, if the gasp reflex didn't kill her when she first went underwater, she could reasonably survive hypothermia for a couple of hours, but only if she didn't panic and shoot her blood pressure though the roof. Yoshi inhaled, kicked off the boots that were weighting her, even though that let the cold in a bit, and tightened her belt and sleeve cuffs. The small layer of water inside her clothes would, oddly enough, heat up a bit and help insulate her as she paddled to safety. Because she couldn't see and she was disoriented from the fall, she had lost all sense of direction. There was no way to tell if she was paddling out to sea or toward the piers.

She could hear people shouting and surmised the voices came from Pier 39. She could swim toward the sound, but the wooden planks of the pier were six to ten feet above the water and no one could reach her from there. The chug of a boat engine reverberated in the background. It was moving and she could not pinpoint its location. She could not count on it being a rescue boat. She only had one option.

Yoshi turned toward the sound of barking sea lions. She tried to remember what she knew about the marine mammals, all of it learned on a trip to Santa Cruz that Velvet had once dragged her on. During the winter months there were almost a thousand of the flippered pinnipeds around the pier. There were perhaps three dozen or so on the floating dock she was swimming to. *They are not supposed to be aggressive, right?* Well, she was going to find out, because if the 700-pound mammals could heave themselves onto the lower planks of the anchored dock, certainly a fit 110-pound private eye could do the same.

She shimmied out of the waterlogged jacket that was also weighing her down. Using the distressed caterwauling of the sea lions as a beacon, she swam with strong strokes and splashing kicks. She thought she heard the chugging sound getting louder but she was not sure.

Deciding that she should alert them to her presence, Yoshi yelled out to them in between inhalations. She heard a heavy splash, likely a sea lion dropping into the brackish waters. She hoped it was not swimming at her. Another flopped into the water, then another. The fear was rising in her chest. The chugging noise had gone quiet. What if the boat was a fantasy and a roving gang of sea lions was about to take her down? *Egads.*

She swam closer. She could smell the sea lions, a combination of freshly caught fish, tidal kelp, and a musty wild-animal scent she remembered mostly from the zoo. Their barking and grunting was louder, the noises echoing in her ears so loud she thought one of the creatures was calling her name.

"Yoshi? Yoshi Yakamota?" The voice floated from the bay waters off to her left. It was not very sea liony, Yoshi thought. Oh no, the hippothermia was setting in. That didn't sound right either. *Hippothermia?* The disorientation had begun.

"Yoshi," the voice called again. "Over here!"

The loud splashing continued in front of her as more sea lions flopped into the water.

She turned toward the voice calling her name and tried to swim toward it. Her arms and legs were so tired they didn't want to cooperate. *Swim,* she commanded. She was not sure if her body ever responded, but a moment later she felt something bump into her. *That is how sharks strike.* She felt herself being pulled in the water. The sounds faded away as though she had hit the sleep button on her alarm and drifted back in. She slid into a dreamlike state and a procession of sea lions—looking suspiciously like a Disneyland version of African lions toddling in the surf—carried her on their backs to the safety of golden sands and the blessed warmth of a tropical sun.

Perhaps this was heaven.

CHAPTER FIFTEEN

Velvet was at the hospital the minute visitation hours began at eight a.m. She'd hardly been able to sleep at all at Ari Fleishman's apartment. She was so worried about Yoshi and Tucker and half hysterical still that the detective had insisted she stay with him and his partner for the night. She still hadn't seen Tucker since before she was abducted, before the Davina interlude.

Velvet wiped the image of Davina from her mind. In all the years she'd been chauffeuring women in and out of her bed, she'd never felt guilty once. Instead she'd always been proud of her prowess. Until now.

It wasn't like she had cheated on Tucker. She couldn't have. The two of them didn't have an exclusive relationship. At least they'd never made any promises. Velvet had made it clear from the start that she wasn't a one-woman type of gal. But the funny thing was that ever since their second date, Velvet had been more interested in trying out new positions with Tucker than new *women*. Without ever consciously setting out to be in a monogamous relationship, she had stumbled into one.

But then came the tailspin that landed her in Davina's arms, and now she was feeling so guilty she hardly wanted to have sex ever again. Especially when she thought about Tucker being *abducted* while *she* was out with Davina. Then there was the crazy guy who attacked Yoshi and knocked her into the Bay. Velvet had just about dove in after her, and would have if one of the undercover officers hadn't dragged her back from the edge of the pier.

All Velvet could think about was Yoshi, and how they had fought recently and never really made up, and now she was going to drown and her body would wash up as a ghostly apparition like Jeff's. Every time she thought of the blame she deserved for this entire fiasco, she started feeling queasy all over again.

By the time Ari Fleishman confirmed that Yoshi had been picked up by the rescue boat and was going to make it, Tucker had already taken to the nearest hospital, and finding out whether she was really hurt or just dinged up a bit was like pulling teeth. Even in San Francisco, seeing your girlfriend in the hospital still brought up the age-old, family-only standby from the staff. As it turned out, Tucker had lost consciousness for a while. It was probably just a concussion, Fleishman said, trying to reassure her as to why the doctors held Tucker overnight for observation.

The detective sauntered into the waiting room on long legs, smiling with perfect teeth. "I hear your friend Tucker is a little thickheaded," he said, sliding into the chair next to her.

Velvet furrowed her brow at his enigmatic comment.

"You haven't heard? When they did the MRI they found out Tucker has a deviated bone in her skull."

That didn't sound good. "Is that bad?"

"No." Fleishman chuckled. "Apparently it's some sort of natural bone variation. Doc says her thickheadedness might have saved her from more severe injuries."

Velvet managed a smile.

"I wanted to tell you in person that we've reclassified Jeff Conant's death as suspicious circumstances and opened an investigation."

"Really? Oh, thank God."

Velvet was so grateful that her eyes pooled with tears. *Finally.* Other people were starting to believe her instead of treating her as just another grieving friend unwilling to face reality. She didn't know if it was the new revelation or the relief that Tucker and Yoshi made it out alive, but something had snapped her out of her funk. Suddenly she was ready to get back in the game.

"What changed your mind?" she asked.

"Well, the whole kidnap thing helped. We got one of the perps."

"Do you think the other one drowned?"

"I don't know. The water's pretty damn cold, but the guys I talked to thought he could've made it to shore. The bigger the guy, the longer he can survive in cold water. For all we know, he could have had a boat stashed down there, tied to one of the posts."

"I want to thank you again for having the water rescue team there. If they hadn't already been on scene…"

"You're telling me. That was just lucky. When the perps directed you to Fisherman's Wharf I thought they might have a watercraft getaway planned. Or even worse, they could have just caused a mass panic and sent a couple hundred tourists jogging into the water. The mayor would have had my ass in a can if that happened. Just to be on the safe side I mobilized our water rescue team."

"Have you found out more about the men who kidnapped Tucker?"

"A little. The guy we arrested, Joey Picarelli, has a sheet, mostly petty theft and assault charges, but the organized crime unit thinks he may be a mob enforcer. I think he at least makes a living providing the muscle for bigger criminals. He hasn't said a word since we picked him up, not even the L-word."

Velvet smiled. Ari was referring to lawyers, not lesbians.

"I think that might change soon though, seeing as how we found his prints all over the DVDs in Conant's office."

"Really?"

"You can thank Yoshi for that bit of evidence. She's the one who insisted I send a CSI team over to dust the DVDs. If there hadn't been so many prints, I might have thought Yoshi planted them."

"So, you think this Picarelli character killed Jeff? Because what, he didn't have this disc they wanted?"

"Honestly, I don't know. Like I said, Picarelli's hired muscle. Whatever he did, it wasn't something he came up with on his own. So far I can't tie him to his puppet master, but I will. At least we got the disc, seeing how it almost ended up at the bottom of the Bay. We were damn lucky. It must have popped out of the laptop when the guy dropped it because the laptop went into the water with him. I've got a tech working on deciphering it now."

Velvet nodded. It seemed like the right time to forward her agenda. "If you're serious about investigating Jeff's death…"

"I am." Ari stared briefly at the ceiling tiles as though he was drawing lines between the rows of dots. "I'm hoping Tucker can remember something that might lead us to the other kidnapper. When we have two offenders, it's usually a race to see who can cut the best deal. Someone will give up the name of their employer."

"I have a good lead for you," Velvet said. "You should subpoena the latest work of James Harden, the filmmaker."

Velvet explained Harden's project, and that he had used hidden cameras to film the Golden Gate Bridge for the past nine months.

"He says he has captured some suicides on film," she said, explaining how the Bridge Authority had slapped a restraining order on Harden that prevented him from airing or discussing the "inflammatory subject matter of the film."

"He had his cameras running the night Jeff was killed?"

"I'm sure hoping so."

"Well," Ari said, standing up. "It sounds like I have my work cut out for me. I'll take up this film business with the DA's office. But only if you promise to bring Tucker around for a debriefing." He slid a business card out of his wallet and handed it to her. "Call me when she's ready to talk."

Velvet shook Ari's hand. If she were straight, she'd offer to marry the man. She was that grateful. Not only had he rescued Tucker from the kidnappers and plucked Yoshi from the icy waters of the Bay, he was going to hunt down whoever was responsible for Jeff's death.

"Thank you, Ari. For everything."

"I'm always happy to help, especially when it *doesn't* involve assisting the prime suspect in a capital murder case."

"Gee, a girl gets arrested and charged with murder *once*..." Velvet felt good enough to tease again. *Phew.*

"Oh, hey, I thought Yakamota might get a kick out of this." Ari unfolded the newspaper he was carrying.

The previous night's commotion had made the news, or some of it anyway. The headline read BLIND WOMAN RESCUED AFTER FALL FROM PIER 39.

❖

The problem with December investigations was that while Yoshi could dictate the holiday hours of her own staff, even if that meant risking their wrath by say making them work on Christmas Eve, she could not do the same for employees and agencies beyond her control.

By Friday, December 22, it had become quite obvious that the district attorney's office would not file the paperwork necessary to obtain a subpoena for Harden's film until after the holiday. The SFPD computer tech who had been working diligently on cracking the remaining files on the mysterious disc had flown home to Boston, so clearly nothing would happen on that front either. Yoshi could only sit back and wait and hope they would get moving after Christmas and not wait for the new year.

"Feel this!" Tucker grabbed Yoshi's right hand and brushed it across stubble. The short hairs were soft and tickled the sensitive skin of her palm. Yoshi pulled her hand away, not knowing if the impish receptionist had just run Yoshi's hand over seven days' growth of leg hair or *what*. Yoshi found stubbly hair a little repugnant, further justification for not dating men.

"She insisted on getting her head shaved," Velvet explained.

Yoshi was happy to hear the warmth had returned to Velvet's voice.

The three of them were at Yoshi's house waiting for AJ and Bud to arrive.

"Yeah, because it looked horrible. They shaved these big chunks in my head, said they needed to pull out glass fragments and clean the wounds, but c'mon, how am I supposed to walk around like that? They probably wanted me to keep that bandage wrapped around my head, too. I looked like a mental patient."

"Well, if the shoe..." Yoshi felt good enough to tease, too, apparently.

"Now, Tuck." Velvet's soothing voice seemed to calm Tucker down. "You know the doctor said you need to rest and avoid any situations where you might hit your head. You shouldn't be walking city streets at this point anyway."

"I can't go to your house, since that's where I was attacked. It's too much."

"Tucker, are you sure you're feeling okay?" Yoshi asked.

"Yes," she replied, drawing the word out. "Fine. I'll sit down. Will that make you happy?"

Yoshi wasn't sure who Tucker was addressing her question to, so she ignored it and posited her own. "I was wondering if you have remembered any more details about the night you were abducted?"

"I was unconscious, remember?" Tucker could still sound like a belligerent teen.

"Come on, Tuck," Velvet chimed in. "Yoshi's trying to help. Anything you remember might help find who did this to you."

"Okay, I woke up and I couldn't see. I couldn't move. I was freaking out. It took me a bit to figure out my hands and feet were tied and my eyes blindfolded. I think I was in a car."

"Did it feel like you were moving or stopped?" Yoshi asked.

"Moving."

"Were you sitting upright?"

"No, lying down on my side, like across the backseat."

"What did it feel like?"

"What do you mean?"

"Did it feel like a bench or bucket seat? Was there a hump in the middle? Was if fabric or vinyl? Did it feel like there was air around you or was it more enclosed like a trunk?"

"It was a bench seat, but one of those that kind of tilts down toward the back. It was definitely covered with some kind of fabric. It felt pretty new, it didn't smell brand new but there were no holes or tears or wear. It wasn't the trunk, I know, because there was a speaker in the side door, they were listening to..." Tucker continued sharing details about the vehicle until she ran out of answers.

From Tucker's recollections, Yoshi deduced that the kidnappers had driven a late-model SUV. Nothing as unique as, say, a Hummer and nothing high end that would have leather seats. Probably something more innocuous, like a Ford or Toyota.

Yoshi moved on to questions about the two men, their size, smells, voices, dialects. Each time she spoke to Tucker, she pieced together more detail. "Is there anything you remember about the drive? Did they stop anywhere?"

"Yeah, I was thinking about that. They did stop once before they got to Fisherman's Wharf. I think we were in a parking garage. You know, they made a turn and then the driver rolled down the window, it was automatic, and rolled it back up again. Then we drove around in circles, you know the way you do climbing floors in a garage? On like the third or fourth, he parked and then got out of the car. The Old Spice guy stayed with me but he unrolled his window and the noises of other cars sort were sort of echoey."

Yoshi resisted the urge to point out that "echoey" was *not* a word. "How long were you there?" she asked, thinking of the parking garage AJ had parked her Escalade in the day they paid a visit to Chase Devlin.

"Fifteen, twenty minutes maybe."

"Was there an attendant? Did they stop and pay someone on the way out?"

"I don't think so."

The garage near Devlin's office used automated vending machines to collect parking fees. Plenty of other parking ventures still employed an attendant.

"Oh, I just remembered, when the guy came back he gave something to Old Spice. Maybe that's where they got the laptop?"

"That's what I am thinking." Yoshi acknowledged. "Do you have any sense of where this parking garage might be?"

"Downtown."

"How do you know that?" Velvet asked.

"Just a hunch. The movements started getting more jerky like we kept stopping abruptly, moving a lot slower, and one time the driver guy hollered something about fucking pedestrians. It all just made it feel like the downtown area."

It was far from scientific, but Yoshi was inclined to believe Tucker's intuition. She would have Bud check if any late-model SUVs were registered to Chase Devlin.

"One of them was on the phone for a few minutes. I couldn't hear exactly what he said. The way he was talking, I think the guy on the phone was their boss."

"What about when you got to the Wharf? They must have taken off your blindfold, right?"

"Yeah, at the car. Told me not to look anywhere but in front of us or they'd hurt me. I was freakin' scared. Sorry."

"Maybe you caught just a glimpse of something, like the car color or part of clothing or something."

Tucker was quiet for a moment as though scouring the recesses of her mind for the answer. "I think the car was a dark color. I can't remember seeing it, it's just a feeling, so it might be wrong.

"There was something else," she rushed to say. "When the guy went to take off my blindfold, he had this pale patch. You know the kind of lines people get around their finger when they've worn a ring for years and then take it off? He had a pale band around his wrist like he usually wore a watch but didn't have it on. Does that tell you anything?"

"It tells me the person of interest usually wears a watch, and must have done so until very recently if the outline was still visible," Yoshi deadpanned. "It leads me to wonder where the watch is now."

Chapter Sixteen

"Hey there, girl." AJ was standing on Yoshi's front steps.

"Hey, AJ, Yoshi's not here," Tucker said, yawning.

"I know. She thought you could use getting out of the house." AJ did not say *Yoshi wants her freaking house back,* although she believed it to be true.

Yoshi had told her that since she was abducted from Velvet's crib, Tucker couldn't go back there. 'Specially not with one of the kidnappers still at large. It didn't help that Velvet had had a professional security system installed. Nor had it helped that Yoshi insisted that the minute the perp's laptop went in the water, Devlin stopped worrying about the computer disc. He thought it was now on the bottom of the Bay. Tucker said she wouldn't feel safe until Devlin was behind bars. For now, she and Velvet were sleeping in Yoshi's guest room and wearing out their welcome.

When Yoshi called AJ, she said Velvet would be gone all day, hanging out in the Haight-Ashbury hood looking for some kids that ran away from some strange ex-gay camp. She wanted Tucker to get out of the house, too, before she developed some kind of agoraphobia and could never leave.

"She told me not to be taking no for an answer," AJ said, holding her ground. "Get dressed or I'll take you out in your PJs."

Tucker stormed off muttering curse words under her breath. It made AJ laugh.

Fifteen minutes later, they were in the Escalade heading up Nineteenth Avenue. "Where you wanna go?" AJ asked.

"The Golden Gate Bridge."

"Why? Ya not gonna jump, are ya?"

"No way. I just want to go up there. You know, they could've made me jump, too, but they just kidnapped me instead. I'm always the lucky one that way and I feel like there must be a reason, you know? Like I'm here for a reason, only I don't know what it is. I want to see where he died."

"Okay, kid. You know you don't have to feel bad for being alive, right?"

"Don't you? Sometimes, when you think about Katrina? Like why did the people die that did? Do you ever feel like you owe them?"

AJ didn't have any words to answer a question like that.

They drove over the bridge in silence. AJ pulled into the Vista Point parking lot. Tucker pulled a camera from her bag, stuffed the bag under the seat, and bounded out of the Escalade like a pent-up puppy. AJ pulled on her hoodie and jacket, hugging them close to block out the cold wind.

"I don't get why they call it Golden Gate," AJ said. "Looks like orange-red to me."

Tucker waited at the edge of the parking lot. "Yeah, I thought it was weird, too, but then I found out it's not the bridge that's the Golden Gate, it's what the bridge spans."

"I don't get it."

Tucker motioned with her hands. "The physical space below the bridge, where the Bay drains into the ocean? European settlers named *that* the Golden Gate."

"Huh." It still didn't make sense to her, but then a lot of shit the Pilgrims did didn't make sense either.

They rounded a little hill and found themselves on the bridge proper. AJ just about turned around right then. The walkway looked wide enough to fit two people side by side, but it was separated from oncoming vehicle traffic by nothing more than a calf-high guardrail and twelve inches of pavement. AJ stuck to the left side of the walkway where there was a waist-high rough plywood barrier suggesting something under construction. Given the recent bridge collapse, these renovations didn't fill her with confidence.

They'd only covered about twenty feet when the plywood barrier ended abruptly and Tucker was left looking over a hundred-foot drop. A waist-high metal fence painted to match the other elements of the bridge protected pedestrians from plummeting over the edge. At least there was still earth under their feet. Over the railing, she could see the rocky hillside disappearing under the bridge. Above them an enormous tree-trunk-diameter cable swooped up toward the first of the bridge's two towers, looming in the distance with traffic passing like Tonka toys between its steel legs. Smaller cables ran in twins from the deck of the bridge to the large cable. To the left, the skyline of San Francisco sparkled above glistening water.

They walked on. AJ stuck to the right of the walkway while Tucker was so far to the left that she was running her hand along the steel barrier. Every few steps, she would lean over the railing and look down. AJ wondered how she could be so fearless in this environment yet afraid to return to Velvet's house. Sure 'nough, her own stomach was churning and she could feel her heart rate increasing.

They reached the tower. Tilting her head back, Tucker looked up at the iron giant. From this perspective, it looked as though it could be the bridge between heaven and earth. The perspective was dizzying. It was hard to imagine that this had been built by people her size, dwarfed as she was by the massive structure. The wind blew in strong gusts, spattering them with a mist that seemed drawn from the clouds by the hulking bridge tower.

Raising her voice against the wind, Tucker expressed her desire to tour Alcatraz. AJ acknowledged her own interest by bobbing her head.

They had reached the end of the land and from here on out the bridge would be surrounded by nothing but air. AJ was hit by a wave of nausea and thought about turning back. She belonged on the ground or in the water, not up here suspended a hundred feet over water. Still, she didn't want to leave Tucker out here on the bridge alone.

Tucker leaned out over the railing again. AJ hazarded a sideways peek and decided she was checking out the section of the bridge a few more feet to the left, a narrow gangplank from which to stand or jump. AJ wondered if Tucker was looking for something in particular, maybe hoping Conant had marked the spot he'd jumped from, or been pushed or thrown. The waist-high railing wouldn't be much of a deterrent for a suicidal jumper or a someone lifting a body to drop over the edge.

AJ certainly could not imagine dragging a body all the way from the parking area, even if there'd been two or more people involved. If he was already dead, they would have just stopped on the bridge and pulled the body out. Wouldn't that kind of thing draw unwanted attention? Even after dark? So they probably didn't do that either.

She'd bet that even if Conant wasn't murdered, he'd walked out here on his own two legs. Maybe they had a gun to his back or threatened someone he loved. Whatever they'd done, it had to be one hell of a motivator, at least for her. She didn't think you could walk this far out on the bridge and still think they were going to let you walk back. Dead man walking.

"Oh, my God, oh, my God, AJ, look, look!" Tucker was jumping up and down, pointing at something over the edge of the bridge. AJ took a deep breath and hazard a glance. All she saw was water. And a very long way down.

"Right there." Tucker pointed just left of her feet.

AJ pulled her gaze in closer. She glimpsed a flash of light as though something reflected sunlight back toward them.

"What is it?"

"I think it's a watch."

The next instant, Tucker was on her knees and then laying flat on her stomach, shimmying toward the edge of the bridge like a snake.

"What the fuck you doing?" AJ moved to stop her but Tucker got stubborn.

The slatted pedestrian barrier ended about eighteen inches above the pavement. Tucker's shoulder was pressed against the bottom of the barrier and her arm stretched out under it, her hand inching along on fingertips. A white handkerchief held by the short fingers trailed behind like the train of a wedding dress.

"Am I even close?" Tucker asked.

AJ gritted her teeth and leaned over the railing. Below her and beyond the edge of the pedestrian walkway, she could see three narrow, shallow troughs and a gutter three fingers wide. In the gutter was something shiny and gold.

See, AJ thought for no reason, *that is what* gold *looks like*.

Tucker's marching fingers had made it out to the edge of the second trough but no farther.

"You're about three inches too short."

"Shit." Tucker got back on her knees. She looked AJ up and down. "How tall are you?"

"Five-ten."

"Oh, cool. I'm only five-eight. I bet your arms are longer." She stood up and handed AJ the handkerchief. "Will you try it?"

"Don't you think we should just report this and let the bridge people get it?"

"No, I don't. You know what that is? That's the watch of one of Jeff's killers."

"How could you possibly know that?"

"Because one of the guys who attacked me had this ring around his wrist like he usually wore a watch, only something happened to it."

"That don't prove anything."

"That watch might be my only chance of identifying who attacked me. If I ever want to stop looking over my shoulder or worrying every guy is him, I need to do this. Can you please try?"

"Fine." AJ glanced at the approaching pedestrians. She better get this over with before someone reported them for suspicious behavior. She knelt on the pavement, the pebbles digging into her hands and knees. This was probably going to ruin her shirt. She kissed the pavement and stretched her arm out.

"Right, up, farther right." Tucker offered directions. "You're almost there, really. Just a little bit more."

AJ strained to stretch farther. She stretched until her shoulder and arm muscles complained and threatened cramping. She glanced down toward her feet and saw that the pedestrians where almost on them, and she scrambled to get out of their way. The Asian couple looked at them quizzically but did not voice their question.

AJ watched them walk away. A ringing noise pulled her attention back to Tucker. AJ gasped and lunged toward the younger girl, who was straddling the pedestrian railing like a cowboy. Tucker was out of her fucking mind. AJ fought the urge to scream, afraid any outburst might surprise the crazy chick and send her plunging over the edge.

"Tucker," AJ warned. "Don't."

Tucker dropped her other leg over the railing.

AJ's mouth was dry. She reached out toward Tucker but didn't dare touch her.

Holding on to the railing with her hands, Tucker put one foot down. Then she put the other down.

"AJ?" Tucker's voice cracked. She had not looked up.

"Yes."

"Grab hold of my jacket."

"Jesus, Tucker this is crazy."

"I need your help."

AJ put her right hand gently on Tucker's back and slid it down. She could feel Tucker shaking. Or maybe it was her hand that was shaking. AJ got a handful of Tucker's jacket. With her other hand she grabbed the waistband of Tucker's jeans. Her hands were sweating.

She braced herself against the pedestrian barrier and tightened her grip on Tucker's clothes. She could not bring herself to look at anything beyond the back of Tucker's head, her whole skull visible under the tightly cropped hair. AJ could see where they'd removed glass embedded in her scalp. The scabs were healing.

"Am I close?" Tucker asked. "I can't see."

Damn. AJ did not want to look. She was afraid she'd get vertigo or something and accidentally let go. She forced herself to watch Tucker's fingers. She was bent nearly in half, as though touching her toes. Or doing one last stretch before taking a dive.

"You're close. Just a little to your right. There."

The handkerchief closed around the shining object. "Got it." AJ pulled Tucker tight against the barrier.

"Now what?" Tucker asked, panic creeping into her voice.

AJ could see the dilemma. Efforts to lift a leg over the barrier would swing her torso out over the abyss. Tucker was starting to cry. "I'm scared."

"It's going to be okay." AJ noticed a change in the sound of traffic behind her. A car was idling near them. A car door opened and closed in quick succession. AJ recognized the aura of law enforcement and shouted, "I need help."

The officer came to her side and assessed the situation. "You hold her from the left and I'll get the right."

AJ nodded.

"Okay, ma'am," he said to Tucker. "We're holding you from either side. We're going to lift you up. When I tell you, I want you to sit on the top rail."

On their first try they got Tucker back onto her butt on the rail and then carefully helped her turn around. She jumped down and crumpled into AJ's arms.

"Thank you, thank you, thank you."

AJ untangled herself. And Tucker rushed to the officer and gushed profuse gratitude. "I'm so sorry."

"Thank you, Officer," AJ added. "We don't need to take up more of your time."

He snorted. "I don't think so. You girls just won yourselves a ride down to the station and a mandatory fine."

AJ glared at Tucker.

When the CHP officer opened the back door of his black-and-white squad car and ushered them inside, AJ vowed to never cross the bridge on foot ever again, regardless of how long she lived in the Bay Area. Some experiences you never need to relive.

As the officer slid into his seat and addressed the radio mic, Tucker furtively pulled something from her pocket, wrapped in a white handkerchief. AJ had almost forgotten about the gold watch that initiated Tucker's near-fatal insanity.

One gold watch...*priceless.*

CHAPTER SEVENTEEN

Bud rubbed his eyes with his fists. God, he was tired. He'd been staring at the screen for hours. Even when he shut his eyes, a ghost image remained as though burnt into his retinas the way they said something could burn into the computer screen if it was left on one image too long.

He was sitting in the closet-sized audio-video room at SFPD's Mission precinct. He shared the space with a pimply-faced recruit who'd been assigned the task of controlling the remote control and verifying that Bud was never alone with the film. As though he'd have the skill set to alter the images on the screen or something. Or maybe the kid was there on the filmmaker's behest, making sure Bud didn't steal his film and try to pass it off as his own.

Like anyone would want it. In its unedited version, the film was hour after endless hour of the same view of the Golden Gate. On fast forward, the cars rolled briskly across the span and the fog drifted in and out, but nothing else changed. Then the sun would go down and there'd be the lights of cars zipping across less regularly and then hardly at all. The section they were reviewing right now was even more pointless because it came from the camera placed farthest away and was primarily for what Harden called macro changes.

There were four cameras total. From each side of the bridge, one captured wide landscape views and one captured zoomed-in views of the pedestrians and vehicles crossing the bridge. The cameras were on timers, and every four hours the recording would switch from one camera to another.

Harden had given them two weeks' worth of images captured around the time of Jeff Conant's death. For Harden this was a miniscule selection, culled from the nine months of irrelevant material. For Bud Williams it was like a haystack, and he was looking for a needle, for a few critical moments amidst 14 x 24 hours of crap.

The AV kid had the long view flashing by on 8x and didn't notice when it switched back to the relevant close-ups.

"Hey," Bud called and pointed at the screen.

He wished the kid would just let him operate the remote control. He was a grown man for, godssakes.

The kid stopped fast-forwarding and flipped it into rewind instead. He overshot the spot and was about to push it up to 8x again when Bud growled at him to leave it at 4x. Another hour slipped by and Bud's eyes were starting to close when he saw a bird dive from the bridge like it was after a fish in the water below. He snapped awake and demanded, "Go back, go back."

The image stopped and slowly scrolled backward. A dark, ghostly figure rose from the water's surface and flew in a jerky reverse swan dive up to the bridge.

The image switched direction and the dark figure stepped off the bridge and dropped, flailing arms and legs. It hit the water and disappeared below the waves. *Jesus.* It was a jumper.

"Was that just—" The kid looked at Bud, his face pale. When he found the answer in Bud's eyes, he looked down at his feet, avoiding the screen. "Oh."

"You want to get some air?" Bud asked, giving the kid a way out. "I can handle this myself."

"Yeah." The kid handed Bud the remote and fled the room.

Bud played the scene once more. It was a suicide, but it was not Jeff Conant. The time of day was all wrong, it was too light out, and this jumper looked like a woman. He flipped the speed up again, watching the day pass by in a few moments. He wasn't sure Harden should get permission to show this as a movie. It was a snuff film. That jumper had been some guy's little girl.

The screen grew darker as it slipped into the evening, then lit up again as the bridge's many lights came on and illuminated the passing cars and occasional pedestrians—mostly couples after dark, he'd noticed, randy bucks taking their girls up to a romantic spot in hopes of short-wiring her judgment. Since he had to pay more attention, the nights passed slower than the days, but the sun did rise without another idiot trying to grow wings and fly.

He sped through the next day at the highest speed, telling himself he'd only do one more night before he took another break, went outside and smoked a bowl. It wouldn't be long before he'd forget his promise to himself. At first he didn't notice. Then he didn't know what he'd noticed. He hit the rewind and went back a few frames, forward and back. There it was a clumpy shadow that inched along, noticeably slower than the occasional vehicle. The digital clock read after midnight. As the shadow advanced toward the middle of the bridge, and closer to the camera lens, it slowly resolved into pedestrians. Bud could distinguish three separate heads.

When they stepped under the next streetlight, something shiny caught the light and reflected it back. Bud squinted at the screen and replayed the scene trying to see what it was: gun? knife? glasses? He couldn't tell. Still, he was entranced. This was the most viable image he'd seen in seven days of film. He fought the urge to fast-forward ahead to be sure. The figures stopped walking. They stood in one place as the seconds ticked by. Bud felt his body tense waiting for…something. The way stillness can be like a snake, coiled and ready to strike.

What were they waiting for? Were they talking? The seconds spread into minutes. Bud threatened the film with a thumb on the fast-forward button. Suddenly the figures sprang into action. There was a jumble of movements and then everything stopped again. Bud stared at the screen unsure what he'd just seen. He rewound, put the play on slow motion, and sat back to watch.

The three figures were standing, then one jumped away from the other two as though trying to get away. The two sprang into action. The three were pressed together in an indistinguishable but kinetic form, like cartoon cat-and-dog fights. The fighting ball moved up and down the walkway and then the motion stopped suddenly. Bud let the film play on in slow motion, still not sure what happened. The figures moved under a streetlamp and Bud *knew.*

There were two figures on the bridge. Where there had been three heads, now there were two. The angle of this camera prevented him from seeing the body fall or hit the water, but what he had seen was someone going over the bridge. Jeff Conant had not been alone on the bridge that night.

Bud let the film tick forward at 2x normal speed. The figures slowly disappeared from view. Perhaps fifteen minutes later headlights alerted him to an approaching vehicle, returning to San Francisco. Bud paused the film and stared at the screen. He'd be willing to bet the dark SVU he saw there was registered to Chase Devlin. Likewise, he was nearly positive one of those technical geniuses could clean this image up enough to read the license plate. Maybe even pull mug shots off the suspects.

❖

Yoshi was fuming. She had come down to the police station to meet with forensic technician Lincoln Nebraska after Ari Fleishman called to tell her he had news. She had not gotten to hear any of that news. Instead she had gotten an earful from the chief of police, a ranking military officer, a National Parks ranger, CHP officer and local representative of Homeland Security. All of them had explicitly expressed their dissatisfaction at the behavior of her associates, whose careless actions had disrupted bridge traffic, disturbed tourists, and almost caused a panicked shutdown of the entire bridge when one passerby claimed that a skinhead and angry black man were attaching some type of incendiary device to the underside of the bridge.

As someone who by most accounts had just attempted suicide, Tucker was undergoing a required psychological evaluation.

"I am very disappointed in your lack of judgment in this situation," Yoshi informed AJ. "I hope you realize that this little escapade could jeopardize your entire career."

AJ did not say anything.

"What were you thinking? You could have been killed, both of you. What could have *possibly* been the motivation for pulling such a dangerous stunt?"

"Just a watch."

"I beg your pardon?"

"Look, it ain't a smoking gun, and what Tucker did was totally *whack*, but I understand her wanting to catch the guy who attacked her. I get that you gotta do what you gotta do, so if you want to rescind your offer—"

"So it wasn't your idea?"

"Of course not. I tried to stop her. That didn't work. So, yeah, I kept her a little safe when she did what she was determined to do. That's all."

"Then I owe you an apology, AJ, I am sorry to have doubted you. Did Tucker succeed in retrieving the item?"

"Sure 'nough. I got it right here."

"Good. We're going to turn it over to Detective Fleishman."

They found Ari standing in the doorway to the AV room. "You got to see this," the detective called to them.

Yoshi flinched but didn't reveal it in her voice. "What have you found?"

Ari stepped back and AJ went inside. He narrated what was playing out on the screen.

"Can y'all clean that up 'nough to distinguish faces?" AJ asked.

"That's what Bud asked, too," Ari answered. "I think, since it's digital, they should be able to. Maybe not *that* frame. I understand if it's dark they can pull out hidden information, but if it's too bright or washed out, there's nothing they can do."

"So maybe not the license plate, then?" Bud asked.

"Probably not," Ari admitted.

"Did you try going back to when it arrives?" Yoshi asked. "Then you wouldn't have to contend with headlights." She tugged on Fleishman's shirtsleeve and they backed into the hallway. Ari shut the door.

"I have a present for you." Yoshi held out the watch AJ had given her. "Apparently my receptionist risked life and limb for it, so please treat it accordingly."

Ari accepted it gingerly. "It's got the kind of band that might attract DNA."

"That's what we're hoping."

"This belong to the one that got away?"

"I think so. Tucker and AJ found it up on the bridge. From what I understand, not the sort of place that a casual passerby would lose their watch. Especially if the clasp isn't broken."

"I'll have that checked, too."

"Thanks."

"You ready to meet with Nebraska?"

Ari led the way to the tech guy's computer-cluttered cubicle.

The were greeted by a nerd who acted like he only saw daylight once a year if there was a partial eclipse to witness or the building had to be evacuated. After they shook hands, he started to ramble on about the technical obstacles he'd conquered in his quest to decipher the files on the disc, and how incendiary the contents appeared to be, not that he was reading them.

"What we have here is leverage," Ari said. "Anything Devlin needs, he's got dirt on someone in a position to smooth his path. Politicians, celebrities, religious leaders."

"He's been spying on these people?"

"The disc looks like a backup copy from Devlin's laptop," Ari said. "It doesn't just incriminate other players. There's a whole file of Devlin's activities, including pics. Don't view it before a meal."

Yoshi could understand why Devlin had wanted the CD back so desperately he'd paid the likes of Joey Picarelli to recover it. "How did it fall into Jeff's hands?" she wondered aloud.

"Maybe Tyrone Hill was trying to get himself an insurance policy," Ari said. "He could have stumbled onto it, or maybe Devlin was using it against him and Tyrone got a hold of it to protect himself. Or Devlin was going to threaten Jeff. We might never know."

"Did anything on it tie Devlin to Jeff's killing?"

Ari shook his head. "For that, you'll need get Devlin running off at the mouth."

Yoshi nodded. That seemed like a possibility.

CHAPTER EIGHTEEN

"Yoshi Yakamota." Chase Devlin pulled her hand into a shake. "It's so good to see you again." His clammy hand and the tenor of his voice belied his words. "Please, have a seat." He accompanied her to the chair she'd sat in on her previous visit, then settled into his own. "What brings you by?"

"I can't help but notice Simon is not joining us," Yoshi said, playing a hunch.

"Well…" For once Devlin seemed to struggle for words. "You're right, Miss Yakamoto. This is Gregor."

A low rumble of a voice came from behind Devlin's desk. "Pleased to meet you."

Judging by Gregor's accent and his Scottish name, Yoshi pegged the bodyguard as hailing from the Mid-Atlantic, probably directly from New York City, which had one of the largest populations of Scots.

"I hope Simon is not sick."

"Simon is no longer with us."

"Oh, my God." Yoshi made a shocked face. "You had him killed?"

"No." Delvin sneered. "I had to let him go."

"Oh, that is a shame. Can you tell me how to get in touch with him?"

"Why?" Devlin sounded belligerent and defensive. A lovely combination in a man.

Yoshi was pleased at his irritation. She was going to break him.

"Why not? I may be in the market for a bodyguard," she said innocently. "Particularly one with Simon's skill set. Let's see—breaking and entering, theft, assault, kidnapping." She paused for effect. "Oh yes, and *murder*."

"Gregor, would you mind waiting outside?"

"Yes, sir."

Devlin waited until the door closed before speaking. "I don't know where you get your information, *Ms.* Yakamota, but I can assure you that if my former employee was involved in some kind of criminal activity, it was unbeknownst to me."

Yoshi snorted. "Listen, *Mr.* Devlin, I know I am being a little blunt, but I see no reason to waste time pretending I do not know what I know. You are not as innocent as you would like others to believe. Please reserve your performance for your courtroom audience. It is wasted on me."

"Why are you here? What do you *really* want?"

"Actually, I am here about something *you* want."

"Oh?" Devlin was doubtful. "And what would that be?"

Yoshi reached into her purse and retrieved an unmarked CD jewel case. She waved it languorously.

"What's that supposed to be?" He laughed, sounding genuinely relieved.

"Something you never intended to give away. Something you went to a whole lot of trouble to get back. Something worth…*killing* for."

"You're mistaken."

"No. *You* are. You must have been relieved when Simon made it back. Sure, you had to worry about bad, bad Joey Picarelli spilling his guts, but you had something on him that bought you his silence. And Simon *assured* you that you no longer had to worry about that incriminating material falling into the wrong hands. Unfortunately for Simon, he did not realize that meant he had become expendable. He was too easily traced to you and he knew both your password and how to decipher your encryption. He probably never realized how dangerous that knowledge was."

She waited for an outburst or the sounds of a man breathing unevenly. Chase Devlin was so silent he could only be sitting rigidly, forcing himself to remain calm.

"I am interested," she said in a pleasant tone. "Did you retire Simon yourself or make Gregor do the dirty work? You don't seem like the type to get your hands bloody."

Devlin did not bother to answer her question. "Let's pretend your crazy theory is right."

"No, let's pretend you are writing a book titled *If I Did It.*"

"I don't think so. If you intend to blackmail me with that"—Yoshi assumed he was pointing at the disputed CD—"you'll need to convince me that what you say on it is on it."

"All right. Let's see, does *Captain Blackdong* ring a bell?"

Devlin was dumbstruck. She wondered if his face had lost color. "I—I. Uh, of course it does, that's one of my titles."

"Sure that's all it is?"

Like a jack-in-the-box, Devlin sprang out and snatched the disc from Yoshi's hand. She heard him fussing with the jewel case. He cracked it open and shoved it in his computer.

"See," she said, hoping to conceal the triumphant smile she felt pulling at the edges of her mouth.

Devlin typed in his password.

"I don't know if he told you this, but Simon *dropped* the laptop," Yoshi said. "To be fair, he foresaw the police ambush a little late and needed both hands to take me hostage. And he did make it up to you, grabbing the computer like that and pulling it with us into the Bay. Brilliant. Except when the laptop hit the beams of the pier, the force knocked the CD loose. It's rather amusing if you think about it."

Devlin was opening one of the disc files. Back at the Blind Eye office, Bud and Tucker would be glued to the computer screen, waiting anxiously to see if they got lucky.

Detective Fleishman had personally come by the Blind Eye office yesterday to inform her that the DA was not pushing forward on indicting Chase Devlin. They were hesitant to publicly reveal the "politically sensitive" contents of Devlin's disc, and they insisted that there was simply not enough physical evidence to tie Devlin to the crimes committed on his behalf. A judge said they didn't even have enough for a search warrant. They had enough to charge Joey Picarelli with kidnapping and assault charges relating to Tucker's attack. The DA had offered Picarelli a reduced sentence if he would finger Devlin, but Picarelli's lawyer—hired, incidentally, by Chase Devlin—advised him against taking it.

They had hoped to tie Simon, who they were certain had been the other kidnapper, to Jeff through the watch, which had yielded DNA from Simon *and* Jeff, but Simon could not be found. He had disappeared. Either he was on a beach in Mexico drinking cocktails on Devlin's dime or, more likely, his body was decomposing somewhere in the bay.

Ari Fleishman had been frustrated, to say the least. Like a lot of good cops, he wanted justice. But he wouldn't break the rules to get it. The rules said he couldn't search Devlin's office without probable cause. He couldn't turn Yoshi into an agent of the law and charge her with getting the information he legally could not. But there was nothing in the rules that said he couldn't introduce the detective agency to Nebraska or for Nebraska to do some outside consulting, explaining how a certain program worked.

Right now, while Devlin was verifying the contents on his disc, he had unleashed a friendly spyware virus that would allow Blind Eye access to Devlin's computer to browse through Devlin's files. Being good citizens, if Blind Eye investigators stumbled upon any evidence of criminal activity, they would report it to the relevant law enforcement office.

Yoshi sat in Devlin's office with a demure smile on her face, ready to trick Devlin into revealing his secrets. She still had a few tricks up her sleeve.

"Did you find what you were looking for?" she asked nonchalantly.

Devlin shifted in his chair. "Let's say this is what you think it is. Why bring it to me?"

"Should I have taken it to someone else? If you think someone else would pay more…"

"Pay?"

"Of course. This is a business proposal, after all."

"And why would I pay you?"

Yoshi affected a laugh. "You're joking, right? We've both seen what is on that disc. And you were willing to kill for it, after all." She chuckled. "Of course, we both know I need not worry about *that*."

"Oh? What's to prevent me from killing you? I know you don't have a copy of the information on this disc. It's protected. You're the last person who can tie this to me. I could kill you—"

"Oh, of course you could." Yoshi acted like she was talking to a silly child. "You are a big boy. But we both know you do not have the guts to do that kind of thing yourself. I'm sure Conant's murder made you look tough to your friends, but you and I know the real story. You never intended for Beavis and Butthead there to kill anyone. They were just supposed to scare Conant, weren't they? Get him to give up the disc? Only he didn't know he had it. That is ironic, eh? They could have tortured him all night and he could not have told them what you wanted."

Yoshi tapped the side of her head. "Nothing upstairs. Which smart-ass had the brilliant idea of hanging him over the bridge? I would put my money on Simon. You were right to have him killed for that. The police would have had him dead to rights. They were just waiting for the DNA to come back on the watch they recovered and"—Yoshi leaned forward over his desk like he was her confidant—"they were caught on *film*."

Devlin's breathing had suddenly changed. It was subtle, but Yoshi was certain she had found a chink in his armor. "Oh, yes, the whole sordid incident. Turns out this documentary filmmaker John Harden has been filming the bridge for nine *months*." She shook her head. "Can you imagine? I understand that the police are working to enhance certain elements—like the vehicle license plate. For your sake, I hope you buried Simon *in* that SUV. You know, so it won't be traced back to you. As your new business partner, I think I should take over hiring security."

"We're not partners, and I am not going to pay you *shit*." He stood up. "I think you should leave."

"It is so cute that you think that. Maybe I should not have used the word 'partners.' Let me make it clear to you. You are going to pay me fifty thousand dollars and give me a share of the profits from your little side business. If you refuse, then I will go to the police and you can play Captain Whitedong in prison."

He stepped around the desk toward her. "What do you think you're going to take me down for?"

"Killing Jeff Conant, and probably killing Simon, too, when we find his body.".

"Make up your mind. I thought you said I didn't get my own hands dirty."

That was true, but the wheels in Yoshi's head were turning. She did not know where they were going. Until that became clear, she needed to stall. She pushed back her chair. "Are you wearing a watch, by any chance?"

"Why?"

"Can I examine it?" She strode toward him.

He stepped back. "Look, you crazy bitch, I don't have time for your fucking mind games. Leave now or I'll have Gregor escort you out."

"Give me your watch and I *will* leave."

"No way. I'm not falling for that. Get out before I call the police."

Yoshi smiled. "Please do. In fact," she pulled out her cell, "I'll call for you." She flipped it open. "It's still nine-one-one, isn't it?"

"Put it *down*." The menace in his voice sent a shiver down her spine. He yanked open a desk drawer.

She punched in Nine and searched with her fingertips for One.

He dug in the desk. Something metal clanked against the drawer.

She finished dialing, pressed Send, dropped the phone, and raised her hands at shoulder height, palms facing out. She wanted to keep them close to her chest. "I should really be going," she said. "I think I am late for a meeting. That is why I asked if you had a watch, I wanted to know what time it is."

"Liar," he spat at her. "You *know*."

"What do I know?" she asked, hoping he would spell it out.

"Stop playing games."

But I like games, she thought. *Let's play cat and mouse.* Or was it pig and rat?

"When did you figure it out?"

"Oh, I admit you had me for a while. I really bought the Simon diversion. But it was you on the pier that night."

"No. That really was Simon."

"You borrowed his watch."

"Yes, earlier that morning. I couldn't find mine. I'd looked everywhere. I needed to be sure what time it was."

"It was perfect, because Tucker managed to see Simon's wrists when he took off her blindfold. So when she found the watch on the bridge, we all thought it was his."

"What gave it away?"

"You reacted to my mention of DNA. I started to think about the watch. Gold, flashy, expensive. Not the kind of accoutrement a bodyguard would usually wear."

"Smart thinking. That's the kind of thinking that gets broads like you killed."

"Can I ask you a question? Was it an accident? Were you just trying to scare Jeff?"

"Hmm." Devlin was quiet, as though considering his motivation. "I don't know, maybe at first. But when he still wouldn't give, I knew he had to go."

Yoshi swallowed. The more freely he spoke, the more likely it was he didn't plan to let her leave his office alive. "But he didn't know he had it."

"You know, that thought never occurred to me until the memorial service," Devlin admitted. "One of his coworkers said something about him taking screeners home to watch. Then I knew. But you got to it before I could."

"How did it come to be in his possession?" Yoshi asked.

"Tyrone forgot himself. He thought he could control *me*."

"Was he blackmailing you?"

"Oh, please. Do you think he's smart enough for that? He couldn't even think of a smart place to hide it. All along I thought Jeff was in on it. Shit happens."

Yoshi heard light footsteps in the hallway outside Devlin's door. She tried to act nonchalant. "When did you know Simon had to die?"

There was a sharp noise in the hall. She dove toward the floor as the door splintered open. Having misjudged the distance to the floor, she slammed down hard and cried out. Her whimper was lost behind the rush of heavy-booted feet, the smell of leather, sweat, and gun oil. Shouting rang out.

"Put it down. Don't do it, Devlin!"

Shots fired, echoing in the room. Hands pulling her up, running across her chest, her back, her legs.

Someone repeated, "Are you hurt? Are you hurt?"

Stumbling to keep her footing, Yoshi pulled at the buttons of her striped dress shirt. "Was Devlin shot?"

"He was, but he'll live." Ari Fleishman reached in her open shirt. "You'll feel tugging," he said as he yanked the tape from her skin.

She yelped when it pulled all the fine hairs from just below her bra line. It was a huge relief to have the recording device off. Yoshi didn't even mind if she was walking around her bra showing. She was slapped on the shoulders again.

"Nice work. You really got him." It was one of the female police officers congratulating her this time. "He said more than enough for a search warrant."

Ari slapped her hand and joked, "You ever think of becoming a PI?"

It took another twenty minutes to get clear of the scene and make her way to the foyer of the building.

"Yoshi!"

As footsteps strode toward her, she braced herself for Velvet's embrace. Velvet wrapped her arms around Yoshi and held her for a long time.

When Yoshi started to squirm, Velvet whispered in her ear, "Thank you." Then taking her hand and pulling her into the late-December air, she added more loudly this time, "I knew I could count on you."

Epilogue

New Year's Eve

Velvet walked into Mecca feeling almost like a brand-new person. The depression she'd battled through the holidays was finally lifting, thanks in large part to the Blind Eye team and, of course, a prescription for Celexa from her shrink. She was back at work on a juicy investigative article: kids missing from an ex-gay program north of the city. And she and Tucker had finally come clean with each other. Well, it was she who had to come clean, about Davina. But Tucker 'fessed up some things, too, mostly about her childhood and the issues the kidnapping brought up for her.

She spotted Yoshi and Tucker and practically ran toward them.

"Vel!" Tucker was the first to embrace her.

"Happy New Year, both of you," Velvet said, trying to be heard above the clatter of the rest of the room. It was good to be back in the land of the waking.

AJ arrived with a hottie named Maria. Velvet had almost forgotten that AJ and Yoshi had decided they would be friends instead of lovers. She'd been so wrapped up in her own head for weeks now…or was it actually months?

"Where's Bud?" Tucker sounded genuinely disappointed.

"Oh, you know Bud." Yoshi consoled her. "He's not one for social gatherings. He's probably at home with a bottle of gin, watching old episodes of *Ironside*."

Velvet interjected, "Hey, I loved *Ironside*."

"Is there anything on TV you don't love?" Yoshi was genuinely curious.

"*Survivor*. I don't need to watch people eat rats and fight over shelter. Okay, so let's talk New Year's resolutions."

AJ went first. "I'm gonna get to know this breezy on my arm." She smiled at Maria, who positively beamed in reply. "And I'm taking a new job."

"You are? Where?" Yoshi sounded perplexed.

"Wit' you."

"You're accepting my offer? You'll join Blind Eye? What led you to that decision?"

"When I looked at Tyrone at the hospital after they got him stable. I realized all I wanted to do was help him kick his addiction. As a cop, all I'd get to do was arrest him or maybe turn him into a snitch and use him to make a bigger bust. I'd like to experience helping people instead of arresting them."

"That is wonderful, AJ. Welcome aboard."

Everyone foisted hugs on AJ, and now it was Tucker's time to beam. She and AJ had become fast friends in the last two months, and knowing she'd be a fixture in her life next year made her recognizably jubilant.

Tucker was jumping out of her seat at this point. "I'm so excited. My resolution is to see a shrink so Velvet gets off my back about the whole post-traumatic stress disorder thing. Geesh, I just got kidnapped once. And…I'm also going to get back on my bike and do the AIDS /LifeCycle ride this year. And…" She paused. "I'm going to make an honest woman of Velvet."

Velvet smiled. "We're moving in together."

She thought she caught a wink from Yoshi, something she hadn't seen in years. Yoshi actually approved. Velvet felt at peace with the decision, a far cry from the usual trapped feeling she got when she made any sort of romantic commitment.

AJ turned to her new boss and spoke proudly. "Before you spill it, boss lady, the three of us have a little gift for you. It's kind of a thank you for everything."

Maria pulled out a large square box from her oversize fuchsia tote and handed it to AJ with a knowing grin. AJ put it rather gingerly into Yoshi's open arms.

"What is it?" Yoshi asked, not moving.

"Open it!" all four women chimed in.

Yoshi tore open the box, getting a little help from Tucker with the heavy tape and the enormous inner Styrofoam squares. She pulled out what looked like some sort of mysterious black plastic electrical equipment. Yoshi moved her fingers for a moment over the raised plastic parts and then looked up, puzzled.

"Surprise!" Tucker exclaimed. "Do you know what it is?"

Yoshi was reticent. "I'm not certain."

"It's a PowerBraille Display Unit." Tucker was triumphant as she read directly from the outer box. "It translates what's on the computer screen into Braille so you can now surf the Web and read e-mails yourself."

Yoshi smiled broadly. "Color me very grateful. This must have cost a fortune."

"We split the cost. Even Bud chipped in," Tucker effused. "This will make us a lot more efficient now, too. Very PI-like of me, don't you think?"

"Very PI of you, Tuck."

"Does it read porn?" Velvet brought the conversation back from the realm of sappy, as usual.

As everyone chortled, no one actually answering her query, she continued to wonder if there were ways to translate actual erotic images into Braille. Probably not.

"Okay," Yoshi said, still flush with appreciation. "My new resolution is to learn how to use this thing. I have a feeling it may just change my life."

"Speaking of life changes, I have one, too," Velvet said.

"Me too," AJ interjected. "You first."

Velvet told everyone the news she had been sitting on. The board of directors of *Womyn*, the lesbian magazine she'd founded with Rosemary Finney so many years ago, before the court battles, before Rosemary's murder, had asked her to step back in and take the reins as publisher and editor in chief. She was a bit terrified to be back at the helm of a magazine, but she was thrilled, too. *Womyn* had always been her baby and she was ready to start nurturing it again.

"I've decided to take the job after I finish this story about the ex-gay programming camp."

"Wow, Velvet, that's great," Yoshi said.

Of all people, Velvet had let Yoshi know how much she'd suffered after being torn from *Womyn*. She was glad Yoshi approved. It meant leaving a plum job at the *Chronicle* for a lower salary, fewer benefits, and longer workdays. But for Velvet it also meant reentry into the only world that had ever felt truly, uniquely her domain.

"What will Marion think?" Yoshi asked the question Velvet was dreading.

Marion Serif was another of her dear friends, and now she would also be her closest competitor. She wanted to forge new territory as competitors; she wanted to remain friends. But she was afraid Marion wouldn't want the same.

"I don't know yet. I'm going to talk with her soon. So, enough about me," Velvet said, suddenly aware of the extra attention. "What's your news, AJ?"

"I don't know how to go 'bout sayin' this, so I'm just gonna come out with it," AJ said, in a way that made everyone know this was not any sort of laughing matter. "I think I might not be a lesbian after all."

Tucker giggled. "Right. 'Cause you're straight? You almost had us there!"

"Naw, y'all. I'm serious. I ain't got no beef with dykes. I'm just thinking I might be transgender. Ya know, more like these FTM trans guys than other lesbians, even aggressives."

"Whoa. Dude." Tucker was wide-eyed.

Everyone else was silent for a moment. Velvet, who had sensed the wheels turning for AJ in the last few months, was glad she was broaching the subject of gender identity. Velvet had slept with her share of studs and aggressives, terms black butch lesbians used to identify themselves, and she'd never thought of AJ as one of them. Velvet wanted to react positively before anyone lamented the lesbian community's loss of "another good butch," a comment that seemed to cut particularly to the bone when it was thrown about. San Francisco seemed to be on the verge of a transgender moment. From literature to activism to arts, suddenly trans folk were popping up all over the place. Velvet supposed that for dykes who had never really felt like women, they might find themselves reflected more in the trans experience.

"Congratulations, AJ." Yoshi had beaten her to the punch. "I believe that is in order? We are certainly honored that you feel comfortable sharing this with us, as it can be such a difficult decision to come to."

"Wow, that's *huge*," Velvet added. "What's it mean for you? Are you thinking the whole nine yards? Name change, testosterone, surgery…"

"Whoa, there." AJ smiled, pleased with the support. "I got a lot more thinkin' and investigating 'fore I know what's right for me. I just wanted to tell y'all. It's a big thing and y'all like my dawgs."

AJ held up her fist and Tucker raised hers to punch it. Velvet had never been a fist puncher, so she'd leave this to the butches. Er, one butch and one FTM? Oh, well, more proof this would take some getting used to for all of them.

Tucker, who had been relatively quiet throughout, piped up sounding like an eager eight-year-old. "Can we call you Pops now? Or Puffy J?"

"Um, I think I'm gonna keep rollin' with AJ if y'all don't mind."

"Okay, Papa J, whatever you say."

Velvet excused herself to take a cell phone call. She could hear Tucker pelting AJ with questions. *God, please don't let Tucker decide to become a man.* She was having a hard enough time dealing with this whole monogamy thing, she didn't want to add turning hetero on top of it all.

"Hi, Stan, what's up?" A call from her editor was not always a good thing, so she awaited his reply cautiously.

"The paper just got word from the directors of the Golden Gate Bridge, Highway and Transportation District," he said. "They voted in favor of accepting bids for a feasibility study."

"Yeah? Oh. Oh, my God, that's great news. Wozlawski, I could have your baby right now!"

She asked Stan a few more questions, then practically sprinted back into the main part of the bar. On four-inch Pucci cork platform heels, it was no easy feat.

"Guess what!" Velvet demanded immediate attention. "That was Stan the man Wozlawski, and there's going to be a feasibility study for the bridge barrier."

Yoshi jumped to her feet. "Excellent. Do you know details?"

"Yeah, as long as bridge district funds aren't used, the board agreed to authorize a two-year study. And here's the best part. This time the bridge directors decided not to burden the feasibility study with the requirement that any suicide barrier be foolproof."

The group shared a toast and did some hooting and hollering, except for Yoshi, who wasn't the hooting type.

Velvet felt a sense of joy she hadn't experienced since Jeff died. She had closure. And she had a big undercover assignment, a new job, and perhaps scariest of all, a live-in girlfriend. She also had the sense that this coming year would be an interesting one for all of them.

Authors' Note

On a September morning in 2000, a few days before his birthday, Jacob received news that his brother-in-law Tom Sherwood had committed suicide in Pocatello, Idaho. Two days later, a Bannock County coroner ruled Tom's death a homicide. The early misidentification hampered the investigation and the case remains unsolved. Although his death was not a suicide, the deaths of others close to the couple have been; most recently, Jacob's cousin Jeremy. Suicide's victims—including the friends and family struggling in the wake of these losses—weighed heavy on our minds while we were writing Blind Leap.

Because this book touches on the issue of suicide, we want to remind readers that outreach can mean the difference to a person on the edge. If you or someone you know is in that lonely place, we recommend Kate Bornstein's wonderful tome *Hello Cruel World: 101 Alternatives to Suicide For Teens, Freaks and Other Outsiders.* Or call the National Suicide Prevention Lifeline at (800) 273-TALK. Somebody does care. Seriously. Step back from that ledge. The world can't afford to lose you.

About the Authors

Diane Anderson-Minshall is the executive editor of *Curve* magazine, the country's best-selling lesbian magazine. The cofounder and former executive editor of *Girlfriends* magazine and the cofounder and former editor/publisher of *Alice* magazine, Anderson-Minshall focuses her writing primarily on lesbian life, popular culture, travel, entertainment, and celebrities. Her works have appeared in *Passport, Film Threat, Utne Reader, Wine X, India Currents, Teenage, Bitch, Seventeen, American Forests, Femme Fatale, Diva, The Advocate, Fabula, Bust, Natural Health, Venus*, and numerous newspapers.

Her essays have also appeared in *Reading The L Word: Outing Contemporary Television*; *Bitchfest: Ten Years of Cultural Criticism from the Pages of* Bitch *Magazine*; *Body Outlaws*; *Closer to Home*: *Bisexuality and Feminism*; *Young Wives Tales: New Adventures in Love and Partnership*; *50 Ways to Support Gay and Lesbian Equality*; and *Tough Girls*. Anderson-Minshall coedited the anthology *Becoming: Young Ideas on Gender, Race and Sexuality* and coauthored *Blind Curves*, the first in the Blind Eye mystery series. Diane was named one of PowerUp's 2006 Top Ten Amazing Women in Showbiz, for her work with lesbian filmmakers. And in her spare time, she performs with a fat-girl burlesque troupe in Portland, Oregon, as Bang Bang Betty and Dirty Diana.

Jacob Anderson-Minshall is a former park ranger and peace officer who now spends his days penning queer novels and riveting essays on the politics of gender, disability, feminism, and popular culture. He cofounded *Girlfriends* magazine and served as the publication's first director of circulation. Now the transgender writer's weekly syndicated column, TransNation, runs in LGBT publications from San Francisco to Boston, and he is a frequent contributor to the country's best damn feminist publication, *Bitch* magazine. His work appears in the forthcoming anthologies *Trans People in Love* and *Men Speak Out: Views on Gender, Sex, and Power*.

Originally from Idaho, Jacob and Diane have lived in the San Francisco Bay Area for fifteen years in the company of several fur kids. They divide their time (not evenly, of course) between Idaho, California, New Orleans, and their newest home in Portland, Oregon.

Books Available From Bold Strokes Books

House of Clouds by KI Thompson. A sweeping saga of an impassioned romance between a Northern spy and a Southern sympathizer, set amidst the upheaval of a nation under siege. (978-1-933110-94-3)

Winds of Fortune by Radclyffe. Provincetown local Deo Camara agrees to rehab Dr. Bonita Burgoyne's historic home, but she never said anything about mending her heart. (978-1-933110-93-6)

Focus of Desire by Kim Baldwin. Isabel Sterling is surprised when she wins a photography contest, but no more than photographer Natasha Kashnikova. Their promo tour becomes a ticket to romance. (978-1-933110-92-9)

Blind Leap by Diane and Jacob Anderson-Minshall. A Golden Gate Bridge suicide becomes suspect when a filmmaker's camera shows a different story. Yoshi Yakamota and the Blind Eye Detective Agency uncover evidence that could be worth killing for. (978-1-933110-91-2)

Wall of Silence, 2nd ed. by Gabrielle Goldsby. Life takes a dangerous turn when jaded police detective Foster Everett meets Riley Medeiros, a woman who isn't afraid to discover the truth no matter the cost. (978-1-933110-90-5)

Mistress of the Runes by Andrews & Austin. Passion ignites between two women with ties to ancient secrets, contemporary mysteries, and a shared quest for the meaning of life. (978-1-933110-89-9)

Sheridan's Fate by Gun Brooke. A dynamic, erotic romance between physiotherapist Lark Mitchell and businesswoman Sheridan Ward set in the scorching hot days and humid, steamy nights of San Antonio. (978-1-933110-88-2)

Vulture's Kiss by Justine Saracen. Archeologist Valerie Foret, heir to a terrifying task, returns in a powerful desert adventure set in Egypt and Jerusalem. (978-1-933110-87-5)

Rising Storm by JLee Meyer. The sequel to *First Instinct* takes our heroines on a dangerous journey instead of the honeymoon they'd planned. (978-1-933110-86-8)

Not Single Enough by Grace Lennox. A funny, sexy modern romance about two lonely women who bond over the unexpected and fall in love along the way. (978-1-933110-85-1)

Such a Pretty Face by Gabrielle Goldsby. A sexy, sometimes humorous, sometimes biting contemporary romance that gently exposes the damage to heart and soul when we fail to look beneath the surface for what truly matters. (978-1-933110-84-4)

Second Season by Ali Vali. A romance set in New Orleans amidst betrayal, Hurricane Katrina, and the new beginnings hardship and heartbreak sometimes make possible. (978-1-933110-83-7)

Hearts Aflame by Ronica Black. A poignant, erotic romance between a hard-driving businesswoman and a solitary vet. Packed with adventure and set in the harsh beauty of the Arizona countryside. (978-1-933110-82-0)

Red Light by JD Glass. Tori forges her path as an EMT in the New York City 911 system while discovering what matters most to herself and the woman she loves. (978-1-933110-81-3)

Honor Under Siege by Radclyffe. Secret Service agent Cameron Roberts struggles to protect her lover while searching for a traitor who just may be another woman with a claim on her heart. (978-1-933110-80-6)

Dark Valentine by Jennifer Fulton. Danger and desire fuel a high-stakes cat-and-mouse game when an attorney and an endangered witness team up to thwart a killer. (978-1-933110-79-0)

Sequestered Hearts by Erin Dutton. A popular artist suddenly goes into seclusion, a reluctant reporter wants to know why, and a heart locked away yearns to be set free. (978-1-933110-78-3)

Erotic Interludes 5: Road Games, ed. by Radclyffe and Stacia Seaman. Adventure, "sport," and sex on the road—hot stories of travel adventures and games of seduction. (978-1-933110-77-6)

The Spanish Pearl by Catherine Friend. On a trip to Spain, Kate Vincent is accidentally transported back in time—an epic saga spiced with humor, lust, and danger. (978-1-933110-76-9)

Lady Knight by L-J Baker. Loyalty and honor clash with love and ambition in a medieval world of magic when female knight Riannon meets Lady Eleanor. (978-1-933110-75-2)

Come and Get Me by Julie Cannon. Elliott Foster isn't used to pursuing women, but alluring attorney Lauren Collier makes her change her mind. (978-1-933110-73-8)

Dynasty of Rogues by Jane Fletcher. It's hate at first sight for Ranger Riki Sadiq and her new patrol corporal, Tanya Coppelli—except for their undeniable attraction. (978-1-933110-71-4)

Running With the Wind by Nell Stark. Sailing instructor Corrie Marsten has signed off on love until she meets Quinn Davies—one woman she can't ignore. (978-1-933110-70-7)

Burning Dreams by Susan Smith. The chronicle of the challenges faced by a young drag king and an older woman who share a love "outside the bounds." (1-933110-62-7)

Promising Hearts by Radclyffe. Dr. Vance Phelps lost everything in the War Between the States and arrives in New Hope, Montana, with no hope of happiness and no desire for anything except forgetting—until she meets Mae, a frontier madam. (1-933110-44-9)

Innocent Hearts by Radclyffe. In a wild and unforgiving land, two women learn about love, passion, and the wonders of the heart. (1-933110-21-X)

Justice Served by Radclyffe. Lieutenant Rebecca Frye and her lover, Dr. Catherine Rawlings, embark on a deadly game of hide-and-seek with an underworld kingpin who traffics in human souls. (1-933110-15-5)

Justice in the Shadows by Radclyffe. In a shadow world of secrets and lies, Detective Sergeant Rebecca Frye and her lover, Dr. Catherine Rawlings, join forces in the elusive search for justice. (1-933110-03-1)

A Matter of Trust by Radclyffe. JT Sloan is a cybersleuth who doesn't like attachments. Michael Lassiter is leaving her husband, and she needs Sloan's expertise to safeguard her company. It should just be business—but it turns into much more. (1-933110-33-3)

Storms of Change by Radclyffe. In the continuing saga of the Provincetown Tales, duty and love are at odds as Reese and Tory face their greatest challenge. (1-933110-57-0)

Distant Shores, Silent Thunder by Radclyffe. Dr. Tory King—along with the women who love her—is forced to examine the boundaries of love, friendship, and the ties that transcend time. (1-933110-08-2)

Beyond the Breakwater by Radclyffe. One Provincetown summer, three women learn the true meaning of love, friendship, and family. (1-933110-06-6)

Safe Harbor by Radclyffe. A mysterious newcomer, a reclusive doctor, and a troubled gay teenager learn about love, friendship, and trust during one tumultuous summer in Provincetown. (1-933110-13-9)

Honor Reclaimed by Radclyffe. In the aftermath of 9/11, Secret Service Agent Cameron Roberts and Blair Powell close ranks with a trusted few to find the would-be assassins who nearly claimed Blair's life. (1-933110-18-X)

Honor Guards by Radclyffe. In a wild flight for their lives, the president's daughter and those who are sworn to protect her wage a desperate struggle for survival. (1-933110-01-5)

Love & Honor by Radclyffe. The president's daughter and her lover are faced with difficult choices as they battle a tangled web of Washington intrigue for…love and honor. (1-933110-10-4)

Honor Bound by Radclyffe. Secret Service Agent Cameron Roberts and Blair Powell face political intrigue, a clandestine threat to Blair's safety, and the seemingly irreconcilable personal differences that force them ever farther apart. (1-933110-20-1)

Above All, Honor by Radclyffe. Secret Service Agent Cameron Roberts fights her desire for the one woman she can't have—Blair Powell, the daughter of the president of the United States. (1-933110-04-X)